Lucy Ashford studied English and History at
Nottingham University, and the Regency era is her
favourite period. She lives with her husband in an old
stone cottage in the Derbyshire Peak district, close to
beautiful Chatsworth House, and she loves to walk in
the surrounding hills while letting her imagination go
to work on her latest story. You can contact Lucy via
her website: lucyashford.com.

Discover more at millsandboon.co.uk.

THE WIDOW'S SCANDALOUS AFFAIR

Lucy Ashford

MILLS & BOON

First Published in Great Britain 2020
by Mills & Boon, an imprint of HarperCollins*Publishers*
1 London Bridge Street, London, SE1 9GF

© 2020 Lucy Ashford

ISBN: 978-0-263-27736-4

MIX
Paper from
responsible sources
FSC® **C007454**

This book is produced from independently certified FSC™ paper
to ensure responsible forest management.
For more information visit www.harpercollins.co.uk/green.

Printed and bound in Spain
by CPI, Barcelona

Chapter One

May 1794—London

It was past nine o'clock by the time Serena, swathed in a dark hooded cloak, paid off the hackney cab driver at the corner of Henrietta Street and headed towards Covent Garden. The crowds that gathered nightly here were in search of pleasure, but she felt as if she was heading straight into her worst nightmare.

Overhead a full moon rode high in a pitch-black sky, but its silvery glow was nothing compared to the bright lamps that beckoned from the many taverns and gaming houses. The May night was warm and women in scanty attire paraded themselves brazenly in front of the piazza, exchanging banter with the young bucks who'd stopped to ogle them. Hucksters roamed the streets, selling food, flowers and fruit they'd scavenged from the day's market, while by the church a fiddler played lively tunes and some men—clearly inebriated—attempted a clumsy jig. Serena had to jump aside as the dancers flung themselves about.

I am late, she chided herself desperately. The meeting was supposed to take place here, at the corner of King Street, but so far there was no sign of the man she expected to see. She tried to fight down her rising panic. Whatever next? Perhaps he'd changed his mind…

Hope rose and was dashed. If he didn't turn up she would face shame. Dishonour.

She let out a low cry as a rough hand tugged at her shoulder and a man pulled her round to face him growling out, 'You the lady who's come to meet Mr Silas Mort?'

'I am.' Serena pulled out of his grasp, her heart hammering painfully. 'And please don't touch me again. Do you understand?'

He laughed. He did more than that—he sneered. 'Strayed a bit far from your fancy home, haven't you, my lady? This is a different world to what you're used to, eh?' He jerked his thumb in the direction of a narrow passageway. 'Mr Mort's down there. And he don't like to be kept waiting.'

He set off along the alley, not even bothering to check if Serena followed. And of course she did. But she held her head high, because even though she was terrified, she knew she must not let the man know it. She'd learned that, if nothing else. Fear made you weak. Fear made you a victim.

She realised she was being led towards three men lurking in the shadows of a tavern and found herself wrapping the cloak she'd borrowed from her maid even more tightly around her shoulders, trying to ensure its hood covered her striking blonde hair. Though what was the use of attempting to disguise herself? They knew exactly who she was—and anyway, the minute she opened her mouth to speak she would give herself away as someone who just didn't belong here. *You might as well have worn your best satin cloak and silk bonnet, Serena, you fool.*

'I have an appointment with a man called Silas Mort.' She was amazed that her voice sounded so calm. 'Which of you is he?'

'Which of you is he?' one of the men jeered, mimicking her educated tones. 'Well, our Silas has picked himself a fancy piece to keep himself warm this time, hasn't he, lads?'

Her heart lurched as his meaning struck home. 'No,' she began, 'you don't understand—'

Then she broke off, because she recognised the black-clad man with the scarred face who was limping towards her.

'So you're here, then?' He nodded in approval.

'As well for you, my fine lady, that you decided to keep our appointment.'

With a flick of his hand, he beckoned to his three comrades to stand back, giving Serena time to reassess the grim welt of the scar that ran from his forehead down across one eye to his cheekbone. Her pulse was pounding dizzily. 'Mr Mort,' she began, 'I have come to pay you the money you demanded. I must also inform you that if I hear any more from you after tonight, I shall most definitely set the law on you. Do you understand?'

She hoped she'd sounded confident, but all Silas Mort did was burst out laughing. 'You'll set the law on me, will you, Your Ladyship? That's a likely tale. So you're saying, are you, that you're ready to squeal to the magistrates about this meeting of ours tonight? Oh, I think not. Because if you do, the whole world will know about the rather juicy piece of scandal you're so eager to hide.' He jabbed a finger at her, not laughing now, but snarling. 'So let's have no more of your threats.'

He turned to his comrades. 'Such a sad picture, eh, lads? A pretty little widow, still grieving the loss of her hero of a husband over two years ago...' His gaze swung back to Serena. 'You'd better pay up, my lady. And fast.'

Serena already had her purse in her hand. 'Here

are twenty guineas,' she declared. 'And in return, Mr Mort, I expect a complete end to your greed.'

He snatched the purse and examined the coins inside. 'Looks like it's all here. But are you accusing me of greed, milady? You, with your fine house and carriage and jewels?' He thrust his face close to hers. 'Just for that, I think you owe me rather more, don't you? Another twenty guineas at least.'

Serena closed her eyes for a moment. Taking a deep breath, she said, 'Oh, no. I absolutely refuse to pay any more. You are a crook and a scoundrel—'

Silas Mort lifted his hand and his three companions surged forward to surround her. One tugged her hood away and she felt her pinned-up blonde curls falling loose. 'Pretty,' the man murmured lecherously. 'So pretty...'

Desperately she tried to push him away. She thought she'd learned some sense in the past few years, but surely she'd been the stupidest person on earth to fall headlong into such a nightmare. She struggled to break free, but her enemies were too many and too strong.

Only then, from behind her, came another voice. An upper-class male voice with just a trace of a foreign accent saying calmly, 'Gentlemen, pray pardon my intrusion. But do you know, I rather think you've made a mistake here.'

The next minute a tall man wearing a plain, dark coat and a hat that shadowed his face was ambling towards the ring of men. Putting one hand possessively on Serena's arm, he looked round at her startled enemies. 'Perhaps I should explain,' he went on, 'that this particular lady happens to be under my protection. So I'd be mightily obliged if you'd leave us to enjoy our *rendezvous.* I'm sure you understand.'

There was something lurking in his polite declaration—a hint of steel, Serena felt—that made Mort's men hesitate. But even so, he was one against four. *They'll kill him*, was her first thought. *Dear God, they'll surely kill him.*

They didn't. But neither did they retreat. The newcomer tugged Serena closer, his hand firmly round her waist. 'Say nothing,' he ordered in a low voice. Again, the hint of steel. 'Leave this to me.'

She couldn't have spoken if she'd wanted to. In fact, shock had robbed her of her voice. Because now—now that she dared to look up at him properly—she realised who he was.

His name was Raphael Lefevre. He was a French nobleman who'd come to England last year to escape the aftermath of the Revolution that had engulfed his homeland. As had many of

his countrymen; but Lefevre was different, because instead of declaring his horror at what was
happening in France, instead of giving aid to the
victims and doing anything he could to stir up
public awareness of his countrymen's plight, he
cheerfully announced that he would be pleased
if he never returned to his native land.

'In heaven's name, why should I?' he'd drawled.
'London suits me perfectly.'

Which he made all too apparent.

Thanks to an English education—for his father, the Marquis of Montpellier, had sent him
first to Eton, then to Oxford—his command of
the language was almost perfect. On returning
to England a year ago at the age of twenty-eight,
he'd met up with former friends and made many
more, not least because of his wealth. He'd stirred
up plenty of criticism also, especially since he was
often seen in the company of London's most notorious pleasure-seekers, but he could be utterly
charming when he chose and by many he was
described as handsome, with his thick dark hair
and strange, silvery-grey eyes.

Indeed, Serena herself had once almost fallen
for his honeyed words and devastating smile.
Never again, she'd vowed; but unfortunately they
were too often forced into one another's company
at society's most exclusive events. And those eyes

of his—mocking, laughing—seemed to follow her everywhere.

Only a few days ago at Lady Sunderland's ball, she'd had the misfortune to be standing near to him when the subject of loyalty to one's country came up. He'd made some cynical dismissal of the subject and she couldn't help but retaliate. 'Of course, we all know where your duty lies, Monsieur le Marquis! Many of your fellow countrymen stayed behind in an attempt to restore order to your sad homeland. But you have made pleasure-seeking in London your chief priority!'

There had been some murmurs of agreement, but Raphael Lefevre's usually languid voice had hit back at her with blistering speed. 'Ah, *madame*. Such a fiery temper! Long may you remain content to be a widow. You see, I might lack sympathy for my homeland, but not for my fellow men.' He'd gazed at her assessingly. 'It would be a brave suitor indeed who took you as his wife.'

The barely stifled laughter from his companions had been burning in her ears ever since. And now he was here, the detestable Marquis who took nothing seriously, holding her close to his side. Was this another game of his?

'The lady and I,' he said calmly to Silas Mort and his crew, 'have an appointment to meet here because she expressed a wish to explore somewhere a little livelier than her usual haunts. Ours is a rather private affair, you understand? Though I'm afraid I was late in arriving—and for that I must beg Her Ladyship's forgiveness.'

'No,' Mort began, 'look here, she came to meet *me*!'

'Really?' Lefevre raised his eyebrows in disbelief. 'My good man, you'll forgive me if I find your claim rather bizarre. Wouldn't you say so, Serena?'

He looked down at her then, his voice mild, but his hard-angled jaw somehow dauntingly uncompromising. Giving silent orders to her. *Ours is a rather private affair*, he'd claimed—yes, he'd actually said it aloud. Was he crazy?

He was mocking her, of course. Getting his revenge for her past taunts. But she was aware that by now a small crowd of passers-by were gathering, eager for fresh entertainment. Gambling dens and cock-fighting pits were common fare round here, whereas the humiliation of a fine lady was rare indeed. Serena guessed that if the hateful Raphael Lefevre sauntered off as casually as he'd arrived, then absolutely no one else would lift a finger to help her, and Silas Mort's crew would have her at their mercy again.

Could there be a more unlikely knight in shining armour than the vain and idle Marquis? He gambled, he took part in all the wilder sports going and he lavished his wealth on fripperies. The younger men of the *ton* foolishly aped the careless way he wore his expensive clothes and they copied his every mannerism, even his faint French drawl. At this precise moment, though, he was her only hope of protection. And Serena was aware of a most peculiar sensation. As if it would only be natural for her to surrender to his tempting embrace...

You let this man make you a public laughing stock once before—surely that was enough?

Tonight his clothing was surprisingly sober, but those silver-grey eyes that glittered above his razor-sharp cheekbones were as sinful as ever. And at this very moment Silas Mort was limping forward, puffing out his chest. Talk about being caught between the devil and the deep blue sea.

'Now see here.' Mort was wagging a gnarled finger at Lefevre. 'It ain't wise to go interfering in what's none of your business.'

Lefevre's grip on her never wavered. 'But it is my business. I told you.' His words were precise. Steel-edged. 'Anyone who insults this lady insults me. And that most certainly would not be wise.'

Her senses tingled, this time not from fear of Silas Mort and his crew, but from something entirely different and far more shocking. *Anyone who insults this lady insults me?*

Lies, of course. He was lying—again. She shivered.

At least his words made Mort hesitate. But then, in a sudden wave of rebellion, Mort's men were urging their leader forward. 'Take him on, Silas!' called one. 'He's all fancy talk, the gent. Our money's on you!'

'Tell him to leave the pretty widow to us,' jeered another. 'Tell him we have first claim on her, right?'

As Serena felt Lefevre's strong arm tighten around her she tried to push him away, but then she heard his voice in her ear and the rich, husky depths of it smouldered through her veins. 'Stop fighting me, Lady Serena,' he murmured. 'If I leave you with them, don't you realise what they'll do to you?'

The blood was rushing to her face now and her mouth was dry. They'd clashed often in London's richest drawing rooms, but she'd never before realised how powerful a parcel of sheer, outrageous masculinity he was. And as she lifted her head she found herself fascinated by his firm yet sensual mouth...

Do something, Serena. You cannot let yourself be indebted to Raphael Lefevre!

But Mort and his crew still surrounded them. What could she do except hiss out, so only Lefevre could hear, 'I do not belong to you. I don't know why you think you have the right to interfere in my life, and—'

She broke off because Lefevre was cupping her face almost tenderly with those strong hands of his and murmuring, 'Stay close, *ma chère*, and I'll take care of you.'

Ma chère? I'll take care of you? No. No! What was he saying? What was he doing? He must be mocking her, as he'd done so often before! Yet suddenly his thumbs were softly caressing the sensitive hollow below her earlobe, sending some dark and dangerous message to the very heart of her. And then—unbelievably—he was lowering his mouth to hers and the fiery impact of their mouths coming together caused heat to surge like a furnace inside her. She wasn't pushing him away now. She was melting into him, becoming one with him. For those few moments, there was only the shocking intimacy of his lips branding hers in a firm declaration of ownership. Dear God. No one else existed…

Until she realised more men had drawn near. The kind of rich wastrels who—like Lefevre himself—amused themselves by visiting the night-time dens of Covent Garden—*dipping low,* it was called. She knew the names of them all. Lord Giles Beaumaris, the son of a duke. Callum Finlay, who owned vast swathes of land in Scotland. And Sir Simon Hawkesworth, who bred racehorses at his country estate in Berkshire.

'Hey there, Lefevre!' Beaumaris called. Along with his friends, he was already assessing the hovering menace of Mort and his band. 'What's going on? You need a hand here?'

As the three men drew closer she whipped up her hood so her face was half covered, but Lefevre's newly arrived allies weren't looking at her. Instead they'd strolled towards Mort's crew and were clearly flexing their muscles beneath their expensive clothes. 'A fine night for a fight, wouldn't you say, my friends?' Finlay drawled to the other two. Finlay was a noted boxing enthusiast; the others were equally strong and fit and Mort's men were wise enough not to take up the challenge. 'Looks like reinforcements have arrived, lads,' Mort muttered as he and his cohorts slipped away down the side alley into the darkness.

Now, Serena told herself, her pulse pounding. *Now is your chance to escape.*

She tried. She really tried to break free, but Lefevre held her tightly as his friends attempted to peer at her cloaked and hooded figure. Beaumaris raised his eyebrows. 'What the devil have you been up to, Lefevre, you rogue? I thought all four of us agreed to meet here to search for entertainment, but it looks like you've already found yours with this little lady.' He was staring hard at Serena and she pressed her face into Lefevre's shoulder, begging him mutely. *Please don't betray me. Please don't tell them who I am.*

'Lady?' Hawkesworth was scoffing. 'Since when did they start calling the bits of muslin round here "ladies"?' He pointed at Lefevre. 'And watch yourself, my friend. It looks like this particular one would have got you into a spot of trouble if we hadn't come along, so make sure you get your money's worth. On that note, we'll leave you to it.'

They strolled away, making even coarser jests. Serena's cheeks burned anew. *If only I can get home,* she prayed. *Then I shall put this whole, horrible nightmare behind me and do my best never to be within a mile of Raphael Lefevre ever again.*

But the Marquis clearly had other ideas, since he still had a firm hold of her and was steering her off in the very opposite direction. That was when she did indeed try to break away, but, undaunted, Raphael Lefevre marched her steadily onwards. 'No escape for you yet, my lady,' he declared. 'Eventually, I'll take you home. But right now, it's time you and I had a serious talk. One that we've been putting off for a little too long.'

Her heart sank even further.

Chapter Two

Raphael led her down a narrow cobbled lane to a tavern just north of the piazza, though with hindsight he reflected that he should have headed for somewhere a little more respectable, for shady-looking characters still loitered in the shadows and at every corner prostitutes looked for customers. Indeed, one of them called out to him, 'Special price for a handsome gent like you, darling!'

'No thanks,' he called back. 'I've already got what I need.'

He drew Serena close again. Which was the moment he realised she was shivering badly.

Was it with shock, after her encounter with that gang of ruffians? Though he guessed that were he rash enough to ask her, she'd probably declare she'd prefer their company to his any day. *Too bad.* Once inside the tavern, he led her to a corner well away from the smoky light of the

cheap tallow candles and noticed that her hood
had once more slipped down, causing him to catch
his breath at the sheer perfection of her face. Pale
and distraught she might be, with her fair hair
falling from its pins, but she was one of society's beauties without a doubt. She had a lovely
oval face and a full mouth, with thick-lashed eyes
that were like the colour of the ocean on a summer's day.

And what had just happened in these mean
streets had clearly shaken her badly.

'Why doesn't she marry again?' people asked.

*'Because she loved her husband, the Honour-
able Lionel Willoughby,'* was always the answer.
*'He died a war hero and there can never be any-
one else for her...'*

He realised she was speaking to him, in a voice
that combined both contempt and defiance. 'Is
this another of your attempts to humiliate me,
Monsieur le Marquis? Bringing me to a place like
this?'

He thought reflectively that the arrogance of
the English upper classes matched that of the
French aristocracy any day. 'As far as I can see,
your own attempt to humiliate yourself tonight
could not be surpassed, Lady Serena—even by
me.' He beckoned to a waiter. 'Wine, if you please.
And make sure the glasses are clean.'

She looked round in some agitation. 'The last thing I want is wine!'

'Really?' He shrugged. 'I thought you might need it. What were you playing at back there? And don't tell me it's none of my business, because I rather think it is—since I came to your rescue.' The bottle of wine arrived and he half filled the two glasses. 'What's more, I actually thought you might express a little gratitude.'

'Grateful? Monsieur le Marquis, was it my gratitude you were hoping to provoke, with that display of...of sheer masculine vanity back there in the street just now?'

He remembered all too clearly the evening he'd been introduced to her last November at a society ball. 'She's a real beauty,' he'd been told by Giles Beaumaris. 'Just wait till you see her!'

Yet what had struck Raphael wasn't her beauty as much as her vulnerability. His first thought on seeing her in the crowded ballroom was—*She looks very, very lonely.*

Then he'd asked her to dance, but he'd had no chance to discover what had caused that bereft look in her eyes, because after that just about everything had gone wrong and there was no hope of redemption for Raphael Lefevre in the eyes of Lady Serena, oh, no. Since that disastrous meeting, the haughty widow with the dead war hero

husband had decided to pick him out for her wit-
ticisms, which he'd been able to swiftly slap down
thanks to his own dry humour and his popularity
with the fashionable set. But just lately, her comments had started to become damned dangerous.

Raphael's mouth curled cynically as he watched
her push her glass of wine away. Now, if only
kisses were the answer. In his arms tonight she'd
felt soft and yielding, and when their lips met
she'd actually tasted rather delicious. What was
more, he could swear he'd felt her silken mouth
actually *welcoming* him…

He guessed she'd been aware of it, too, and
hated herself for it—but not as much as she hated
Raphael Lefevre.

He drained his glass and reached for the wine
bottle to pour himself more. Lady Serena clearly
felt the cheap liquor was beneath her contempt,
just as he was. But at least she appeared to have
regained her composure; though he couldn't help
but notice that in sharp contrast to the lady's gla-
cial expression, some rather enticing locks of her
pale gold hair had escaped to cluster in charming
fashion around her slender neck.

And how she would hate the fact that he'd noticed. *Be careful,* he reminded himself harshly.
All right, so she was a beauty, but *Dieu,* she hated
him. He said, mildly, 'So you call my rescue of

you a "display of masculine vanity", do you? Strange, but I was under the impression I was saving you from a bunch of villains who were about to turn rather nasty. Surely you realised the danger to your reputation, let alone your physical safety, of entering such a notorious quarter by night?'

'I could ask you the same question!' she said, but then he saw her blush. Even she, refined as she was, would know why men like himself and his dissolute friends visited Covent Garden. They came in search of rather earthier pleasures than were available in the refined atmospheres of Almack's, or in Mayfair's aristocratic drawing rooms.

'I'm a man, in case you hadn't noticed,' he said softly. 'I can take care of myself on meaner streets than these—and as for my reputation, I'm reliably informed it has no further to fall. You, on the other hand, are the sister of a peer of the realm, the Earl of Stainsby no less. Yet you came to this district unchaperoned. Unprotected. Why?'

He saw something like panic briefly flutter across her face. Once more she appeared—unusual for her—to be struggling for words. Then she said, without expression, 'My business here was completely private. And I must make it clear that I took strong exception to the way you—you...'

'Claimed you as mine?' He flicked his fingers in the air as if thoroughly dismissing the incident. 'Pardon me if you had other plans to deal with that rather menacing crew. Do you have a pistol beneath your cloak? Or—now, here's an idea—were you going to slay them with words, maybe?'

She looked a little wildly towards the door, but he lazily lifted one curling finger and drawled, 'I wouldn't recommend flight. Not hereabouts, at any rate. Lady Serena, why are you objecting so strongly to the fact that I came to your aid tonight?'

To Raphael's experienced eyes, only the tiniest pulse fluttering in her throat betrayed her inner turmoil. 'There was no need,' she said at last, 'for you to—to *maul* me as you did in front of all those people. To make it look as if—as if...'

'As if we were lovers? But I'd explained to those louts that indeed we had an assignation. And since I was outnumbered at the time, I had to leave them in absolutely no doubt that I would protect you come what may.' He studied her, allowing a smile to play around his lips. 'Don't you agree?'

The colour stained her cheeks again. 'You, *monsieur,*' she said in a slightly less steady voice this time, 'are an unscrupulous rogue.'

'Oh, undoubtedly,' he agreed. 'But you, Lady Serena, are far too proud.' He found himself fascinated by the way that her luscious lips, like her cheeks, seemed to turn pink as she struggled to reply and he almost felt sympathy for her predicament, until he reminded himself that only a week ago, in his full hearing, she'd remarked how odd it was that the Marquis had abandoned his fellow countrymen. 'His friends and his family, too,' she'd added, 'for all we know. Yes, he left them all, in order to live the kind of life here that caused a revolution in France!'

The remark had been made at a fashionable party, in a crowded salon. Her words had made him angry, yes indeed, for one moment. Just the one.

Now, in this dingy tavern, he made himself relax and pointed his finger towards her untouched glass. 'Are you sure you don't want any of that wine?'

She flashed fire again. 'Of course I don't! I never wished to come in here in the first place, with you, of all people!'

He kept that faint half-smile on his face, because he guessed his calmness drove her wild. *'Mon Dieu,'* he said. 'It must be very lowering for you, I'm sure.'

He sipped at his own wine and noticed that her

cloak had fallen back from her shoulders a little, allowing him a glimpse of the pale green gown she wore beneath. It was high-necked, demure even; but he wondered if she realised how tightly the soft fabric clung to her breasts. Briefly he recalled the impact of her slender yet womanly figure when he'd held her close and clamped down on the tingle of arousal.

Remember that she despises you. She's also dangerous to you. Now's your chance, so for God's sake take it.

'You, Lady Serena,' he went on in companionable tones, 'must realise that the best way to deal with those ruffians who threatened you is to report them to the law. May I ask if you intend to do so?'

She was silent just for a moment. 'I—I couldn't report them,' she said at last. 'Because it concerns a matter that I prefer to keep private.'

'Ah.' He nodded his head wisely. 'Could it be that my Lady Serena's gleaming halo has slipped in some way? *Quelle surprise.*' He lifted one admonishing finger. 'Here's a suggestion. Maybe you should consider dealing with the flaws in your own life, before launching yourself so bitterly at mine. Except—oh, dear me, Lady Serena has no flaws. Lady Serena is perfection itself. And yet...' he leaned closer '...and yet I can't help but think, from what I saw tonight, that those unsavoury men you came to meet were out to blackmail you.'

He saw her catching her breath.

'And,' he pressed on, 'here's another word of warning. Blackmailers always come back.'

'But I gave them the money they wanted…' Her voice trailed away as she realised what she'd said.

'Dear me,' he said softly. 'So I'm completely right. That halo of yours is in danger, isn't it? Here's my proposal, my lady. I deal with those men. And in return, you—as of now—will stop trying to blacken my reputation in public.'

'I can deal with those rogues. I told you, I *have* dealt with them!'

He shook his head, almost in sympathy. 'And as I told you, blackmailers always want more. Which could mean you making a few more night-time trips to Covent Garden with a purse full of coins to hand to them—at the very least.'

'They wouldn't dare. I've seen the last of them, I assure you!'

'You think so?' His voice was cold. 'But two of them have been following us. I spotted them twice on our way here as I looked back, so believe me, they haven't finished with you yet. There's also something else you should consider. What if you were recognised tonight, by those acquaintances of mine?'

'No,' she declared. 'It's impossible. With me in this old cloak, they surely couldn't have…' Her voice faded. She caught her breath. '*Monsieur.* Those men. You wouldn't tell them, would you? I thought even you couldn't stoop so low!'

'Your opinion of me never ceases to entertain me,' he said almost with amusement, 'but you've no need to worry. Why on earth should I bother to spread the tale? Though as I say, any of them could have glimpsed your face, in spite of your cloak and hood. You are, after all, quite distinctive. And they would wonder—"Why on earth was Lady Serena Willoughby skulking around the piazza in a manner no lady of the *ton* would contemplate, with Raphael Lefevre of all people?"'

She was silent. Unable to respond.

'I think,' he said at last, 'that you need to consider your position a little more carefully, especially if the word does get around. I suggest that I call on you, tomorrow afternoon.'

'Why?'

'Because, Lady Serena, I still believe you might need my help.' He held out his arm to escort her to the door. 'One way or another.'

'Never,' she declared a little shakily. 'Besides,

tomorrow afternoon is impossible. I have other plans!'

'Then in my opinion, you would be wise to cancel them. I'll see you around four.' He pointed to the door. 'Shall we go?'

Chapter Three

As if in a dream—a very bad dream—Serena let Lefevre guide her towards the Strand. It had begun to rain and her cloak was quite damp by the time he succeeded in hailing a passing cab.

'You'll want my address,' she said to Lefevre.

His response was curt. 'I know your address.' And indeed, after he'd helped her climb in she heard him instructing the driver, 'Curzon Street. Here's money for the fare.' Then without another word he was off, striding down the street through the rain with the arrogance that came so naturally to him.

Serena leaned back rather weakly in her seat as the carriage moved off. He'd told her two of Mort's men had been following them. He could have been lying. He most likely *was* lying. But, oh, what a disaster of an evening. As if her pre-arranged meeting with Silas Mort hadn't been bad enough, Raphael Lefevre had turned up and added to her confusion by calmly offering her his protection. But his kiss had warned her just how dangerous he could be, even when he was pretending to be on her side.

Such a proud man. So utterly impervious to the gossip that trailed in his wake wherever he went—gossip that would envelop her, too, if the word were to spread about their encounter tonight. She felt dizzy at the mere thought.

'I still believe you might need my help,' he'd said as they left the tavern. 'One way or another.' And he'd threatened to call at her house!

She clasped her hands tensely in her lap. Surely he would change his mind. She reached desperately after that faint glimmer of hope. He'd had his fun with her tonight and he'd seen her humiliated—wasn't that enough for him?

Yet he and she were bound to meet again. At society gatherings, society balls… Oh, Lord. She fought for a solution and had found absolutely none by the time the cab jolted to a halt outside her Mayfair mansion.

She hurried up the pristine marble steps, thinking that all she wanted now was to be alone, but of course already the front door was being opened by a footman, and her housekeeper, Mrs Penney, was coming towards her in a flurry. 'My lady!

Fancy being out in all this rain. Your cloak is soaking wet!'

She allowed Mrs Penney to strip off her cloak and forced herself to give a cheerful smile. 'It was my charity work, of course. Didn't I warn you I'd be late? The meeting lasted longer than I expected.'

Oh, these lies.

Kind Mrs Penney shook her head in disapproval, but her tone softened. 'Now what you need, my lady, is a nice hot bath. There's a fire already lit in your room and I'll send Martha to help you out of those wet clothes.'

Her older brother George had asked her to view this house a year and a half ago, when Serena had returned to London after a period of solitude at the family home in Yorkshire. 'The place is yours if you wish,' George had said in his usual shy way. 'You'll be ready to move on with your life, I know. Hope it suits, m'dear Serena.'

From the first she'd loved the house, absolutely loved it, with its high ceilings and large, light-bestowing windows. The furnishings, which George informed her with pride he'd chosen himself—well, they were a different matter. Oh, dear. George might be a distinguished and dutiful earl, but his taste in decor was startling. *Never mind*, Serena had told herself. Striped chintz sofas and

gilded jardinières she could cope with. Just about.
There was one problem, though. 'George,' she re-
minded him, 'you know I've still got the house in
Dover Street where I lived with…'

Where she'd lived with Lionel, her army officer husband.

'Lionel's gone,' George had said. 'It's time for
you to start afresh. Terminate the Dover Street
lease and start to enjoy yourself, that's my advice—clothes, parties and so on. Oh, and I know
you'll wish to carry on with that little charity
affair you and your friends are always talking
about—'

'George,' she'd interrupted, 'darling George,
it's not just a "little charity affair"! My friends
and I are trying to provide an education for children who've not been as fortunate as us and to
give them the chance of a better future. But thank
you so much for the house and *everything*. You
are a dear.'

After that she'd hugged him and he'd looked
a little embarrassed, but pleased, too. Poor
George—since their father's death some years
ago, he'd never ceased to take his duties as head
of the family extremely seriously and often she'd
wished he would enjoy himself more. But that was
her only complaint about her older brother, who'd
shown his affection for her in numerous ways.

And so she re-entered London society as a twenty-three-year-old widow, with a beautiful if oddly furnished house in Mayfair and the belief that she'd learned some of life's hardest lessons. But tonight it seemed that maybe she'd learned nothing at all. Silas Mort and Raphael Lefevre—oh, Lord. Which of them posed the greatest danger?

She scarcely registered a word as Martha, her maid, chattered away. There was indeed a hot bath ready for her in no time, after which Martha brought out an ivory satin night robe for her to wear. But all the time Raphael Lefevre's taunts were ringing in her ears. *'That halo of yours is in danger, isn't it?'*

'There, my lady.' She realised Martha was still talking cheerfully to her. 'Fancy getting yourself wet through in the rain like that! Now, I'll just put a few more coals on the fire and you can have a nice read before you go to bed, like you usually do.'

And Martha left Serena sitting in a chair by the hearth with a cup of hot chocolate at her side and a copy of Mary Wollstonecraft's book—*A Vindication of The Rights of Women*—in her hand. But Serena didn't feel like concentrating on that learned volume in the least. In fact, she felt rather more like having a good cry. She pulled out her handkerchief and dabbed furiously at her eyes. *Stupid. So stupid of me.*

She'd had such a privileged life, enjoying an idyllic childhood on the family's ancestral estate in Yorkshire; though there had been great sadness, too, for her mother had died when Serena was fourteen, just after George had gone to Cambridge. Their father never recovered from his wife's death and died a mere three years later—which meant that George became the new Earl of Stainsby at the age of twenty-one, while Serena, thanks to a legacy from her mother, was wealthy in her own right.

So Serena had grieved, but she'd also striven to lead the life her loving parents would have wanted for her. And when she was nineteen, George had taken her to live in the family's grand town house in Clarges Street so she could have her first Season. Even though George didn't like London at all, he was determined to do his duty and find his sister a good husband. Poor George, that was yet another of his schemes come to naught, for she'd fallen in love, or imagined she had, with a twenty-five-year-old army officer called Lionel Willoughby, who was the third son of a viscount.

Serena was entranced by his charm. She was in awe of his tales of the countries he'd visited with his regiment and the battles he'd fought in.

Though for the first two years of their marriage he was based in London, occupying a senior post at the barracks in Knightsbridge, which, he explained, meant that he often had to work long into the evening. Serena believed him—until she discovered that his so-called official business was a lie to cover up his gambling and drinking in the taverns and gaming dens of low-life London.

Yes. Lionel had been a pleasure-seeking wastrel, just like Raphael Lefevre—and she had been drawn to the handsome young officer like a moth to a candle flame. Once reality set in, she'd been too deeply ashamed to admit her mistake to anyone. Outwardly she maintained that theirs was a happy marriage, but her love for him was dead. Her brother had always disliked Lionel, had even tried to forbid the marriage, but Serena had pleaded with him. 'George, I shall never, ever be happy with anyone except him, I swear!'

Soon enough she'd realised George wasn't mistaken at all. But then Lionel's regiment was called to the war in India, where two years ago he was killed in battle. He'd died a hero's death, she was assured. Amid outpourings of sympathy, she moved back to the family home in Yorkshire for the usual period of mourning. Everyone assumed she was stricken with grief, but Serena was using that time of isolation to prepare herself.

Strengthen herself. She'd resolved that her youthful errors were behind her now and she'd vowed to never willingly surrender her freedom again.

But Lionel's past still haunted her. Indeed, it was because of Lionel that she'd been forced to meet Silas Mort tonight.

It was only a week ago that she'd been out walking in the park with Martha when a shabbily dressed man with a scarred face had limped up. 'Money for an old soldier, lady?' he'd whined. Martha would have shooed him off. But the man drew closer and whispered, 'I've things to tell you about your husband, Lady Serena. You'd be wise to listen.'

So, already gripped by a premonition of dread, Serena had waved Martha away—and she had listened.

The man's name was Silas Mort and he'd been a soldier in India two years ago, he told her, under her husband's command. 'People say he died a hero when we fought against the Sultan of Mysore and his men,' Mort went on. 'But I tell you, my lady, as soon as the Sultan's men opened fire on our lads, your husband panicked and ran for his life. There was lots of smoke from the guns and cannon and he made the mistake of running towards a bunch of the Sultan's men who were waiting to attack our flank. They killed him, of course. Afterwards, the word got round that he was bravely attacking them. Like hell he was. He was running for his life—thanks to the smoke, his officer friends didn't notice, but the lads and I saw it all. After that, my knee was smashed by a bullet and I finally got home to London with no money and a near-useless leg. But I'd fought for my country, see? And when I heard that Willoughby had been hailed as a hero for running like a rat from the enemy, well, I said to myself, "That's not right, is it?"'

So even Lionel's death was a lie. The scarred soldier's tale rang all too true—she'd always suspected that her husband was the last person on earth to act so bravely. He'd died a coward, but Serena had reeled at the thought of the world knowing it all.

Proud, Lefevre had murmured. *You, Lady Serena, are far too proud.* Yes. She was. And that was why, when Silas Mort demanded money to keep quiet, Serena had agreed to meet him tonight in one of the liveliest, bawdiest haunts of the city.

She'd trained herself to live an independent and full life and her friends always murmured, *So brave! So sensible!* But she'd been neither this evening when she'd stood there on that dismal street with shadowy figures lurking on every side, no, indeed—her heart had thundered and her throat had gone dry.

Only then she'd felt safe because Raphael Lefevre had appeared. He'd silenced Mort by warning him that Serena was his—in other words, she'd been claimed by the man she despised most in all of London.

The lady and I have an appointment, he'd said, in that elegant, slightly accented voice of his. She'd wanted to shrink into the ground. Though what occurred next was even more appalling, because when he wrapped his arm round her and drew her close to his strong, hard body, something had happened to her, something wild and wanton and terrifying in its unexpectedness. With his kiss, it was as though all her carefully built defences had been demolished in one lightning assault.

Her body had betrayed her in a few moments of stupid, shameful weakness. She couldn't deny she'd felt a throb of physical desire that had frightened her almost more than Silas Mort and his threats. Had the detestable Marquis realised her vulnerability? Had he guessed? It was rather likely, to judge by that all too knowing smile as he'd gazed down into her eyes.

Whatever spell he'd cast over her tonight, he was an expert. No wonder women threw themselves at him. But she wasn't that sort of woman! She knew better—or did she? Oh, my. She sat by her fireside, but it wasn't the flames that brought a simmering heat to her body. No, it was the thought of Raphael Lefevre holding her in his arms. The thought of his mouth wickedly—*knowingly*—caressing hers. He'd offered his help, but dear Lord, he was quite possibly the most dangerous man in creation for her. He'd guessed she was being blackmailed, but he must never know why, or it would give him a weapon with which to make her life unbearable.

Abruptly she put down her book and walked across the bedroom to her gilded mirror, intending to brush out her long fair hair in a sequence of strokes that usually soothed her. Yet tonight even her familiar image in the mirror shook her, because somehow she looked different. Her blue-green eyes seemed almost haunted. Her lips were surely fuller, as if they were reliving that rogue's kiss. And on smoothing down her satin night robe, she realised her skin was acutely sensitised, her small breasts warm and somehow heavy. Never, ever had she been so aware of her body's vulnerability.

Lefevre had insisted he would call on her tomorrow, therefore she would make very sure she was out. Problem solved—and as for that kiss, no true gentleman would betray her by talking about it! Surely even he knew that! But what if— as Lefevre had suggested—she'd been recognised by one of his friends?

She climbed into her four-poster bed and thumped her pillow, struggling to get comfortable. Oh, Lord, the news of their kiss would take London by storm.

Lefevre had been causing something of a stir ever since his arrival here last year, thanks to his title and his wealth; for unlike many of his fellow compatriots who'd fled the chaos that followed the Revolution, he'd somehow managed to bring a large part of his fortune with him. His popularity was not lessened by his striking appearance and caustic wit, all of which meant he'd been quickly taken up by the fashionable set. Indeed, Monsieur le Marquis was generally in such demand that when he'd asked Serena to dance at a party five months ago, she'd been surprised.

She was rather more surprised to find him polite. Pleasant, even. 'I've heard you lost your husband during the fighting in India,' he'd said. 'He gave his all for his country, I'm told. You have my sympathies, *madame*.'

She found his slightly husky French accent beguiling and his presence curiously disturbing. But then, at the end of the dance, one of his drunken cronies had staggered up and clapped him on the shoulder. 'Damn it, Lefevre, you've won your bet! You managed a whole dance with the woman we call "the iceberg". I owe you ten guineas, you scoundrel!'

A wager. The hateful Marquis had asked her to dance for a ten-guinea wager.

She'd lost sleep over that. And now, as she lay in her luxurious bed, once again the longed-for oblivion refused to come to her rescue; the candles were extinguished, the coals in the hearth gave out only a faint glow, but still she was awake, listening to the rain pattering against the window panes and the occasional rattle of a carriage going by.

Why, when every sensible urge in her brain told her to avoid Lefevre as if he were the devil incarnate, did his embrace tonight linger in her thoughts and her body like some fiendish spell he'd laid on her?

She turned restlessly in her bed, fighting to resist the memory of his firm lips plundering her mouth. To banish the recollection of his wicked hands holding her close. Her blood ran hot, then cold again when she realised that if that kiss became public knowledge, she would be a complete and utter laughing stock. Beaumaris, Finlay, Hawkesworth—those three men who'd seen them tonight were Lefevre's friends, but they certainly weren't hers.

She rose abruptly from her bed and walked rather shakily to the window, pushing the curtains aside a little. Pressing her forehead against the cold glass, she gazed out, feeling as if her very heart was chilled. All her friends thought she was in charge. In control. But maybe this evening she'd met her match in Raphael Lefevre.

She couldn't rid herself of the memory of the way he'd pulled her against him with such strength, yet such surprising gentleness. And his voice, for once, hadn't been mocking, but had been protective: caring even, in a way that had curled like liquid honey inside her, somehow melting the aching loneliness deep in her heart...

Dear God. How could she have been such a fool?

She looked up at the night sky, where between the drifting clouds the full moon hung high above the chimney stacks. At least, she reminded herself, Lefevre couldn't possibly know the reason for Mort's threats. He couldn't know that her husband had died a coward's death. Tonight the mocking Marquis had seized an opportunity to humiliate her, that was all—and his offer of protection had to be a joke. Silas Mort would stay away from her anyway, for not only had he received his money, but he'd been reminded that she had powerful acquaintances. Yes, she had to put the incident behind her.

It was then that a slight movement in the street below caught her eye.

A stray dog, maybe? For a moment all was still again. But then a shadow moved on the opposite side of the road and she realised a man was standing there, gazing up at her window.

A gasp of horror almost choked her. Black hat, black coat, scarred face… It was Silas Mort. She jumped away, heart hammering, but it was too late; he knew she'd seen him, because he'd tipped his hat with an evil leer, as if to say, *I'm not done with you yet, my lady.*

Chapter Four

$\sim\!\!\sim\!\!\sim\!\!\sim$

At around half past ten the same night Raphael Lefevre arrived at his Piccadilly club to find the popular haunt of the rich as crowded as usual at this hour of the evening. Beneath the glittering candelabras, older men sat in leather armchairs while liveried footmen hovered close by with drinks. Through a gilded archway, a score or more of gamesters crowded round the green baize tables and studied their cards with feigned nonchalance. Young bucks dressed in the height of fashion stood in groups discussing the latest scandal to engulf one or other of the King's wayward offspring, or the merits of the newest opera singer to catch the *ton's* fancy. The heat, the chattering voices, the scent of hair powder and pomade all engulfed Raphael as he entered. And paused.

Because he'd already heard his own name among the babble of male voices.

'So here he is, our Marquis.' One man was nudging to another. 'Up to his tricks as usual. Have you heard? I got the news an hour ago from Giles Beaumaris—bumped into him on my way here. This time Lefevre's been caught in a rather compromising situation with Lady Serena Willoughby, of all people.'

There were gasps. 'No. Lady Serena? Beaumaris must have been lying!'

'He's not,' the man answered with satisfaction. 'He said Finlay and Hawkesworth saw it, too—and he swore blind the Marquis was kissing the lady! Now, we all know Lady Serena has a sharp tongue; but, my friends, perhaps Lefevre can teach her to put that tongue to better use!'

His voice faded as he spotted Lefevre looking straight at him.

'Good evening, gentlemen.' Raphael gave the man and his companions a brief nod. 'How fascinating that my supposed exploits are offering you entertainment yet again.'

The man was already backing away. 'I'm sure no offence was meant, Monsieur le Marquis,' he stuttered.

'I suppose you're afraid I'll challenge you,' Raphael said casually. 'Pistols at dawn, maybe.' The man paled and Raphael laughed. '*Monsieur*, you may breathe easy. Believe me, you're not worth the trouble.' And, without a second glance at all the others warily watching him, Raphael strolled past them towards the billiards room.

So Giles Beaumaris had indeed recognised Lady Serena. Raphael had suspected he would, since he'd developed a *tendre* for her until she'd replied quite cuttingly to his advances. Trust Beaumaris, the wounded suitor, to spread the news. Lady Serena would be upset, to put it mildly. Well, well.

In the billiards room, only one person awaited him—Sir Dominic Southern, with whom he'd arranged a game. But Raphael was late and Dominic, who was one of his more respectable friends, was watching him with a mixture of concern and irritation as Raphael nodded a casual greeting and picked up his cue.

'I don't know,' Dominic said finally, 'whether to applaud you or to weep for you, Raphael. You do realise that the entire club is bursting with the news of your encounter tonight with Lady Serena? In Covent Garden, of all places! Well, man? What have you got to say for yourself?'

Both men were the same age, but Dominic was as blond as Raphael was dark. Dominic's clothes—brown coat and knee breeches—bore the slightly faded, almost rustic look of a decade ago, whereas Raphael set the fashions for the *ton*.

Many described Dominic as the perfect English gentleman—and since Raphael was considered by quite a few to be the perfect French scoundrel, it often occurred to him that he and Dominic made an odd pair.

Raphael started chalking his cue carefully. 'Perhaps,' he said, 'I've decided to make it my life's occupation to entertain the gossips.' He studied the table, gauging the lie of the balls. 'And aren't I making a success of it?'

'So what Beaumaris said is true, then?' Dominic shook his head in exasperation. 'Tonight, Raphael, I feel you've gone a bit far. I happen to rather like Lady Serena.'

'Do you?' Raphael raised an eyebrow. 'There are some who are of the opinion that the woman's a shrew. But if you want to know all of it, she'd got herself into difficulty with a gang of louts and I told them to leave her alone.' He sent an ivory ball rolling across the baize, then looked up. 'I know you're a Member of Parliament and you feel you have a public duty to uphold the law, so wouldn't you have done exactly the same?'

Dominic gave an exasperated sigh. 'But you embraced her, man! You were actually seen kissing her! What's going on? Don't say you're halfway to seducing her! My God, if I were a gambler, I'd say your chances were nil!'

Raphael straightened and blew chalk dust from the tip of his cue. 'You do gamble occasionally, *mon ami*. And you nearly always lose, so, going by that logic, I'd say my chances of seducing the lady are actually quite good. That is,' he added thoughtfully, 'if I wanted to.' He gestured towards the table. 'It's your turn.'

Dominic didn't move. 'Good Lord, Raphael, you know I'm forever defending you. But Lady Serena has powerful friends, as well as wealth. She also has a highly respected older brother who happens to be an earl, so be very careful. That's all I can say.'

'In that case, can we proceed with the game? As I said, it's your turn.'

Dominic surveyed the table gloomily. 'You've left me in a difficult spot.'

'Look there.' Raphael pointed. 'You could always try a cannon off the cushion.'

Dominic tried, but failed miserably. Raphael took over and they played on in silence for a while.

The two had met at Eton, where Raphael had been sent by his father. 'It was to get me out of the way,' Raphael always sardonically explained. 'My older brother, Guy, was the dutiful heir. I was trouble.' Dominic had been Raphael's reluctant accomplice in many a scrape at school and after that at Oxford, but it was true that loyalty was

Dominic's overriding virtue. When the Marquis died eight years ago, Raphael's older brother inherited the title and the estates in southern France, while Raphael chose to become an officer in the French army. He kept in touch with Dominic by letter and Dominic even came to visit the family estate one summer when Raphael was home on leave. But after that, Raphael's letters ceased.

'No point,' he'd explained to his old friend at their reunion in London last year. 'I was abroad with the army most of the time. And then came the Revolution—so do you really think anyone had time to write letters? Or that there was any chance of them getting through?'

Nevertheless, when Raphael arrived in England Dominic had been one of the first to greet him, delighted that his old comrade was alive and well. Dominic also knew better than to ask Raphael about the bloodshed he must have seen, or the friends he must have lost.

By then Raphael had inherited the title, because his brother had died—murdered, he told Dominic briefly, by a Revolutionary mob. But Raphael spoke rarely about the past and he knew Dominic was disappointed by the way he'd so rapidly immersed himself in the pleasures of London, finding himself a fine mansion in Grosvenor Square and becoming a member of all the best clubs.

Quite a few people complained that while France was drowning in the blood of its people, the Marquis of Montpellier seemed miraculously consoled by the delights of upper-class English society. But most of the *ton* enjoyed his sense of fashion and his dry wit, which was aimed especially at the earnest folk who took life too seriously. His forays into the London underworlds of cockfighting, gambling and the demi-monde in general were dismissed merely as evidence of his Continental heritage. Certainly they did little to diminish his popularity either with London's young blades or with the fairer sex.

But what about Lady Serena Willoughby?

She had always appeared impervious—indeed, hostile—to Raphael's charm and, lately, her enmity had started to become a problem. Tonight, Raphael had most definitely gained the upper hand. Though did he feel a sense of satisfaction? *Dieu*, he ought to! But instead he kept seeing her face, her delicate, vulnerable face as she shivered in his arms. And the expression in her rather lovely blue-green eyes as he leaned in to kiss her...

Dominic said, frowning, 'Your turn again, Raphael—didn't you hear me?'

'Of course. My apologies.'

The trouble was, Raphael had never really been able to put Lady Serena out of his mind since their very first meeting last November. Which had been, quite simply, a disaster. He'd already heard all about her, of course; knew that she and her three close friends had been labelled 'the Wicked Widows' by some wag who'd fallen on the wrong side of that wealthy and aristocratic quartet. All four had lost their husbands at a relatively young age; all four were targets for suitors, fortune hunters especially, but the women were united in their declaration that they had no need whatsoever of new husbands.

Raphael had expected the four of them to be a bunch of harridans. But when he first actually spoke to Lady Serena at that ball last November, she'd taken him by surprise.

He had no difficulty even now picturing the diaphanous peach gown she'd worn, which was high-necked but close-fitting and sewn with sequins and seed pearls. Her arms had been sheathed in long cream gloves that ended high above the elbow, leaving a tantalising few inches of bare flesh that made his mind rove instantly into dangerous territory—*lovely arms.* Which meant, in his experience, that her legs would be long and slender, too, and would start to become deliciously curvaceous in the forbidden realm above her gartered stockings…

He remembered how he'd clamped down hard

on his illicit imaginings, fully intending to move on; but then fate took a hand. Disastrously. Because just at that moment he'd heard the comments of some spiteful matrons from nearby. *Such a scandalous gown,* they were saying. *Why, you can almost see through it. Women like her are a menace. They either steal the attention that should be paid to our daughters, or they are out to lure our husbands into mischief.*

And Serena had heard them also. He knew it by the sudden set of her slender shoulders, the defiant tilt of her chin. It was then that he'd approached her.

'What a set of old dragons,' he'd said cheerfully to her. 'And I think your gown is rather marvellous, actually. My name is Raphael Lefevre. I know it's somewhat unconventional of me to announce myself like this when we've not been formally introduced, but I hope you'll do me the honour of dancing with me, Lady Serena?'

When he'd taken her hand and led her into the dance, he'd felt he was in contact with something very unusual, almost precious. A lady of independence and integrity, not to mention beauty. It was her eyes that had struck him first, those blue-green eyes that were translucent like the sea, so thick-lashed and expressive; then his gaze had flown unbidden to her lush pink mouth. And gradually he'd realised that, quite contrary to his expectations, she was shy, even vulnerable.

'I will not be cowed by them,' she'd told him. 'I will not.'

'Bravo,' he'd answered with a smile.

He knew she'd been married to a high-ranking army officer who'd died a hero in battle. He'd also heard that after the set period of mourning, Lady Serena had made it plain she had no wish to marry again. Was her heart broken? So people maintained; indeed, during that dance Raphael thought he sensed some undefined emotion she was trying, he guessed, to hide with her witty talk. He'd been glad to make her smile a little with his droll comments about the assembled company and he'd felt a kind of connection between them that made him want to linger when the dance ended.

But the encounter turned to disaster all too swiftly. Thanks to that comment about a wager, she'd condemned him out of hand and their mutual enmity became a public entertainment.

'Men like Raphael Lefevre,' she'd said soon afterwards at a fashionable party, 'with their gambling, their drinking and their habit of treating women as playthings make one realise why there was a revolution in France.'

Raphael, who'd been passing by at the time, had gracefully bowed in her direction. 'I treat women as playthings sometimes, *madame*,' he'd agreed politely. 'But only if the ladies in question ask me nicely.'

There had been gasps of shock, together with not a few chuckles. Raphael had strolled on past them all, aware that his retort would quickly spread around town; indeed, the very next afternoon while riding in Hyde Park he had encountered no less a personage than the Prince of Wales, who'd beckoned Raphael over to his carriage with a merry grin. 'Heard about your quip last night, Lefevre, you devilish fellow! *Only if they ask me nicely.* Oh, dear me! My friend, you are priceless—France has lost an impeccable wit! And do tell me—' the Prince pointed a finger at Raphael's chest '—where did you get that elegant waistcoat?'

Yes, Lady Serena's initial attacks on him had done Raphael no harm at all. But recently she'd gone one step too far and begun to ask questions about his former life. She also had one or two suitors whom he suspected could prove equally problematic if they, too, joined in her enmity against him and a line had been crossed. The time had come to take more decisive action—and tonight had offered him his chance.

The game of billiards didn't last long, since Raphael was very much on form. Afterwards he and

Dominic joined more of their friends in the card room, but Dominic was rather quiet. Doubtless he was disappointed, not for the first time, by his friend's behaviour. Shortly afterwards, Dominic left, but Raphael stayed on to play several hands at piquet while lightly fending off further questions about his encounter with Lady Serena—until a young viscount, rather drunk, blurted out, 'Does this mean we'll hear no more of the rumours that you'd really prefer a French girl to warm your bed, Lefèvre?'

There were several indrawn breaths, but Raphael merely smiled. '*Quel absurdité.* What nonsense.' He splayed his cards out on the table. 'I have the trick, I believe. Would you care to deal, Monsieur le Vicomte?'

Once the game was over he downed the last of his brandy, gathered up his winnings and announced it was time for him to leave. Some demurred, asking him to stay, but others said nothing, though they were watching him closely. No doubt several of them thought he'd gone too far tonight, toying with a lady like Serena Willoughby. But unlike Dominic, they were careful to keep it quiet.

He went outside. It was late, but instead of heading homewards he turned in the direction of Leicester Fields, where several of the taverns were still open. And in one of them, he found his manservant, Jacques.

Raphael sat down next to him. 'Well? Did you manage to track down Silas Mort?'

Jacques wiped some beer froth from his lips and answered gruffly, 'I did. He and a couple of his friends have rooms in a lodging house near here and I followed them to a drinking hole they're fond of. One of them was drunk and I got him even drunker. He blabbed about how Mort is blackmailing a grand lady. And it's exactly as you guessed, my lord.'

Raphael nodded. *'Bien,'* he said softly. 'Very good, Jacques. And what about the other fellow I asked you to investigate? Mr Jeremy Wolverton?'

'Wolverton is a church-going businessman who's made a fortune in importing expensive fabrics. And he happens to be one of Lady Serena Willoughby's most ardent admirers.'

Jacques was a Breton, not tall, but wiry and strong. He'd been known to say he would die for his master, but he wasn't afraid to speak his mind to him. And he spoke his mind now as he went on, 'You took a risk, my lord, tangling with that woman tonight. You need to silence her, not seduce her.'

Raphael took a long drink of the ale the landlord had brought over and contemplated his manservant in silence for a moment. He answered softly at last,

'But what if the two coincide, *mon ami*? What if seduction is the only way to silence her?'

Jacques gave a sigh. 'A lady as virtuous and as privileged as her? You're on dangerous ground, my lord. Don't say I didn't warn you!'

Raphael regarded him steadily. 'Any further news of our other search? Our main purpose here in London?'

'No, my lord. I keep asking—carefully, like you said—but there's no news at all. And now I'd guess even you would agree it's time to retire for the night. Shall I find you a hackney cab?'

Raphael examined his pocket watch. 'No. It's not raining so I'd rather walk.' *And clear my head,* he added to himself. In fact, it would take them a mere twenty minutes to reach the mansion that Raphael rented in Grosvenor Square, where Jacques, at his own insistence, slept in an attic room above the stables. 'I prefer to keep an eye on those valuable nags of yours myself, my lord,' he'd once said. 'I don't trust these English grooms one bit.'

Raphael didn't trust them either. Didn't trust anyone, come to think of it, except Jacques and his old friend Dominic.

As if sensing his master's mood, Jacques spoke not a word all the way home and in the silence

Raphael was aware that above them the moon shone bravely from between the rain clouds to miraculously paint the damp rooftops and pavements with gleaming silver. But his mind was filled with darkness. *I thought even you couldn't stoop so low*, Lady Serena had told him.

'Your opinion of me,' he'd replied smoothly, 'never ceases to entertain me.'

How much further could he fall in Lady Serena's eyes? Tomorrow she would realise that she'd been recognised in his arms tonight by people who knew them both. People who mattered.

Thanks to Jacques, who'd been on her trail for weeks, he'd known about Silas Mort accosting her in the Park the other day. He'd learned the details of her planned assignation with Mort, again thanks to Jacques. He'd arranged to be in the vicinity of the piazza himself, watching from the shadows, and—now this was the riskiest part of the plan—he'd suggested to his three regular companions in revelry, Beaumaris, Finlay and Hawkesworth, that they all meet up there a little after nine, to see what entertainment was on offer.

Serena had been a few minutes late. That had worried him at first, but fortunately his friends had been late, too. He'd taken her in his arms the minute he saw them approaching in the distance. And he'd offered them entertainment indeed—for they'd witnessed one of the haughtiest ladies of the *ton* in Lefevre's embrace and the news was spreading like wildfire.

He wondered what her reaction would be, were she to find out that this was exactly—*exactly* what he'd planned.

Chapter Five

The next day—two p.m.

There was no hiding it.

Serena realised from the minute she entered the room that her friends must have heard every detail of last night's excruciating encounter with Raphael Lefevre. Poor Beth looked decidedly shocked. Lady Joanna's eyebrows were raised, as if to ask, *My dear Serena. Whatever have you been up to this time?* Even Mary, who claimed to despise gossip, was sitting on the edge of her chair, tense with expectation.

They met like this regularly at one another's homes and this time it was Lady Joanna's turn to host at her house in Brook Street. Normally the greetings they exchanged were relaxed; it was never long before the wine started to flow as well as the conversation and, in this particular draw-

ing room, Serena loved to feast her eyes on all
the exotic mementoes that Joanna's husband, a
wealthy East India merchant, had brought home
from his travels. Twenty years older than Joanna,
he'd died three years ago, but the large room was
still a vivid reminder of his journeying, scattered
as it was with Hindu statuettes, Oriental porcelain
and silk tapestries.

Though clearly, all these treasures were as
nothing compared to the novelty of having someone in their midst who had been kissed by the notorious Raphael Lefevre.

It was Joanna who was the first to speak. 'Well,
Serena darling!' Joanna was the granddaughter
of a duke and pronounced her words with aristocratic relish. 'What an absolute scandal broth
this is, to be sure. Now tell us, do—how exactly
did you come to be in the company of the rather
delicious Marquis?'

Serena tried to wave one hand airily. 'Goodness me. You know how the gossips exaggerate!'

Beth's eyes were round. 'But, Serena—did you
truly let that dreadful man actually kiss you?'

Oh, Lord. Serena's heart fluttered in panic now.
And what a kiss... She was saved temporarily,
because it was at that very moment that a pro-
cession of footmen entered, bearing platters of

tiny salmon sandwiches, asparagus tartlets and chocolate eclairs.

Serena ate very little. She knew she was safe while the footmen were here serving the refreshments, thus ensuring the rest of the conversation could only be small talk, but soon enough they'd be gone and then three pairs of inquisitive eyes would turn on her once more. How on earth could she explain last night's horrendous events without betraying the story of her blackmailer, Silas Mort?

These women were her dearest friends. All wealthy and well born, the four of them had always moved in the same social circles and Mary had drawn them even closer by asking if they would help her with a charity school she'd established in Spitalfields, one of the poorest areas of east London.

'How can we best help these deprived children?' she'd said to Serena. 'By making sure they get an education, that's how. Education is the key to everything!'

Possessed of a dry sense of humour along with considerable wealth after her businessman husband's death, Mary was a natural leader who was determined to put her brains and her money to good use. Serena, though her own husband was still alive then, had embraced the cause wholeheartedly. *At least,* she'd thought, *I can put some of my time to good use.* Then Beth had joined them and finally Lady Joanna. 'We need to educate these girls so they can work out what lies men are going to spin them,' Joanna had declared in her forthright way.

But then Lionel Willoughby was sent to the war in India, where he died. Serena often thought it was the loss of their husbands that had formed the real bond between the four friends, especially as many married women shunned their company.

'As if I would be interested in any of their dreary menfolk!' Joanna had once exclaimed with a peal of laughter. 'But I could definitely be tempted by a rake. Yes—by a handsome, daredevil rogue. I am determined not to give up on my life just because my husband's in his grave!'

Beth had been slightly shocked. She'd loved her husband dearly—he'd been a kind-hearted Hampshire landowner and she'd been devastated when he'd died of a fever two years ago. 'Joanna,' she'd protested. 'You can't mean it, surely? A *rake*?'

'Oh, but I do mean it.' Joanna had plied her fan. 'Just give me a chance. Take the Marquis of Montpellier, for instance. I'd dance with him any day and more.'

They'd all gone a little silent then because Monsieur Lefevre, though he'd only recently arrived in the country, had rather taken society by

storm. And even Serena, who hadn't yet had her
fatal dance with him, had to admit to a certain
interest in the man. Yes, that was the word. Interest. That was all.

Soon the four of them were firm allies who enjoyed meeting every week with refreshments of
wine and cake. They always paid close attention
to Mary's reports about the Spitalfields school's
progress, but there was also time to discuss society news: the marriages, the courtships and, of
course, the latest scandals.

Mary, with her sometimes acid wit, had once
offended a ridiculous dandy who belonged to the
Prince's set and the dandy had promptly chris-
tened the four of them the 'Wicked Widows', a
name that spread around town. 'But we're not
wicked at all!' Beth had exclaimed.

Joanna, on the contrary, had found it amusing,
as did Mary, who'd said to them all, 'My dears, I
take it as a great compliment that a fool like him
sees us as a threat!'

In fact, many people admired their spirit and,
if anything, their invitations to society events increased. But now Serena had shocked herself and
her friends with that kiss and she had to think of
some way to explain it. She sipped the last of her
delicately scented tea and drew a deep breath.
The final eclair had disappeared, the footmen

were leaving the room and she felt her remaining shreds of courage departing with them. Three pairs of eyes turned on her.

'Well?' said Joanna.

Serena's attempts to explain were, in retrospect, quite feeble. Indeed, how could they be anything else? She couldn't give the reason why she'd been in Covent Garden last night, all alone. And she could not deny that Raphael Lefevre had taken her in his arms and kissed her. Had she fought him off? On the contrary.

Beth still looked utterly bewildered. 'But what a terrible thing that he should take advantage of you when you were alone and unprotected, Serena! And, Joanna, how can you find it amusing?'

'Beth, darling,' chided Joanna, 'you're a lovely person, but sometimes you're so naive. It occurs to me that our Serena may have had a secret assignation with Monsieur le Marquis. After all, we're the Wicked Widows. Can't we live up to our name just once in a while?'

Beth flushed, touching the silver locket she wore that contained a miniature portrait of her husband. 'I'm sure we're not wicked in any way at all. And I, for one, don't wish to be!'

Mary put in calmly, 'Nor do any of us.' She turned to Serena. 'My dear, you really must report Lefevre to the authorities. If the man believes he can insult a lady in public, you must make an example of him, for all our sakes.'

Joanna had been watching Serena curiously. 'Come now, Serena,' she chided. 'We've observed for weeks how you and the rather dashing Marquis have been sniping at one another. Could it be that for some reason you've decided to kiss and make up?'

What could Serena say? She could tell them the truth—well, at least a portion of it. 'I'd rather unwisely gone out on my own,' she said.

'To Covent Garden, at night?' Mary sounded sceptical. 'Surely your coachman didn't agree to drive you there?'

'I took a hackney cab,' said Serena. 'I didn't intend to—well, I wasn't really thinking where I was going.' Oh, dear. All this sounded dreadfully lame. 'I dismissed the cab and walked a little, but some rough men challenged me near the piazza. And Monsieur Lefevre happened to be passing by.'

Mary pursed her lips. 'And what was the Marquis doing in Covent Garden?'

What did gentlemen usually do in that area? Visit the taverns and gaming dens. Consort with the ladies of the night. *Oh, dear.* She said, 'I didn't ask him why he was there, Mary.'

'But Monsieur Lefevre arrived just in time

to rescue you from these ruffians?' asked Beth rather breathlessly.

'Yes. He did. And he apologised afterwards for his—his somewhat forward behaviour.'

'The kiss, you mean?' Her friends' eyes were widening, but Serena struggled on.

'Yes. The kiss. Monsieur Lefevre pointed out, you see, that he needed to make it absolutely obvious I was under his protection. Otherwise, those men would never have believed him.'

Silence reigned and Serena's heart sank still further, especially when Mary said a little crisply, 'Such a shame you had to let that man humiliate you so.'

But Beth came to her rescue. 'Mary,' she protested, 'it doesn't sound as if poor Serena actually had much choice! She was in mortal danger. Whatever else could she have done? And I've never heard any tales claiming the Marquis mistreats women. Indeed, he's very popular with them, isn't he?'

'Popular? I should think so!' Joanna's eyes suddenly sparkled. 'Why, I heard from a lady who knew him in Paris that when he makes love to you, he uses his—'

'Joanna!' Beth had looked scandalised and Joanna sighed.

'Darling Beth, don't be so strait-laced. We've

all been married so we know the reality. I'm sure we've all suffered a husband's drunken fumbling, so aren't we allowed just a few delicious fantasies about the Marquis?'

Mary frowned her disapproval. As for Serena, she just sat there because she knew this was only the start of it. She would have to face these insinuations from all corners of society now, from her enemies as well as her friends. And always at the back of her mind, she would hear Lefevre's ominous final warning: *Blackmailers always want more.*

The thought terrified her. But who could she turn to for help? To her brother George? Even if he could track down Silas Mort, he would do it in such a righteous, heavy-handed way that there might well be a formal prosecution and a court case. The newspapers would leap on the story and the full reason for her meeting with Mort would be salaciously exposed.

'Dead War Hero Actually A Coward', the headlines would run. Yes, Silas Mort would be punished—but it was Serena who would have to live with the shame of it, for ever.

Last night Raphael Lefevre had suggested he could keep her blackmailer at bay and she'd done nothing but think about his ominous offer half the night and all this morning. Yet to rely on him for help was inconceivable. What exactly would he do to silence Mort? And what price would she, Serena, have to pay?

It was impossible for her to accept his offer. Impossible!

She realised Mary was talking once more. 'Serena, you really must show the Marquis that you're in charge. But you'll have to decide quickly on your plan of action, because I'm afraid other people are going to be questioning you about this. The story of last night's incident will be all around the town by now.'

As if Serena didn't realise that. 'Surely people will just as quickly forget,' she said as lightly as possible. 'After all, there's always some new scandal coming along.' *Though not as good as this,* she told herself with a sinking heart. *Oh, no. Not nearly as good as this one.*

'But, Serena,' Beth pointed out, 'since Monsieur Lefevre rescued you from dreadful danger, surely you will have to be nice to him from now on?'

'I don't think,' she began, 'that I could ever bring myself to actually be nice to him—'

'I could,' murmured Joanna. 'Oh, indeed I could.'

Serena endeavoured to ignore her. 'Although last night, naturally, I had to admit I was grateful to him—'

'For the rescue?' broke in Joanna archly, wag-

ging one finger. 'Or for the now famous kiss? Just
tell us, darling. What was it like to be in the arms
of Raphael Lefevre? Did you simply melt with
longing? Because I'm sure I would!'

Mary turned on Joanna. 'Really! This is no
time for levity!' Beth, too, was shaking her head
in disapproval. As for Serena, she reached for her
glass of wine, because her throat had gone suddenly dry.

How had it felt, to be kissed by the notorious
Marquis?

It had felt like heaven, something deep and
shocking inside her replied. Yes, the answer
was…heaven. She stamped the treacherous inner
voice down and looked round at them all with
something like desperation. 'Listen. Last night
was an entirely unpleasant experience which I
really don't wish to talk about any further. So
please may we turn to the subject of the school?'

At which they all took pity on her, even Mary,
who said, 'Of course.' She reached for her spectacles. 'And, Serena, we ask these questions only
because we're concerned about you. It must have
been an absolutely shocking experience!'

Beth was nodding earnestly. 'Serena, we all
love you. Whatever life throws at you—and last
night was surely one of your worst ever ordeals—
you always set us such a strong example!' She

rose to hug Serena, then the other two came over to embrace her as well.

'So now,' Mary continued, returning to her chair and rustling her papers purposefully, 'on with our business. I'm still endeavouring to renew the school's lease, which expires in three months. But unfortunately the landowner, Lord Gardner, is proving a little difficult.'

Joanna spoke up. 'Is it a question of money? If so, I'm sure I can help.'

'Money isn't the issue, Joanna. No, I'm afraid it's pure arrogance on Lord Gardner's part. He's been heard publicly saying he doesn't see the point of educating the lower classes—and he isn't alone.' Mary looked round at them all. 'We need people of influence to speak up for our cause. Mr Jeremy Wolverton has recently spoken to Lord Gardner on our behalf, but with no success, I'm afraid.'

Serena and Joanna exchanged glances. 'Your fervent admirer,' Joanna whispered.

Serena shook her head hastily. She knew that the rich Jeremy Wolverton donated regularly to their cause and his success as a businessman gave him considerable influence, but his tendency to sermonise on the value of hard work was tedious.

'Poor Wolverton. He's smitten with you,' Joanna had recently warned her. 'There'll be a proposal some day soon.'

Serena had laughed. 'At least I'll have no problem in declining. He is so very...*worthy.*'

Once again Mary was summoning their attention. 'So, ladies, we need as much public support as we can get. And, on a much happier note, you'll be pleased to hear that the new teacher I appointed, Miss Murphy, has settled into her duties very well.'

'The French children,' Beth burst in. 'How are those poor French children, the ones whose families have only just arrived in the area?'

'You mean the refugees? Poor things. There are seven children so far and fortunately Miss Murphy speaks some French so she's making every effort to help them feel at home. Now—' and Mary adjusted her spectacles '—let us proceed with the monthly accounts...'

To Serena's relief, Lefevre appeared to have been forgotten—but not by her, because the clock on the mantel told her it was well past four o'clock. The hour at which Lefevre said he would call at her house. And so? she told herself defiantly. He would find her gone. He'd be angry, but her absence would speak for itself. He had to learn that she was not his to be manipulated. She was just beginning to breathe a little more easily when a footman entered with a note on a silver salver.

'A foreign personage called at the front door just now, ma'am,' he announced to Joanna. 'A man dressed like a lackey. I told him that if he was a tradesman he should have used the side door. But he insisted he had a message to be delivered.'

Joanna held out her hand. 'For me, I assume?'

'No, ma'am. He requested that this missive be delivered to Lady Serena.'

Joanna frowned. 'This sounds most odd. Let me see this letter. It could be a trick—'

But Serena had registered one word—foreign. 'No,' she broke in. 'No, Joanna. I will read it.' As the footman handed it to her, Serena took one look at the bold masculine handwriting declaring her name and she knew. Swiftly she opened and read it.

You no doubt remember I promised to call on you this afternoon at four. Your servants told me where you could be found and at this precise moment I'm waiting in my carriage a little way down the road. You will oblige me by joining me.

It was from Lefevre, of course. His faithful manservant, whom everyone knew as Jacques the Breton, had delivered it. A fresh flood of panic almost made her feel sick. If she didn't obey, the Marquis might well come here directly and shame her in front of her friends. What on earth was she to do?

Rather stupidly, she decided to lie.

'I'm afraid I must take my leave,' she announced. She tried to laugh. 'So foolish of me!

You see, I almost forgot that I have an appointment with my costumier. She sent her messenger to my house and the servants directed him here.'

'Of course,' they chorused, her kind, lovely friends, as she headed for the door. 'But we'll see you on Thursday night at the Duke of Hamilton's ball, won't we, Serena?'

She stopped in her tracks. *No.* Lefevre would be going. His friends, Beaumaris and the others, would be going… 'Oh, didn't I tell you? Unfortunately, I have other plans for that evening!'

She barely had time to register her friends' astonished faces before she was hurrying down the stairs to the hall, where a footman waited with her pelisse and bonnet. Telling lies to her dearest companions. Whatever next? Raphael Lefevre's voice from last night curled through her veins, rich and husky. *I still believe you might need my help. One way or another.*

She'd resolutely refused. 'Never,' she'd declared. But last night Silas Mort had been outside her house, watching. Gloating.

Lefevre and Mort—my God, she was truly caught between the devil and the deep blue sea this time. She took a deep breath and braced herself to face the man who was quite possibly the more dangerous of the two.

Chapter Six

Lefevre was standing beside a curricle a little way down Brook Street. As she might have expected, his vehicle was of the finest quality, made of polished ebony with buttoned seats of dark red leather.

'Lefevre's rigs are always the best in town,' she'd heard her brother, George, say with reluctant admiration, 'even if the man himself is a scoundrel.'

Lefevre's small but burly French manservant was holding the heads of the pair of matched bays and the look he gave her was hostile. Serena remembered he was rumoured to always carry a pistol beneath that shabby coat of his—as if the Marquis needed protecting from anyone! She felt her stomach pitch a little as Lefevre strolled casually towards her, looking effortlessly elegant in his dark green topcoat and buckskin breeches. His white cravat was carelessly tied, but its loose folds dramatically emphasised the chiselled perfection of his suntanned face—dagger-sharp cheekbones, square jaw, piercing grey eyes and thick black hair.

For a moment she felt like a debutante facing her first dancing partner at some grand ball, except that her nerves were in no way softened by any anticipation of pleasure. It was her misfortune that her enemy was so ridiculously handsome. It was even more disastrous that his sardonically curved mouth reminded her all too vividly of last night's kiss.

He took her hand and bowed. 'Lady Serena,' he murmured. 'Good day to you.'

It was not only his looks, she realised, but his voice that always shook her to her core. His command of the English language was all but perfect—his years at Eton had seen to that. But there were still those undertones of his native French that curled their way through her like some seductive perfume.

She hated this man. Yes, he'd saved her from Silas Mort last night, but at such a cost! Yet somehow she managed to answer calmly, 'I wish it were a good day, Monsieur Lefevre, but it has not been made any the better by seeing you here. You will oblige me by stating your business, since my own carriage will be arriving to collect me in half an hour, and—'

'It won't,' he said.

Then he smiled. That smile played about his firm yet sensual mouth, but didn't touch his eyes. 'You needn't worry about your carriage,' he continued. 'You see, I informed one of your grooms that I would be bringing you home, so there was no need for him to send it.'

For a moment she was speechless. 'You informed… And my groom *obeyed* you?'

'Oh, yes.' He was casually pulling on a pair of elegant leather driving gloves over his long, supple fingers. 'People usually do, you know. In fact, it was your groom who told me I'd find you here. Tell me, did you and your Wicked Widows enjoy tearing my reputation to shreds at your weekly gossip session?'

Her reply was coldly furious. 'Fortunately, we had more worthwhile matters to consider!'

The man actually chuckled. 'Dear me. I really have offended you, haven't I? But there are several matters we need to discuss, you and I. And I decided a short drive in my curricle would give us the necessary opportunity.' He gestured towards the vehicle with a slight bow.

Serena stood exactly where she was. 'You mean, I assume, that a drive with you will give you the opportunity to remind me once more of the humiliation you inflicted on me last night?'

'Come now, *madame*.' He shook his head in reprimand. 'If my memory serves me correctly, it was actually you who laid yourself open to humiliation by planning to meet with that gang of ruffians. You have no doubt been regretting your decision ever since.'

'Oh, Monsieur Lefevre. You cannot imagine how much!'

'Since it led you to become obliged to me?' She saw a flash of something rather dangerous in those strange silver-grey eyes, but instantly his languid smile was back in place again. 'Maybe I *can* imagine it,' he went on. 'After all, I've heard you announcing your opinion of me often enough—in fact, I appear to have become something of a preoccupation of yours. And you must admit that you have, after last night's encounter, landed yourself in a rather awkward situation.'

She faced him squarely. 'But my blackmailer has been paid off. I only wish I could deal with you in the same way.'

Lefevre actually laughed. 'You still don't like my suggestion that you place yourself under my protection? In a very…*amicable* sort of way?'

'I don't see the necessity of lowering myself to such an extent, Monsieur Lefevre!'

By way of reply, Lefevre pointed back the way she had come. 'I'm sure you'll agree,' he said, 'that we'll have more privacy to exchange insults in my curricle than we do here. Though we actually make quite a fine pair, don't we? Your friends certainly seem to think so.'

Serena's gaze jerked towards where he was pointing. *Oh, no.* At one of Joanna's top-floor windows, she could glimpse three faces peering down at her. And no doubt their eyes were wide with fascination.

Lefevre indicated his waiting curricle and extended his arm. 'Shall we go?'

'You can go to perdition, Monsieur le Marquis!'

'Perhaps. But I'm afraid it really looks as if you shall have to come to perdition with me. You loved your husband very much. Is that correct?'

'Of course! Of course I did!'

'Well, then. This is the difficulty. You see, I need to talk to you about the rather sordid subject of your late husband's reputation...as a war hero.'

So he knew. Oh, God, he knew why Mort was blackmailing her. Feeling as though she'd been trapped into an assignation with the devil himself, she allowed him to help her up on to the passenger seat. Rather dizzily she heard him instruct

Jacques to take up his place on the running board at the back, then Lefevre settled himself beside her and gathered the reins. And all the while her hand burned from where he had touched her. *Ma chère,* he'd called her in front of Silas Mort. *My dear.*

'Monsieur Lefevre,' she began as the carriage moved off, 'I admit I was more than foolish to be in Covent Garden last night. I realise I had put myself in danger and I'm grateful that you rescued me. But please, can this be the end of the matter?'

She saw his lip curl. 'I'd love to oblige. But there is another problem. You see, the rumours are running wild that you and I are having a secret affair.'

'No.' She was panicking again. 'You must silence them!'

His gaze locked with hers. 'Why should I?'

'Because you took advantage of me!'

'Did I?' he said softly. 'Did I really? I think you forget, Lady Serena, that you made no effort at all to resist my embrace. In fact, you settled into it rather nicely, I felt, on recollection of the moment.' He looked thoughtful. 'A recollection that I, personally, shall treasure.'

With a hiss of shock she glanced down at the road, contemplating flight; but his steely voice pinned her to her seat. 'Jumping from a moving vehicle isn't the answer, Lady Serena. No—what we have to do from henceforth is to show the world we've resolved our differences and are currently enjoying a most pleasant liaison.'

She closed her eyes. Opened them and said, 'Dear God. You're joking.'

His gaze never left the road ahead. She couldn't help but notice that he drove with meticulous skill. 'Actually, I'm not,' he said. 'Think about it for a moment. Such a tactic will protect you from further blackmail, since Silas Mort will not come near you while I'm around, nor will he dare to mention the truth about your husband's death. In addition, our apparent fondness for one another from now on will mean that our kiss last night will be fully explained.'

'Never! I will be a laughing stock!'

He glanced at her. 'Really? On the contrary, many people will be charmed by your apparent appreciation of my finer qualities.'

'Of your finer…' She was shaking her head, almost laughing—because otherwise she would be weeping. 'Believe me, I don't need to waste one moment dwelling on your proposal, which can only be a jest. My answer is no. A thousand times, no!'

'Oh?' he said with polite disbelief. 'You have other options?'

At this particular moment, no, she thought bleakly. And then—then, she was turning to face him, her hands gripping the edge of her seat as his fine bays trotted onwards. 'Monsieur Lefevre, this I cannot believe. You said earlier that we needed to hold a private conversation. Do you call *this* a situation of privacy, when we're about to enter Hyde Park at this hour of the afternoon? Do you realise that half the people I know will be here?'

'Half the people I know, too,' he said cheerfully. 'A popular spot, isn't it?'

Serena stared straight ahead. He would know they'd be seen. He would also guess that the topic of that kiss would be resurrected by all who spotted them and they would be the subject of fresh and salacious gossip.

He could not have dreamed up a better way to humiliate her if he'd worked on it all night. Dear Lord, he probably had.

Foolishly, she risked a further glance at Lefevre himself. If she'd been hoping to spot any sign of weakness, she was disappointed. Instead she was reminded of how one of his foolish female admirers had declared he could surely tempt any woman he chose into sin and Serena had laughed dismissively at the time, but now the comment suddenly didn't seem quite so funny. He was distractingly, devilishly male—and unfortunately he had the arrogance to match his looks. She'd always told herself she was repelled by men like him, yet in his arms last night she'd felt *safe*. She'd also felt warm and melting and needful in a way she'd never, ever experienced—and that was the most frightening thing of all.

He was so calm. So confident. And now, watching him control that pair of lively bay mares with the surest touch of any man she'd ever seen, she suddenly imagined his hands on her, just as they had been last night. That strange ache started low in her stomach again...

No. You must not think like that.

But memories of yesterday evening's encounter in Covent Garden kept flooding her mind and body. Memories of that look he'd given her, with his silver-grey eyes almost black in their intensity, his hard face at first forbidding in the ghostly glow of the street lamps, yet somehow so alluring that she'd wanted to reach out and touch his angular cheekbones, his faintly stubbled jaw, his lips...

For Heaven's sake! Serena realised that for a moment she'd stopped breathing and her pulse was thudding unevenly. Yes, he was dangerous, to her senses and her sanity. She'd known it since that ball months ago, when he'd asked her to dance for a wager; no doubt he'd also counted on being able to boast to his friends that he'd had one of the Wicked Widows eating out of his hand. And she'd been so ridiculously hurt, because just for a moment she had imagined he might be the hero she'd once dreamed of, in the days when she'd believed fairy tales could come true.

After that she'd hated him, of course. But how could she shut him out of her life, when he had such power over her? Already they were well inside the Park and men on horseback and ladies in open carriages were turning to stare. Serena could almost hear the sound of jaws dropping. As for Lefevre, the damnable man was at this moment being greeted by a baronet and his wife who were driving by in a barouche.

'Good day to you, *monseigneur*!' the man called eagerly. 'Good day, Lady Serena. It's a fine day for a drive, is it not?'

Oh, how their eyes devoured her. She wanted to jump off this carriage and run, but instead she silently repeated Mary's advice. *Serena, you really must show the Marquis that you're in charge.*

In charge. Right. The words echoed hollowly, as useless as a challenge to an empty room. She suddenly realised Lefevre was speaking to her again.

'The Park,' he was saying in a leisurely fashion, 'is surely at its best on an afternoon like this.

Don't you agree, Lady Serena? How splendid it all is. The trees coming into full leaf, the birds singing, the finest of London's fashionables out enjoying the air...'

'Stop it!' she hissed. 'Whatever game you're playing, stop it, damn you!'

He turned to her with a look almost of wounded innocence, but behind it lurked something much darker. 'I'm living,' he said, 'up to public expectation. Since last night people have formed definite opinions about the two of us. And I fear your situation might only become worse if we denied them their enjoyment, Lady Serena.'

The way he said her name, letting it curl around his mouth. The way he just...*looked* at her. She felt hot and confused and afraid—yes, afraid, even here with the birds trilling their joyful songs and smiling people all around. Indeed, everyone appeared to be smiling except her.

He was right, of course. The linking of his name with hers would be the talk of every fashionable drawing room in London. She could imagine the shocked yet delighted voices even now. 'Have you heard how our French Marquis has made a conquest of Lady Serena Willoughby of all people? Amazing! That he should win over the very woman who is so well known for her scorn of men like him!'

She said calmly, 'You would hate for people to be disappointed? Then I have news for you. They're going to be extremely disappointed, because you are not going to bend me to your will.'

'But we were observed in an embrace, remember?' His voice was equally level. 'To fashionable society, that means a great deal. You are also being blackmailed over your late husband's alleged cowardice, a fact you must be desperate to conceal. Unless you have positive proof that the allegation is a lie?'

Her silence spoke for her, she knew. The anguish gathered in her throat, almost choking her. What could she do? How could she escape this man's hold over her?

'Very well,' he went on. He spoke with a note of strained patience. 'You wish to uphold the story of your husband's heroic death. You also accepted my protection last night, a fact you can't deny. On my part, I want you to stop your denunciations of me in public.'

'I've only said aloud what everybody knows!'

'Ah, but coming from your fair lips, I take the insults rather more personally. So let me repeat that, for our mutual benefit, we both appear in public as allies.' He paused a moment to let his words sink in. 'Perhaps a little *more* than allies.'

Serena felt a fresh and sickening jolt of dismay. She was doomed.

He was guiding his curricle down to the lake now, where the grass verges were thronged with London's elite enjoying the late afternoon sunshine. All of them—from elderly ladies in old-fashioned barouches to bachelors on horseback—took it upon themselves to peer at the Marquis and his companion, some even using lorgnettes.

He doffed his hat to them, politely answering their comments on the weather and acknowledging their compliments regarding his matched bays. After a while, though, he gathered the reins in one hand, put his other very briefly on Serena's and said quietly, 'Are you all right?'

She was almost speechless. Raphael Lefevre— her demon, her nemesis, her ruin—was asking her if she was *all right*? Rather faintly she remembered how less than an hour ago Beth had said, 'I've never heard any tales claiming the Marquis mistreats women. Indeed, he's very popular with them, isn't he?'

And Joanna's response: 'Popular? I should think so. Why, I heard from a lady who knew him in Paris that when he makes love to you, he uses his…'

Whatever else the lady from Paris might have

said it really wasn't wise to think about, because here the Marquis was, with the touch of his hand still lingering and his body far too close, tormenting her with that indefinable charisma that not even she could deny.

He represented everything that was dangerous. He threatened her position in society, her belief in herself even. Here, in the Park on this fine afternoon, with the warm breeze rustling the fresh Maytime foliage and children playing on the green turf, she felt sucked into a vortex of fear and shame. But all the same, just the presence of him here beside her was enough to make her unsteady. She could feel the force of his sheer masculinity tearing down her carefully built defences with every moment that went by.

To be lured into humiliation by a careless rake? Not again. Never again. Desperation made her voice shake as she blurted out, 'You and I cannot be seen together. You've trapped me into this situation, but everyone knows we're enemies!'

Judging by the tightness of his jaw, she guessed he was growing impatient. 'Last night,' he said, his eyes now on the path ahead as his horses stepped onwards, 'means you can no longer maintain your enmity. Last night, as I've just pointed out, your acceptance of my protection—most willingly, it appeared—will make you seem an utter hypocrite unless you agree to my proposition. It shouldn't be too difficult for you. I suggest we appear together at whichever events you normally attend, thus showing ourselves to be a happy couple for a specified length of time. Shall we say four weeks, starting from yesterday? It's true that people will be surprised, since your many caustic comments about me won't have been forgotten. But I am quite popular in most circles, you know. I believe it will quickly be accepted that you've succumbed to my overwhelming charm.'

'I think there's something you've forgotten, *monsieur*,' she said bitterly. 'What about *my* reputation?'

He turned his head to gaze at her. 'You loved your husband, didn't you? Then you must wish to do your utmost to save his heroic legacy, even if it was a lie. So here's my advice, Lady Serena. Make it clear you're enjoying yourself in my company. Show yourself to be revelling in my attention.' His voice hardened a little. 'And whatever else you do, you will stop, from today onwards, making intrusive enquiries about my personal life, both past and present. Do you understand?'

She didn't mean her voice to come out as a gasp, but it did. 'Everyone will think we're lovers!'

'No doubt. But we don't have to go that far in

reality.' He threw her a sidelong smile that almost shook her from her seat. 'Delightful as last night's kiss was, I'm perfectly able to resist your charms, believe me.'

Her heart bumped to a stop. Last night she'd melted in his arms as if she'd been waiting for the moment all her life. She knew that. *He* knew that. Dear Lord, her heart still raced in shame at the memory. 'I detest you,' she said calmly.

'Then nothing's really changed, has it? You can continue to detest me, certainly. But for your own sake, I suggest you keep your feelings to yourself. If you don't agree to my plan, I'd guess it will take Silas Mort about twenty-four hours to contact you again with fresh threats. So we need to let it be known—quickly—that we are more than just friends. This afternoon has been a start, but we must establish something more formal. I've been invited to the Duke of Hamilton's ball in two nights' time and I assume you have, too. So I suggest we arrive together and I'll call on you tomorrow to finalise the details. I take it you agree?'

Devil. Deep blue sea. Lefevre had told her she was too proud and he was absolutely correct. It was her pride that had led her to keep up her pretence of devotion to a husband who was unfaithful and cruel to her almost from the start. And now, that same pride could well be her undoing.

Serena clasped her hands together and took just a little comfort in the fact that they weren't trembling like her heart was. Like her very soul was.

'I have no choice, after all,' she said at last. 'Have I?'

'You have not,' he said quietly.

You have...

Chapter Seven

The Marquis set her down outside her house in Curzon Street where her footman, Robert, was holding the door open for her. No doubt he relished the chance to admire Lefevre's fine curricle and horses, though now, thank goodness, they were disappearing into the distance. She swept inside the house before she realised Robert was saying something. Distracted, she had to ask him to repeat it.

'You have visitors, milady,' Robert announced.

The last thing she needed. 'Visitors? Who are they?' By now Martha had hurried forth to take her hat and pelisse. Serena tried hard to remember if she was expecting anyone, but her brain was still reeling from her encounter with the Marquis.

'Your brother, the Earl of Stainsby, is here, milady,' explained Robert. 'And Lady Joanna also.'

'Together?' She was thrown again, because she knew that Joanna and George clashed whenever they met.

'Your brother arrived first and Lady Joanna a short while afterwards. They are both in the first-floor salon.'

'Very well. Thank you, Robert.' But Serena's heart was sinking further—because earlier Joanna had seen Lefevre driving Serena away from her house in his carriage. She would be here to find out more. And George? He heartily detested Raphael Lefevre. What if he'd heard about the events last night in Covent Garden?

Oh, Lord, what a pickle she was in. And, indeed, on reaching the landing she heard raised voices from the salon—George, exasperated, declaring, 'I've told you, Joanna, I do *not* consider myself to be a staid old bachelor!'

Joanna next, cool and teasing. 'Perhaps to call you a staid old bachelor is a little extreme. But you know, George, you could transform that huge house of yours in Clarges Street! Open up the ballroom and hold parties! Join the fast set!'

Serena, her fingers on the door, heard George practically exploding. 'Me? Are you suggesting I should associate with those frivolous, idle creatures who spend their lives wasting their family's fortunes?'

Joanna gave her bubbling laugh. 'But you *have* no family, George, other than your lovely sister! You rattle around in your London home like a dried pea in a pod. You should either marry and father a dozen noisy children, or become a rake and hurl yourself into society! Just like...'

Her voice faded as Serena entered the room. 'Like Raphael Lefevre,' Joanna completed her sentence softly. 'Hello, Serena.'

Serena closed the door behind her. 'Joanna. And George. How very pleasant.'

George nodded to her brusquely. 'Serena,' he began, 'Joanna is suggesting I should join the company of wastrels and gamblers, like Lefevre—that odious man!'

Once more Serena's heart stopped, though already Joanna was saying mischievously, 'Yes, but, George, some of us ladies do find the Marquis quite entertaining, you know. Don't they, Serena?' She'd drawn close to touch Serena's hand. 'Darling, you left your gloves at my house this afternoon, so I thought I'd call round with them. Oh, and Mary asked me to bring you this copy of the school's accounts also. What a pleasant surprise to find dear George here! He has some family business to discuss with you, he says.'

Family business. Serena was able to breathe again. So George didn't know yet about last night.

It was only a temporary reprieve, but that was something.

'I came,' George was saying stiffly, 'because I wished to consult with you, Serena, concerning some plans for the estate in Yorkshire. But perhaps now is not the time. Such matters may be a little dreary for you, as Joanna suggests.'

'No, George!' Serena was dismayed. 'Dreary, never! You know how I love the Yorkshire house!'

'Another time, maybe.' He inspected his pocket watch. 'I have an appointment shortly. And since you have company, I'll take my leave.'

With his departure he took Serena's last hope of deflecting the curiosity of Joanna, who was watching her now with speculative eyes. 'I thought I'd better get rid of him,' Joanna said, all traces of levity gone. 'Because, Serena, you look quite fatigued, my dear. Now, sit down and tell me. What *is* going on between you and Raphael Lefevre? You detest the man!'

Serena sank into one of the garish pink and green sofas with which George had furnished the room and shook her head. 'Joanna, I can't explain everything to you. Not yet. But I find that I may have to spend a certain amount of time with the Marquis. I may even have to pretend that I like him.'

'Oh, my goodness!' Joanna's hand went to her

mouth. 'Serena, he's not—*forcing* you in any way, is he?'

'Not in the slightest,' Serena said swiftly. 'This is all for outward appearance only. There is really nothing to be alarmed about.'

'No?' Joanna was watching her carefully. 'I'm not going to press and pry. But what's brought this on?'

Serena pressed her hands together in a gesture of appeal. 'You say you trust me, so please trust me *now* when I say that this is something I simply must endure for a brief while. You can help me by accepting it—and making others accept it.'

'But you and the Marquis together? Society will be bursting with the news!'

'Do you think I don't realise it?' Serena's voice held a note of despair.

Joanna looked thoughtful. 'Now, I know you dislike Lefevre strongly, but I must say he rather intrigues me. Take, for instance, all the rumours of his partying and gambling. Indeed, there's no denying he likes his forays with his friends into, shall we say, the murkier corners of London. But his very best friend is Sir Dominic Southern, who is a paragon, is he not? The man lives with his sister Amelia out in Kensington—the dullest of places! Even George could find no fault with Sir Dominic. And what misdeeds has Lefevre actually committed? Have you ever seen him drunk? How many mistresses does he keep here in London? I don't know of any at all. The stories run wild and he does nothing to stop them, but sometimes I wonder if he's just putting on an act.'

Serena was incredulous. 'An *act*?'

'Oh, you might laugh, but I tell you, I think he's just pretending to be a villain. Now I'm not going to press you any more. I'll accept for the time being that whatever you've arranged with Lefevre is very necessary to you. But in your own interests, dear Serena, you must find a reason that explains to everyone why you've had this sudden change of heart about the man. Do you see?'

Serena nodded slowly. 'I do see.'

Joanna was rising now and reaching for her bonnet—which was, as ever, a rather spectacular creation with a wide brim and many ribbons. 'I must be on my way, darling. I have an appointment with Madame Lavergne in Bond Street— she's making me two new silk gowns which are absolutely delightful! But I just had to call in, to see that you're all right. Now, remember what I said. Lefevre is putting on an act, so you must, too. Think of a good reason for your revised opinion of the man and then, my goodness, you must enjoy yourself!'

Joanna kissed her and left. Serena, feeling

rather numb, went to pick up the copy of the school accounts that Joanna had left for her. *The Marquis.* How on earth was she to explain her change of heart concerning the Marquis? She leafed through the accounts listlessly.

And it was then that she suddenly had a rather wonderful idea.

When Raphael arrived at Serena's house the next afternoon he came straight from meeting Dominic for lunch at a sedate club in Piccadilly. 'Could we go to the library, perhaps?' he'd suggested to Dominic after they'd eaten. 'So we can have a little more privacy?'

Dominic, looking wary, had picked up his glass of port and led the way to two secluded armchairs in that almost empty room. 'Well?' he said as he seated himself. 'What trouble are you in this time, Raphael? I've warned you before. You make enemies rather too easily.'

'I also have good friends, I trust.' Raphael looked straight at him. 'Not for the first time, I need your help.'

Dominic was instantly serious. 'You've had more news?'

'Nothing definite, but I may be on to something. Jacques is excellent at ferreting out information— but you, *mon ami,* are in daily contact with a com-

pletely different level of society. You're a Member
of Parliament, so you have access to government
records. Can you obtain for me a list of London
businessmen who keep up a regular trade at the
Channel ports?'

'I'll make enquiries, of course. But the Channel ports! Why?'

'Early days, my friend,' said Raphael. He
downed the last of his port. 'Early days—but I'd
be grateful for your help. As ever.'

It was half past two by the time he reached
Curzon Street and knocked on the door. He knew
Lady Serena had several admirers and found himself wondering if they all received the same chilly
treatment from her butler. Certainly it was with
an air of distinct disapproval that Grinling led
Raphael to Her Ladyship's private study on the
first floor.

'A visitor, ma'am,' he announced. 'The Most
Honourable the Marquis of Montpellier.' He spoke
as if he was announcing that the milk for her tea
had gone sour.

Lady Serena took her time in turning around,
thus giving Raphael several moments in which to
admire the back of her rather striking day gown
of pink taffeta, with its ruff of cream lace that
emphasised the elegant curve of her neck. When

she eventually faced him he saw she was wearing spectacles, which gave her a charmingly earnest look. *Interesting.*

After a moment, though, she took them off and said, somewhat wonderingly, 'Why, Monsieur Lefevre. This is a surprise! What brings you here, I wonder?'

Grinling had left, silently shutting the door behind him. Raphael said, '*Madame.* I promised you I would call. Yesterday, you remember?'

'Slipped my mind,' she murmured. 'Slipped my mind.'

Now *that* he found hard to believe, but he strolled calmly towards her desk. 'You look busy. What with, I wonder?'

'I'm writing letters...' Suddenly she clapped her hand to her forehead. 'But of course! You've come because we made an arrangement to be seen together! I'd almost forgotten. Had you?'

'No,' he said. 'No, I rather think I had not.' Frankly, he'd been expecting to be met with anger or maybe a frosty silence. But this? Whatever was she rambling on about?

He realised she was gesturing airily towards a rather startling chair of bright yellow satin with gilded legs. 'My brother George furnished the house for me,' she explained, as if sensing his surprise. 'So kind of him, don't you think? Sit down and make yourself at home. Now, I remember you said, Monsieur Lefevre, that we had to spend some time with one another—four weeks, I think you suggested. For our mutual advantage.'

She wrinkled her nose a little, as if in slight puzzlement. And he wondered—what the hell had happened to her overnight? Had her wits become addled? Had she completely forgotten about Silas Mort and his blackmail threat? Had she forgotten that kiss?

If so, that was a first among the ladies with whom he'd been acquainted. He found that he was almost amused. He said, 'For our mutual advantage indeed. On your part, to keep secret the somewhat regrettable nature of your husband's death in battle. On my part—to stop you, my lady, from being rather a thorn in my side.'

'Oh, my! A thorn in your side, Monsieur le Marquis?' She laughed merrily. 'How very quaint!' She leaned forward a little. 'But, yes, it's all coming back to me now. Forgive me, but all these letters, these invitations—' she waved at the heap of papers on her desk '—they distracted me. Though I do recall thinking, after our ride in the Park yesterday, that people are going to find it a little peculiar—are they not?—if you and I suddenly appear to be the best of friends, when we've been rather at odds with one another up till now.'

'Stranger things have happened, Lady Serena. But, yes. Some people will be taken by surprise.'

She wagged a finger. 'But they won't be so very surprised,' she said, 'if you and I appear to have become allies in a common cause. Have become…united, so to speak.'

'United?' The wicked side of his mind roved.

'Yes, indeed! Wouldn't our sudden reconciliation appear more reasonable if you and I, Monsieur Lefevre, had apparently resolved our differences because—how can I put this?—because we'd found an area of mutual interest?'

Her breasts looked remarkably pretty beneath the lace of her fichu… *Stop it.* Roving again. He said mildly, 'And that "area of interest" is?'

'You may or may not know that I am involved in a charity.'

Ah. 'I've heard something to that effect, indeed,' he said.

'Good.' She nodded her satisfaction. 'Yes, my friends and I support a school in Spitalfields for the children of the poor. We fund a large proportion of the scheme, but we also receive generous gifts from all quarters. From local churches and businessmen, from peers of the realm and quite a few of our politicians too.'

He thought he could see where this was going. 'Are you suggesting I join their number? But what about my reputation, *madame*? Am I really a fit person to be associated with such a worthy cause as your school?'

She waved a jewelled hand in the air. 'Oh, it's not your moral advice we require, Monsieur Lefevre, but your money! Your support of our cause will doubtless surprise your friends, but in my opinion it gives an undeniable reason why I've temporarily renounced my single status and have decided to—to...'

For the first time she looked lost for words. He helped her out. 'To shock the *ton* by associating with me, Lady Serena?'

'Well—' and she gave a small shrug '—if you care to put it like that, yes. So what do you think of my plan?'

Raphael had to admit it was a neat trick of hers, to turn the tables on him and put him in a good light for once. It did make sense. It would explain to the *ton* why the two of them—hitherto such enemies—were suddenly appearing together with their differences apparently forgotten. And a hefty donation to her charity would be good value at twice the cost, if it meant that her intrusive probing into his past came to an end.

Though he'd rather have silenced her in other ways, he thought suddenly. She was gazing up at him with those innocent-looking blue-green eyes, but he remembered—oh, he remembered—how lushly inviting her lips had been during that kiss. How her body had moulded to his, almost as if it guessed what pleasure could lie in store. For both of them…

He felt desire pulsing at his loins. *Stop that.* Forbidden territory, absolutely—besides, Lady Serena was not his type in the least. 'How much do you want for this school?' he asked flatly. 'Would two hundred guineas suffice?'

She looked startled by the amount, but quickly concealed her astonishment and was all charm again. 'Monsieur le Marquis, that is most generous! Though as I explained, the important fact is that your name will be prominent in our list of donors, which will shortly appear in *The Times*. How inspiring, for such a notorious—I mean, notable personage as yourself to be making this generous gesture!'

He didn't allow his expression to change. 'Yes. Inspiring. No doubt you'll also be announcing it in person, tomorrow night?'

'Tomorrow night?' For the first time she looked slightly flustered.

'I hope you've not forgotten that yesterday you agreed to attend the Duke of Hamilton's ball with me tomorrow evening? I came here to tell you I'll collect you in my carriage at eight.'

She was silent. A little stunned even. Clearly, the reality of her situation was biting home.

He said, gently, 'I could leave now, you know. But I think your servants would be rather surprised if you didn't offer me some refreshment. Tea, for example.'

'Yes. Yes, of course...'

'Allow me,' he said, rising and walking over to the bell pull.

Serena sat back in her chair, to give herself a moment—just a moment—to recover her breath. To recover her *strength*. Since the carriage ride in the park, she'd agonised over how to escape this awful tangle, but she couldn't—that was the simple answer. The Marquis had caught her up all too neatly in his web. But at least, she thought she'd found a way to make their appearances together just a little less of an earthquake-sized shock to polite society.

The idea had come to her shortly after Joanna's visit. *The school, of course. He could pretend to support our school!* Though now it worried her very much that he'd accepted the suggestion with so little argument. What was he plotting now? She glanced at Lefevre as he stretched himself out on the chair in her study—all the long, lean length of him immaculately clad in dark tailcoat, glossy top boots and breeches that hugged his muscular thighs. And it struck her that she was dealing with a highly dangerous enemy.

Welcome distraction was provided by a maid coming in with the tea tray and Serena began to pour, a little too energetically. 'Just think, Monsieur Lefevre! It will give everyone a delightful surprise to learn at the ball that you are supporting our charity venture!'

'A surprise indeed,' he answered. 'Do be careful. I think you've rather overfilled that cup.'

She put the silver teapot down with a hand that shook, aware that he was watching her with those steadfast silver-grey eyes of his. 'I do hope,' he went on, 'that you will appear radiant tomorrow night, Lady Serena. Glowing, in fact, because you will be so happy to be by my side. We are going to convince the *ton* that we are entranced by one another. Remember? Otherwise, I'll remove myself from your life without a moment's hesitation—and I think you'll find there could be unpleasant consequences.'

She held his gaze steadily but felt a cold shiver on her skin. Did he mean from Silas Mort? Or from himself?

She reached calmly for her cup and said, 'My, I do hope you'll be able to adopt a friendlier tone towards me at the ball, Monsieur Lefevre!'

He was still watching her with that faintly mocking smile curving his lips and she felt it like a whisper of warmth over her skin, penetrating her body, teasing her nerve-ends like the kiss of a dark flame.

He continued to lounge opposite her on that gaudy chair and said, 'Friendly? Friendly is not enough. Let me remind you that we're to present ourselves from now on as a couple who are infatuated with one another and the fact that I'm willing to make a generous donation to your school has only increased your affection for me. Every now and then, a light touch, even a caress, will seem only natural. Inevitable, even. Remember, Lady Serena, that you are seeing me in an entirely new light. In fact, you feel you have completely underestimated the nobility of my character.'

She was taking a sip of her tea and almost choked. 'I hope you realise,' she said at last, 'that there are limits as to how far I can disguise my true feelings towards you?'

He finished his own tea swiftly and deposited the cup on the table. 'I accept there'll be no displays of unbridled ardour,' he said gently, 'which is a pity.' He rose to his feet. 'Except when a villain like Silas Mort is around, perhaps?'

She rose, too. 'Believe me, Monsieur le Marquis,' she said in a low voice, 'I shall count the days until this is over.'

'Will you? I, on the contrary, shall relish our time together. Every minute, in fact. Though now, regretfully, I must leave you.' He reached out to let his fingers brush her cheek and when she backed away with a gasp his mouth curled in a mocking smile.

She felt a hot pulse of shame. Silently she promised herself that she would one day get even with him.

He headed for the door then, but at the last moment he turned back and added, 'One other point. Will you please explain to your staff that I shall be a regular visitor from now on? Your butler, when he opened the front door to me, looked as if he'd personally like to shoot me. Have a word, will you? As I said, I'll call for you tomorrow evening at eight.'

Serena stood rooted to the spot as he left. Despicable, hateful man! Yet, at the mere memory of his light touch, she felt her heart pounding. Desperately she tried to calm herself. Yes, he had her trapped completely for now. But he would regret it—because she'd vowed she would never, ever let herself fall under the power of any man again.

When the old nightmare struck again that night, she shouldn't have been surprised. Indeed, it was stupid of her to think she was over it, for she'd accepted months ago that the darkest time of her life would always haunt her.

Lying in her bed, with the heavy silence of the house enveloping her, she remembered her wedding day. Everyone had called them the golden couple—she, the sister of an earl, and Lionel, the grandson of a duke.

Her brother had tried his best to warn her. 'Serena,' he would say, 'I've heard stories about Lionel. I'm really rather anxious about your future with him.'

She refused to believe him, but slowly—day by day, month by month—the truth hit home.

She realised that Lionel's country mansion in Northamptonshire was all but ruined and that his financial situation was precarious, though of course money was a problem easily dismissed by her husband because Serena's fortune had become his on marriage. At that time Lionel had an army post based in London and they rented a smart house in Dover Street, paid for with Serena's money. But soon enough Serena noticed that her fortune was disappearing in other ways, thanks to extravagant army banquets and the many weekends that Lionel spent shooting or hunting with his officer friends in the country. She also began to realise that he gambled heavily.

Within six months of the wedding, she was forced to acknowledge that in her foolish mind she'd made Lionel into the man she wanted him to be, not the man he actually was. Then he was called away to India, to the war the British were fighting in Mysore, and Serena remained in the Dover Street house, at a loss as to how to occupy her time, yet dreading her husband's return. Until one afternoon, at a tea party, she'd overheard a wealthy widow only a little older than herself, Mary Appleby, talking about a charity school she'd started up in the East End of London. Afterwards Serena had approached Mary shyly.

'I wonder, may I visit your school? Maybe even help in some small way?'

Swiftly, she'd become involved with the school. She also met Joanna and Beth and these friends were the only ones who'd guessed the unhappiness of her marriage. The *mistake* of her marriage. But what could be done? She had continued to put on a brave face in society, as was expected of senior officers' wives, especially when their husbands were away on active service. Then, one night, there was a tap at her bedroom door.

'Mrs Penney,' Serena had cried out in alarm. 'It's three o'clock in the morning. Whatever is the matter?'

'Oh, my lady. There's a man downstairs, come from the War Office! And it's about your husband.'

The official had come to tell her that Lionel had been killed in battle while endeavouring to lead his men against impossible odds. For days the house was filled with flowers and cards of sympathy. *So terrible for you, dear Serena,* everyone said. *But at least you have the consolation that Lionel died a hero.*

And so Serena entered her new life as a widow, with much of her fortune still intact. Her brother, George, arranged for her to take possession of the lovely house in Curzon Street and, after spending the required period of mourning in Yorkshire, she was welcomed back into London society.

She'd resolved to say *Never again* to the possibility of allowing any man to woo her, or even come close to it. Only then, Raphael Lefevre had asked her to dance at that fatal ball last November and just for a moment the kind of emotion she'd thought was dead inside her had unfurled like a tiny plant at the first touch of spring sunshine.

But that emotion had been crushed utterly when she realised that he'd approached her merely to amuse his colleagues, which was actually the kind of trick Lionel and his friends might have concocted to make some vulnerable woman look foolish. Shaken and bruised, she'd realised that once more she'd been stupidly deceived by a man's superficial charm. After that she made herself strong again, telling herself that she was perfectly content to live her life alone—after all, she had her three close friends for companionship and she had the charity school to engage her commitment. But now, all her best-laid plans had come to naught. Disaster had struck again.

Because though she could tell herself all she liked that she detested Raphael Lefevre, her pounding pulse whenever he was near told a completely different story. As for that kiss in Covent Garden... *More,* her body had demanded. *More.*

Chapter Eight

~~~~~~

'Lady Serena Willoughby! And the Most Honourable the Marquis of Montpellier!'

The great hall was filled with chatter when Serena and Raphael arrived at the Duke of Hamilton's ball the next night. But as soon as their names were announced, an acute silence descended, apart from what sounded like a collective indrawing of breath. Serena felt her heart tighten painfully as dozens of pairs of eyes fastened on them like a flock of predators.

They had arrived slightly late at the Duke's magnificent house overlooking Hyde Park. The timing, she guessed, was deliberate on Lefevre's part; he'd doubtless delayed their appearance to ensure that everyone else was already there. Indeed, the main hall was packed, the ballroom glittering with showy jewellery and the flashes of gold on military officers' uniforms. But it was

Lefevre, in his sombre but perfect attire, who drew all eyes: Lefevre, wearing a dark grey tail-coat that hugged his powerful shoulders and a cravat that, plain though it was, dramatically enhanced his chiselled features.

'Smile,' he was murmuring at her side. 'Try to look happy to be with me.'

She smiled. But she also said, so only he could hear, 'Happy? To be with you? Surely you ask the impossible, *monsieur*.'

Lefevre increased his pressure on Serena's arm. 'For many months now, my lady,' he said in the same quietly mocking voice, 'you've taken great pleasure in blackening my name. Sometimes, you know, even a low-down scoundrel like me has to take steps to defend himself.'

She was silent. This was his revenge. He'd been waiting his chance to move in on her and crush her—and how he was revelling in it.

Gradually they progressed through the packed hall, each of them acknowledging the greetings that came from all around. Somehow Serena kept her smile fixed to her face, nodding to people she knew while he guided her, guarded her, spoke politely to those who gaped wide-eyed at them. 'Good evening, Sir James. How do you do, Lady Devereau? And my Lord Hastings—yes, it's certainly been too long since we met...'

Soon the string orchestra in the gallery above was striking up a minuet and with a bow Lefevre led Serena into the dance. It was as well the steps were so familiar, because she felt light-headed, feverish almost. *It's lack of sleep,* she told herself. But she knew it was nothing of the sort.

The Marquis, on the other hand, appeared as powerfully in control as ever. He'd called for her at eight as promised and, as he met her in the hallway, he'd bowed over her hand and murmured, no doubt for the benefit of her hovering staff, 'Lady Serena. You look ravishing.'

She'd chosen a gown of rose-pink silk, high-necked as usual. Long cream kid gloves and pink satin slippers completed her outfit; her silk fan matched her gown and her fair hair was neatly coiled on the crown of her head. She'd thought it was a modest look. Subtle, even.

But as they danced and Lefevre examined her with those cool, silvery eyes of his, she felt she might as well have been naked. It had been one thing to agree to their liaison verbally, quite another to actually be here, with his hands possessive on her waist and his strength imprinting itself on her. Somehow, this man compelled her to think of things she'd forbidden herself to ever contemplate again, like his lips on hers and his body pressing close, urgent with desire…

Oh, Lord, she needed to come to her senses. The minuet would end soon, at which point she must look for the opportunity to tell her friends and acquaintances exactly why she was tolerating the Marquis's company—outwardly, at least.

You see, she would earnestly explain, *the Marquis has been most generous to the charity I'm involved with. Yes, I mean the school, of course. So kind of him, don't you think?*

She'd practised the words over and over while Martha dressed her for the ball. *So kind of him...*

She suddenly realised the dance had ended and, almost solicitously, Lefevre was guiding her to a corner of the big room. 'I trust you're enjoying yourself?' he asked.

She shivered a little. 'I think,' she began, 'I would like a small glass of wine, Monsieur Lefevre.'

'Good idea.' A faint smile tugged at the corner of his mouth. 'Though a larger one might help to take that frozen look from your face.'

She struggled to reply. Hateful, hateful man! Only at that minute—'Serena? Why, Serena—you said you weren't coming tonight!'

Turning abruptly, she saw her friends coming towards her. Beth's eyes were wide with surprise, Mary's with disapproval and Joanna's with something approaching delight. She recalled with fresh horror that all three of them had watched her the other day being driven away in the Marquis's curricle, but Joanna was the only one who had the slightest idea what was going on.

Beth had spoken first, but it was Joanna who chimed in next. 'Well, Serena,' she said. 'Aren't you going to introduce us, my dear?'

Serena had to admit that Raphael Lefevre's manners were impeccable. He bowed in turn to each of her friends as she gave their names, murmuring, '*Enchanté*, ladies. I've heard a good deal about you.'

Mary and Beth were clearly unable to speak for astonishment and unmistakable dismay. Joanna's eyes, on the other hand, were twinkling.

'I am delighted,' Lefevre went on smoothly, 'to have the chance to express my admiration for the work you do to improve the lives of those less fortunate in circumstance than yourselves.' Mary's eyes opened very wide. 'I'm speaking, of course,' explained Lefevre, 'about your charity school. Lady Serena?' He turned to her. 'Perhaps you'd tell them?'

The phrases she'd so carefully rehearsed earlier were performing clumsy somersaults in her head. *Most generous...has expressed a philanthropic interest...* 'The Marquis,' she said at last with a stiff smile, 'has kindly agreed to donate two hundred guineas to further the work of our school. He and I have discovered that the education of the less privileged is a topic of mutual interest. Indeed, the subject has quite drawn us together, I find!' She beamed up at him and could have sworn he gave a barely perceptible wink.

Mary was speechless. Beth appeared bewildered. 'But, Serena,' Beth began, 'the other day you—'

Serena saw Joanna dig Beth in the ribs before chiming in, 'Serena! To have engaged Monsieur Lefevre as an ally—how wonderful! Such an unexpected friendship. But such a worthy cause!'

'Indeed,' said Lefevre and Serena registered that the man looked hatefully smug. 'Perhaps,' he went on, 'I should fetch some champagne to celebrate my new acquaintances? Excuse me a moment, ladies. I'll be back soon—you may depend on it!'

He touched Serena lightly on the arm and strolled off through the crowds.

Joanna drew a little nearer to Serena. 'An inspirational idea of yours,' she murmured. 'Money for our school. Well done!'

Mary had been watching Lefevre's departure with some scepticism. 'Well,' she said. 'Let's hope, Serena, that your gratitude to the Marquis doesn't extend too far. I must say I find all this a little surprising. Why didn't you tell us about the Marquis's offer when we were all at Joanna's house, and we questioned you about that unfortunate incident in Covent Garden? And why did you say your dressmaker sent that note, when it was actually Monsieur Lefevre who was waiting down the road for you?'

Think quickly, Serena. 'Oh, dear,' she said. 'I do apologise, Mary. But at that point, you see, I wasn't at all sure that his offer of a donation was certain! And I didn't want to raise anyone's hopes, my own most of all. I must confess that the Marquis has expressed an interest in our school before, but I didn't know whether to believe him. Now, however, in view of his kind contribution, I think there can be no doubt of his good intentions.' She waved her fan to cool her over-warm cheeks. 'And there's something else. He and I have also decided we might enjoy one another's company on such an occasion as this.'

'And so,' said Joanna blithely, 'you find yourself at a grand ball with our notorious Marquis! What fun!'

'What fun,' echoed Serena in a hollow voice.

Beth still looked puzzled, but she tried as usual to be kind. 'Perhaps we've misjudged him, Serena? Perhaps we were all wrong about the Marquis's unfortunate reputation?'

No, thought Serena rather wildly. *No, Beth, we weren't wrong about him in the least.*

'Never fear,' Joanna declared. 'Beth, the Marquis's daredevil reputation remains intact. But, Serena, my dear, he is without a doubt the most tempting man in London—and you must enjoy every minute with him! Mustn't she, ladies?'

Serena shot her a warning look because at that very moment she'd spotted Lefevre returning, followed by a footman bearing a tray of wine glasses. 'Ladies,' Lefevre announced, 'champagne for us all! Here's to your noble charity work!'

'So generous of you, *monsieur*,' purred Joanna as she reached for a glass, 'to be making such a substantial donation to our cause.'

Serena ventured to take a sip of champagne, but she almost choked on it when Lefevre gave a slight bow in her direction and said, 'I must admit that I view most charity efforts as pure self-indulgence, created to salve the consciences of the rich. But how could I resist this particular cause? Especially when such a charming lady begged me for my help!'

He put his hand possessively on Serena's shoulder. It felt warm. It felt strong. It sent her already heated thoughts scrambling into confusion. 'I did not *beg*,' she began. 'You know I did no such thing—'

But just then a crowd of fashionable men strolled by and stopped. 'Lefevre, by God! Here you are, toasting the Wicked Widows—what a caper! Got them all under your spell, have you? But listen, while you're here, what's your opinion on the race tomorrow at Newmarket? Which nag are you putting your money on, hey?'

Lefevre moved away to speak with his friends and Mary, still frowning, drew closer to Serena. 'You know, I believe we agreed the affairs of our charity were meant to be confidential. I really don't like the thought of the school being discussed with the likes of that man, no matter how much money he gives. We can maybe consider it at our meeting next Monday. It's your turn to host, Serena, isn't it? In the meantime I feel you need to have a word with him. And to give you the opportunity, we'll leave the two of you together, since it looks as if the Marquis is about to return.' She looked round at the other two. 'Are you coming, ladies?'

Beth looked torn for a moment, but then she dutifully followed Mary. Joanna patted Serena's hand and whispered, 'I'll visit you soon, darling. I think Lefevre's donation is a brilliant idea of yours. Believe me, I cannot wait to hear more.'

She sauntered off just as Lefevre returned. He smiled down at her. 'Being tactful, are they, your friends? Leaving us together for a romantic interlude?'

Serena felt two spots of colour burning on her cheeks. 'You did that deliberately, didn't you? Shocking my friends with your flippant comment about my begging for your help!'

He put on a look of wounded innocence. 'But it was you who suggested I support this school of yours!'

'I certainly didn't want it to look as if I was… was *pursuing* you,' she replied heatedly. 'Which was how you, *monsieur*, made it appear!'

'*Hélas*. I have to keep up my reputation,' he murmured.

This was too much. 'I'm going,' she declared, turning to sweep away; but his powerful hand on her shoulder stopped her.

'Going where, precisely, my lady?'

'Home!'

'No, you're not.' Lefevre spoke mildly. 'Not yet, anyway. We have an agreement. Don't you remember?'

She looked pointedly at a wall clock nearby. 'I've been here for over an hour with you. I've danced with you and I'll be lucky if my friends ever speak to me again after your flippant comment about charities being an indulgence of the privileged few!'

'And aren't they?'

She felt hot and confused under his steady

gaze. 'Maybe there's a little truth in it. But did you have to actually say so? Haven't you done enough harm for one evening?'

'There's no harm done, as far as I'm aware. And if you leave now, Lady Serena, I'll follow. Everyone will come to the same conclusion— which is, of course, that the two of us can't wait to get into bed together.'

She backed away, feeling dizzy.

That comment should not have come as such a surprise, because of the way he was looking at her. Her attire was modest, but she felt she might as well be naked. She tried to ignore the carnal interest in the depths of his eyes, but as his gaze took in her face and her figure, something deep inside her was unfurling in an almost agonising torment. He shouldn't be doing this to her. She couldn't *let* him do this to her.

'So will you stay on for a while, Lady Serena?' he asked her.

'You are hateful,' she whispered.

'Careful. Smile back at me—that's right. People are watching us and they might be able to tell what you're saying. You need to look as though you can't tear your eyes from me.' He drew closer and whispered, 'Look as if you'd like me to kiss you. Again.'

The man was simply impossible! 'Your vanity never ceases to amaze me, Monsieur Lefevre,' she retorted. 'Put it this way. I'd need to drink a whole bottle of champagne first.'

'Really?' He sounded surprised and impressed. 'Then let me fetch—'

'And that,' she interrupted, 'is not going to happen.' She thrust her still half-full glass on the tray of a passing waiter. 'So, since you're forcing me to stay—shall we dance?'

He took both her hands and drew her near. His smile had gone now, to be replaced by a strange and intent look on his face. *Mine,* it appeared to say. *You are mine now.*

Serena felt a small implosion rippling all through her body and through every limb. She felt rocked by some surge of need that she'd never felt before and that she couldn't name. Didn't even want to name. Still Lefevre was watching her, with just his look tormenting her in a way she feared would render her helpless were it not for the basic warning that drummed in her brain, telling her that if she gave way to this terrifying tangle of emotions, she would be lost. To *him.* The man she despised.

'You must learn to act your part, Lady Serena,' he murmured in her ear as they took their place among the dancers. 'As I have, for many years.'

She looked swiftly up at him. 'You, *monsieur,* might enjoy lying to people and manipulating them. I'm afraid I don't.'

This time he laughed aloud. 'Your opinion of my character never ceases to amuse me. But we made an agreement and I think you'd be wise to do as I say. Or—' and he said it quite casually '—would you prefer the news to be spread of your husband's shameful death?'

To which there was no possible answer.

And so Serena danced again with Lefevre. But as the music played and the couples moved around them in a dazzling display of peacock colours, her heart was bleak indeed, not only because he was right and she could not afford to break their pact, but because she was far too aware of his strength. His smile. His powerful masculinity.

Her body was betraying her.

She'd made a fool of herself once already in her life. *Never again*, she vowed silently. *Never again*. But she had one whole month of this to endure, so somehow she smiled. Somehow she carried on smiling till the dancing drew to its close, when he led her away, nodding his approval.

'Good,' he said. 'Very good. Even I might be fooled into thinking you enjoyed yourself.'

Her smile vanished in a flash. 'I take no pleasure in being completely humiliated, I assure you!'

He'd drawn her into a corner beneath the musicians' gallery, from where they could survey the main throng. 'Many women wouldn't consider you're being humiliated,' he pointed out. 'Look around. You're certainly the object of a large amount of interest.'

She didn't have to look around to know what was going on. Even though they'd been in the ballroom for some time, people were still nudging one another and whispering. *Lady Serena. With the Marquis, of all people!*

She shivered. 'I detest being the subject of common gossip.'

'Welcome to the real world. You'll get used to it. As I've had to.'

Her response came swiftly. 'That's different! You demand attention with everything you do, everything you say. You enjoy it!'

'Do you truly think so?'

Her heart stopped a moment because of something in his eyes.

'You don't know anything,' he went on in the same controlled tone, 'about my life, or about me. I play games, Lady Serena—just as we all do, one way or another.'

She suddenly felt terribly vulnerable, because of the strange and totally unwanted effect he was having on her. 'I've told you, *monsieur*, that I do not like your games in the slightest. Maybe I ought to have dealt with Silas Mort myself—'

'Ha!' he broke in. 'As you did the other night?

In other words, most ineffectively and putting yourself in danger into the bargain?' His lip curled. 'Anyway, there's no need. Silas Mort won't trouble you again.'

Again her heart faltered. 'You've spoken to him?'

He considered a moment and said, 'Certainly, I've made it absolutely clear to him that you are under my protection.'

She bit her lip. *How?* Had Lefevre paid the man off? Had he threatened him? And what words had been spoken between them, about her own foolishness? She felt the sheer humiliation of it scalding her. 'I suppose,' she said in a low voice, 'I ought to thank you.'

'Oh, do, by all means! But I realise it must have been hard for you to have to face the fact that your much-loved husband wasn't the hero you thought him to be.'

She closed her eyes briefly. Opened them wide and said innocently, 'Tell me, *monsieur*. Talking of heroes—did you never feel like staying in France and trying to restore order, as many of your fellow noblemen did? You were a soldier once, I believe. Didn't you want to join the Royalist army, to try to defeat the bloodthirsty murderers who are wreaking such havoc in your homeland?'

He shook his head with mock sadness. 'Regretfully, my lady, I'm no hero.'

She was about to say, *Evidently.* But then—suddenly—she caught something else in his expression that shook her badly. There was a kind of ragged bleakness in his eyes, a hint even of horrors he'd maybe witnessed. It was gone in an instant, to be hidden again behind that mask of decadence, but she felt a deep and shocking yearning to know more of this man.

It was then that she became aware of someone watching her intently from the other side of the room. A man who looked as if at any moment he was about to head in her direction. Quickly she touched Raphael's coat sleeve. 'Monsieur Lefevre, I refused champagne earlier, but now I would be very glad of a drink.'

'Certainly.' He looked slightly surprised. 'Lemonade, or a cordial of some kind? Shall I find you a chair?'

'I don't mind what I have. And I'll find a chair myself!' *Please go. Please go.*

So Lefevre left and just in time, because the man she'd seen looking at her in such a resolute fashion was almost upon her. It was Mr Jeremy Wolverton.

Chapter Nine

'My dear Lady Serena,' Wolverton began, 'the minute I saw who you were with, I asked your friends how this could have happened. And they told me you actually *arrived* with that man!'

Oh, Lord.

Jeremy Wolverton was a worthy churchgoing man who was also very wealthy, thanks to his business as an importer of fine fabrics. His money and his generosity to several charities had brought him an entrée to certain society events, although naturally the higher circles of society were still closed to him. He was thirty-two years old and as yet unmarried. His appearance was every bit as correct as his manners—his brown hair was always neatly cropped and his clothes were immaculate, if severe. Joanna was convinced he had intentions towards Serena, but she, though sorry for the put-downs he received, was careful to give him no encouragement.

'Mr Wolverton,' she replied, 'I appreciate your concern. But I am free to make my own choices as to the company I keep.'

He looked even more worried. 'But to associate with a man of his reputation! My lady, let me escort you home, straight away. My carriage is outside—'

'No!' Serena felt her irritation bubbling up and went on more coolly, 'Thank you. But as it happens, I'm perfectly happy to spend another hour or two at this party and to leave with you would be unspeakably rude to the Marquis.'

'You know my opinion of the Marquis!' Wolverton declared. 'He is nothing but a despicable pleasure-seeker and not worthy of your company!'

Which was unfortunate, because that was the moment Raphael Lefevre strolled up to Serena's side with a glass of lemonade. Handing it to her, he said, 'I assume the Marquis in question is me? It usually is.'

Wolverton coloured. 'I was advising Lady Serena,' he said stiffly, 'that she should take more care of the company she keeps.'

'And who are you to advise her, I wonder?' drawled Lefevre, not at all ruffled. 'Family? Guardian? I thought not. So make yourself scarce, there's a good fellow.'

'I strongly object to your tone, *monsieur*! I am

Lady Serena's friend and I bear her nothing but respect. Unfortunately, I suspect that you have rather different intentions. And I warn you, if you do anything to upset her—'

Serena saw with dismay that Lefevre, by far the taller and more powerful man, was facing Wolverton full on. 'You'll do what? Pray tell me, I'm intrigued. Perhaps you'll challenge me to a duel? You really shouldn't, you know. Whether it's swords, pistols or fists, I think you'll come to a rather unhappy end. In fact, I guarantee it. Let me escort you to the door, Mr... Wolverton, isn't it? No, don't argue. You've had your say and it's time for you to leave. After all, this is hardly your natural *milieu,* is it?'

Wolverton was backing away. 'You arrogant, bullying—'

Lefevre said, quietly but dangerously, 'Time for you to go, Wolverton.'

As Lefevre accompanied Wolverton to the main doors, Serena realised that the dancing had stopped. The talking had stopped. Every single person in that crowded ballroom had been watching—and as soon as the two men were out of sight, their eyes turned on her.

Serena was upset. Humiliated. And something else—Jeremy Wolverton had always been a stalwart friend to the charity school and to her. She knew he would have been delighted to receive an invitation to this ball, so Lefevre's put-down in public just now would have hurt him sorely.

As the Marquis returned to her, she faced him with battle in her eyes. 'My goodness,' she said, 'I must admit I didn't realise when we made our agreement that it included the possibility of you threatening to fight off my male acquaintances.'

That was when she realised the enormous tension that possessed his body. His shoulders were still braced as if for action, his jaw set hard. Serena stepped back. People dismissed Lefevre as a shallow rake, but yet again she felt she was glimpsing something in him that was far more dangerous than that.

But then, slowly, he relaxed. He even smiled that wickedly hypnotic smile of his and said, 'You realise, though, Lady Serena, that I tend to make an impact wherever I go. One way or another.'

'And I hate it,' she said in a low voice. 'Hate it, do you hear?' She was aware that everyone was still watching them and she was suddenly overtaken by an enormous fatigue. 'Please take me home. Now.'

So he did. He led her from the room past all those onlookers with his arm firmly round her waist and Serena felt like his prisoner. But the trouble was, she didn't loathe the feeling as much as she knew she should. He was a man guaranteed to make men envious and women melt, no matter how much they claimed to detest him. So she said nothing as he collected her cloak and wrapped it round her shoulders; but when he led her outside and she saw his carriage waiting with a groom standing by the horses' heads, she whipped round to him, saying, 'How did your groom know to be here so early?'

'I told him to be ready at about this time. You see, I suspected we might be leaving sooner than expected—for one reason or another.'

This man. This arrogant man. 'You have everything planned, don't you?' Serena said bitterly. 'Down to the last detail. I believe you've been determined to humiliate me from our very first meeting!'

He was pointing to the open carriage door. 'People are watching. Best get inside.'

'No. No, I won't!'

He said harshly, 'Get in the carriage and we can have our argument in there. Not out here, where every passer-by can stare at us. And smile at me, for God's sake.'

So she did. She looked up at him and smiled, at the same time aware that her heart was fluttering against her ribs, because, although he was utterly hateful, her eyes were somehow held by his mesmerising silver-grey ones and she felt the heat rising in her body.

Of course, he was right. People were strolling by on the pavement and vehicles clattered along the busy road, so she let him help her up into the carriage and then, when he'd seated himself opposite to her, she looked straight at him and said, 'What a *perfect* evening we have had, you and I! How could I wish for pleasanter company than yours, my lord, ever? Did you take me to this ball tonight for yet another wager? How much will your winnings be this time?'

He rapped on the roof to indicate they were ready to move away. Then he said, 'If you're referring to the ball last November, I did not dance with you for a wager.'

Again, her world rocked. 'You did. I heard what your friend said that night. You cannot deny it.'

'But I do deny it, absolutely. That fool who made the comment wasn't my friend—he was a mischief-maker and a complete liar. There was no truth whatsoever in his taunt about a wager and afterwards I dealt with him accordingly. Unfortunately, the damage had been done.'

She was silent, her mind reeling. *All these months. All these months, I've believed it.* She said at last, 'Why didn't you tell me at the time? Why didn't you deny straight away that you'd danced with me for money?'

'If I remember correctly, you didn't give me a chance. You believed instantly what that ridiculous man had said and you stalked away.'

Much shaken, Serena answered, 'If what you say is true—then why did you ask me to dance in the first place?'

His eyes gleamed. 'Why did I ask you to dance? If you're looking for compliments, then here they are. Was it because of your beauty? Partly, since of course it's exceptional. But since you ask, there was something else. I asked you to dance because you looked as if you didn't care in the least whether or not anyone asked you. In other words, you struck me as altogether different from all the other foolish, flirtatious females there. You intrigued me—and have done since I first laid eyes on you soon after my arrival in the city. But as for tonight, what can I say? I'm sorry you didn't enjoy the occasion. It's not my aim to make the coming month an endurance test for you.'

'You were unspeakably rude to poor Mr Wolverton!'

'As I recall, Wolverton was rude about me. Besides, he's an upstart.'

He spoke so calmly, yet Serena felt anything

but calm, because all night this man had stirred up a confusion of feelings she had no idea how to handle, except with fresh defiance. 'So I'm to reject my friends and look blissfully happy whenever I'm with you—is that correct? Difficult though it is, I really am trying my best, Monsieur Lefevre!'

The carriage was moving at a steady pace now and the streetlights glinting through its windows cast mysterious shadows on his starkly handsome face. He said, 'You really don't need to hate me *all* the time, you know. I can see your scorn churning around inside you, but be careful. Such tension can make you ill.'

'I wouldn't need to think about you at all if you hadn't imposed this ridiculous agreement on me. And let me assure you, I usually have more worthwhile matters to occupy my mind!'

He settled back against the seat and gave her his curious half-smile. 'You're not thinking of marrying again, are you? Of course, you won't lack for suitors, but I sincerely hope you're not going to marry Wolverton. He's rich, admittedly, but what a dreary existence you'd lead.'

'You think so?' She managed a cool stare. 'Even so, it might be preferable to being in your power, Monsieur le Marquis!'

'It's unfortunate for you, then, that you have to remain in my power for some time yet.'

She made no response but sat silent, rigid, until the carriage drew up outside her front door. 'Three days since our kiss,' he said softly as he accompanied her up the steps, 'but quite a number of days to go. And I rather wish you could try to enjoy them. Live for now. That's my motto.' Then he took her hand and kissed it. Only lightly, but she felt the warmth of his lips and suddenly imagined that clever, knowing mouth pressed against other parts of her body…

She shivered a little, not with revulsion, but with some dark craving that made her mind swim. She closed her eyes briefly, her hand still enfolded by his strong one. When she opened them he was watching her carefully.

At last he released her, murmuring, 'Until next time, my lady. *Adieu.*'

And with that, he was gone.

Serena didn't want any more surprises. She wanted to be on her own to nurse her wounds, but the ever-eager Grinling was opening the front door almost before the Marquis's carriage had moved away and Mrs Penney was there, too, swiftly followed by Martha, who helped her out of her velvet cloak.

'Oh, ma'am,' Martha enthused as she followed Serena up to her room. 'Did you have a lovely evening? Such a handsome gentleman, the Marquis!' Martha hesitated as they entered Serena's bedchamber. 'It's so good to see you enjoy yourself for a change!'

Martha had been her maid for years and was one of the very few people who had guessed the truth about her marriage. Lionel had betrayed her countless times and in countless ways, but Serena had always been forced to hide her unhappiness, because society adored him. And he'd died fighting bravely for his country—or so everyone, including she, had believed.

She'd built a new life for herself since then, with no men to complicate her independence, just the company of her true and loving female friends. But now the Marquis of Montpellier had crashed into her world with an impact that had somehow changed everything—because when he'd kissed her the other night, she'd felt such a disturbing rush of pleasure that her insides had melted. Her body had begged for more. And what really, truly frightened her was that she hadn't hated that moment of weakness as she knew she should.

You must stay in control, she whispered to herself. *You're good at being in control.*

But was she?

She'd had to force herself to be strong in order to survive her marriage. At first she'd blamed herself for Lionel's reluctance to spend much time with his new bride and thought it her fault that he was so eager to join his old set of friends once their honeymoon was over. He took up with former mistresses, too—she discovered that soon enough.

But Lionel liked her money, which was clearly all he'd married her for. *I will endure this,* she'd resolved at the time. *I must endure this.* For a woman of her rank to leave her husband was unthinkable.

After he had died in battle she tried to mourn him, or at least to mourn the man he could have been. She blamed herself still for her rash and foolish marriage and resolved that from now on she would live her life in the way she chose. She'd felt free, almost happy—until Silas Mort had approached her in the park.

She should have challenged Mort to tell everyone, then relied on the hope that no one would have believed him. But she hadn't, because she was too afraid that what he said was true and that others might come forward to verify the tale of Lionel's cowardice. Her foolish pride had laid her wide open to blackmail and to Lefevre's devious plans also; but Lefevre carried with him an extra threat.

She'd resolved never to take another husband. Told herself she did not need a man in her life—and her resolve was still steadfast. But when Raphael Lefevre was close, she felt her body was betraying her and always would. She must fight this terrible weakness. She *had* to fight it. And Lefevre must never, ever know her vulnerability—otherwise the mockery in his eyes during the coming weeks would be unendurable.

Chapter Ten

Once he'd taken Serena home, Raphael reached his own house to find Jacques waiting for him. After ordering a groom to put away the carriage and horses, Raphael listened in silence to what Jacques had to say.

'I've been over to Clerkenwell, my lord. Near to where many of the poor French have settled, as you know. There's an establishment in Lay-stall Street that might be worth you looking at.'

Raphael tensed. 'Then I'll go there. Now.'

'At this hour? You do realise it's almost midnight?'

'Midnight might be a good time for my visit, I suspect.'

'Very well.' Jacques looked resigned. 'Do you want me to drive you there, my lord?'

Raphael thought for a moment, then shook his

head. 'No, that would draw too much attention. Find me a hackney cab, will you?'

Inside the house he was met by his English butler, Surtees, who'd worked for many years for the previous occupant. 'My lord,' Surtees said deferentially. 'Do you require any refreshment? Food or brandy, maybe?'

Raphael found the man's respectful manner a sharp contrast to the sometimes critical observations of Jacques. 'No.' He shook his head. 'I'm going out again.'

'My lord.' Surtees bowed and retreated, without a word of comment or rebuke.

Twenty minutes later Raphael, having exchanged his evening finery for a drab overcoat and low-crowned hat, was inside a cab and heading north-eastwards through the city until the driver pulled up in Clerkenwell. Raphael paid him and surveyed his surroundings, noting that the narrow, cobbled streets were lined with tall houses that were all in darkness at this hour—except for one, where candlelight glimmered from behind shuttered windows. Late though it was, two grimy-faced lads appeared as if from nowhere. 'You after some pretty ladies, mister?'

'Maybe,' he answered.

They grinned knowingly and pointed to the

shuttered house. 'Lots of nice ones in there,' the older one said. 'Enjoy yourself, mister.'

Raphael went to rap hard on the door. It opened to reveal a big woman with a fierce face and stout arms folded across her ample bosom. 'Yes?'

'I'm looking for someone,' he said.

'Female, I hope? Well, now. Pray come inside, sir. You like them fair or dark? Thin or plump?'

He followed her along a narrow, dimly lit hallway. And he said, 'Have you any women here from Paris?'

'Ha!' She turned to face him. 'Is that where your tastes lie? Let's see what we can do for you, shall we?'

This place was like all the others he'd visited since arriving in London last year. It contained a series of small curtained chambers that smelled of cheap perfume, yet the madam in charge showed him round almost proudly, tugging back the curtains one by one. The women on display peered up at him, some curious and others bored. One tried to tempt him by tugging down her scanty bodice.

They weren't French, any of them. 'Don't know about Paris,' the madam said when he questioned her again. 'But that one—' she pointed '—knows quite a lot of Continental tricks—if that's what you want.'

'Are you ever offered French women?' Raphael asked curtly.

'I'm offered them from time to time, indeed.' She shrugged. 'But to be honest, I generally turn them down, see, because they're usually scared and silly. Most of them don't speak any English even. Trouble, they are, absolute trouble—believe me, you'd be far better with one of my ladies! Now, here's Susan. She'll keep a distinguished gent like you *very* happy—'

He cut in. 'Do you know the names of the men who offer you these French women?'

'I don't ask their names, mister.' She was looking defensive now. 'But they're doing those girls a favour, I'd say. Because surely those women are better off here than in their own God-forsaken country where innocent folks get murdered by the dozen every day!' She put her hands on her hips. 'So do you want any of my girls, or are you wasting my time?'

Raphael pressed his lips together. He said at last, 'Maybe I've decided I'm not in the mood after all. Here's money for your trouble.'

Her hard face softened only a little as he handed her the coins. She escorted him rather brusquely to the door and he set off towards Theobald's Road in the hopes of finding another cab.

'*Imbécile.* You should have paid your last driver to wait,' he muttered grimly under his breath.

Raphael had never been particularly proud of himself. Born the younger son of a hugely privileged family, he'd risen in rank in the French army without having to fight a single battle. Together with his fellow officers, most of them aristocrats also, he'd been a dissolute pleasure-seeker—until the Revolution overturned the world he'd known. Two years ago he'd travelled home to Montpellier and arrived in time to see his family's chateau engulfed by flames. Jacques, who'd been his servant in the army, had travelled with him; indeed, it was Jacques who had held him back from charging the brutes who'd fired the house.

'No use, milord,' Jacques had hissed in his ear. 'There's too many of the devils, even for you.'

Two long years ago—and still the memories cut through him like a knife. Those devils called themselves Revolutionaries, but they'd been naught but a drunken mob and, after beating his brother without pity, they'd left him to die amid the still-burning ruins.

Last autumn Raphael had arrived in London to be welcomed into the upper ranks of English society; or by most of its members at any rate, since he gave every appearance of being committed to a life of pleasure. He'd pretended not to care one jot for the violence engulfing his own homeland—indeed, he'd let it be assumed that he'd avoided the Revolution's bloody aftermath by travelling through Europe and enjoying the high life in Vienna before moving on to London. Many of his new English friends, rakehells like Beaumaris, chuckled in agreement. 'Wise of you, Lefevre. Very wise.'

Lady Serena had taken a different view, especially after that fateful dance. It was Jacques who'd first warned Raphael that she'd been openly criticising his conduct and asking questions about his past. 'Has the man truly abandoned his responsibilities to his fellow countrymen?' she'd declared. 'Has he no shame?'

That was the moment he realised he had to act. To warn her he would tolerate her troublemaking no longer; hence his resolve to force her into this mockery of an alliance. He knew she would find it humiliating and he'd assured himself she deserved nothing less. But as his plan progressed, he felt several quite unexpected emotions. Sympathy. Admiration for her, even. And…desire?

No, he told himself. Impossible, because Lady Serena's chilly kind of beauty was, he assured himself, something he could easily resist. The fact that she hated him should even afford him some amusement. *Lady Serena!* people would chuckle.

*Lefevre, the rogue, has succeeded in charming
the ice-cold Lady Serena!*

Four weeks only. Yet as he finally managed
to hail a cab and settled himself inside, he once
more felt that tug of regret that they had to be
enemies and she would end up hating him more
than ever. But he warned himself to dismiss any
such concerns as mere emotional nonsense, that
a man who'd sworn a vow to his dying brother
simply could not afford.

So the cab took him homewards through the
midnight streets and he thought not of Serena, but
of girls being brought to London unable to speak a
word of English and ending up...where? In places
like the house he'd just visited. The thought was
unendurable. His resolve was renewed: he had
to press on with his quest and Lady Serena, like
anyone else who stood in his way, could have no
hold whatsoever upon his emotions.

The morning after the ball Serena came downstairs to be greeted by flowers. Not just any flowers, either—it was as if a whole florist's shop had
been raided for its choicest, most exotic speci-
mens. 'Oh, ma'am,' Mrs Penney and Martha exclaimed in delight as they arranged the jungle of
blooms in various vases. 'Aren't they just beautiful? They must have cost a fortune!'

Serena felt as though her heart was beating rather unsteadily. 'Yes. I suppose they must.'

'And look, ma'am—here's a note. Don't you want to know who they're from?'

Not really. Reading the note without expression, she put it down again. Raphael Lefevre, of course. *'Beautiful flowers for a beautiful lady.'* The note was merely folded, not sealed, which was a deliberate ploy she was sure. He would know that all her servants would be aware the gift was from him and the news would spread swiftly around Mayfair.

Last night at the ball he'd said, 'Everyone will come to the same conclusion—which is, of course, that the two of us can't wait to get into bed together.' The flowers would be yet another public confirmation of their mutual desire. Desperately Serena tried to rally herself. She would tell him when he next called that, although she had to endure his company, she didn't want his gifts. She would point out that she disliked the strong perfume of hothouse flowers.

But he didn't call, that day or the next. She had received several invitations for those evenings, but she refused all of them, telling herself she was all too happy to be on her own. Free of *him*. But she thought about him far too much. All the time, in fact.

That damnable, damnable man. What a tangle she was in. How difficult it was to think of anything—anyone—except Raphael Lefevre.

On Sunday she attended church in her brother's company as usual. But as the two of them left after the service, George was side-tracked by the vicar and she realised that Jeremy Wolverton, who attended the same church, was making straight for her.

'Lady Serena,' he began, 'I hope I didn't upset you the other night at the Duke of Hamilton's ball. But believe me, I was only thinking of your welfare! That man…'

'I presume,' she said, putting up her parasol against the midday sun, 'that you are referring to the Marquis of Montpellier?'

'Indeed. Who else? I apologise for briefly losing my self-control. But to see him in your company! Don't you realise the risk you're running?'

'I thought,' she replied, 'that you might have heard by now how generous he's recently been to our school.'

'I did! But doesn't this mean you are letting Lefevre *buy* your approval?' Wolverton must have seen the sudden frostiness in her eyes because he went on quickly, 'I'm sorry. I apologise. It's only because my own feelings are involved that I—'

He broke off and shook his head. 'At the risk of offending you yet again, I feel duty-bound to tell you that I consider Lefevre is not worthy to be seen in your company!'

'I think your sense of duty is exceeding the bounds of civility,' she answered. 'Mr Wolverton, I really must move on, since I see my brother is waiting by his carriage to take me home. So unless there's anything else...?'

He bowed. 'My lady, I only wanted to assure you of my ardent friendship. Please remember that you can turn to me any time. Any time at all.'

She was aware of him watching her as she walked steadily over to George's town carriage. Often she took Sunday lunch at her brother's house, but today she asked him to take her straight home. 'I hope you're not seeing that fellow Lefevre this afternoon,' said George as he settled inside the carriage with her.

'No.' She spoke tightly. 'No, George, I'm not seeing him today.'

'Or ever again, I hope.' He was easing himself into his seat, then looked directly at her. 'I heard some news about your friend the Marquis. He is, as I suspected, a cheat and a liar.'

Please, no. First Wolverton, now her brother. Her heart sank, but she managed to lift her eyebrows in mock amusement. 'Why, George, isn't that exactly what you've always thought him to be? This is hardly news, surely?'

George pointed a finger at her. 'Listen, sister mine. Have you ever asked the man what kind of life he was living before he arrived in London last year? He abandoned his family estate years ago—everyone knows that.'

'He was enjoying himself, I presume,' she answered lightly. 'I've heard that he spent some time living the high life in Vienna.'

George shook his head. 'Not true!'

'And how do you know that, pray?'

'Because I was talking last night to a prominent Austrian nobleman, von Heidig, who's here at present as a guest of Austria's ambassador. He said that although many French aristocrats sought refuge in Vienna after the Revolution, the Marquis of Montpellier was definitely not among them. "Such a distinguished gentleman," he said to me, "would surely not have escaped my notice." Distinguished! Ha! So where was he, Serena? What other lies has he told everyone? How can you fall for his tricks?'

'George,' she said with a great effort at calmness, 'I've no intention of falling for any man's tricks, let alone Lefevre's. He amuses me, that's all.'

'Very well. But I must express my strongest

concern that you are associating with such a rogue and in my opinion—'

'What is this?' she broke in. 'Why assume that the time Lefevre was supposed to be in Vienna was spent in knavery?'

'Because the man is a scoundrel!'

'I've seen no sign of it myself,' she said quietly. She folded her hands over the reticule in her lap. 'In addition to which, he's been most generous to our school.'

'Oh, so that's how he's getting around you, is it? I can't believe you're defending the man.'

She found she was trembling slightly. 'I'd rather not speak of him any more. Please, George?'

George pressed his lips together and the rest of the journey to Curzon Street passed in silence. Serena was secretly horrified. *Defending the Marquis.* Was she really? She could hardly believe it. First Jeremy Wolverton and now her brother had told her this morning that she must not associate with Lefevre—and she'd defended him to both of them. She had to, she told herself rather shakily. She was in his power, because he knew about Mort's blackmail and the reason for it. But there was something else.

She'd come to believe that she could reject any man's advances without a second thought, but the Marquis was different. His kiss that night in Cov-

ent Garden had kindled something deep inside
her, stirring up feelings of confusion and heat
and, yes—need. At the ball, just his lightest caress
had made her all too aware of the kinds of things
she knew a woman should want from a man. And
from the mocking curl of his lips whenever he
looked at her, it was as if he knew it.

She reminded herself that she would survive
this humiliation. She had faced worse, after all,
thanks to the mistake of her marriage, which she'd
endured for two long years without anyone except her closest friends guessing how unhappy she
was. Lefevre told her she was too proud, but her
pride was also her strength. So accustomed was
she to guarding her emotions that she'd come to
believe she was unassailable as far as men were
concerned.

Until Raphael Lefevre had come into her life.

As soon as her own front door was closed
behind her, she told Mrs Penney and Grinling,
'Please inform anyone else who calls that I have
a headache.' But no one did call. The afternoon
passed slowly; she found she could settle to nothing. And all day, the scent of those wretched flowers seemed to mock her.

The next morning she settled in her sunny
front parlour and began the usual task of open-

ing the day's invitations, but her heart bumped
to a stop when she opened a thick cream en-
velope and found inside a note from Raphael
Lefevre. *I trust you will accompany me to an
exclusive event on Wednesday afternoon. Make
sure you look your very best. I shall call for
you at two.*

She put it down on the table with a sharp snap.
So he planned on another all too public display of
their supposed infatuation, did he? And he was
commanding her to look her best? She rose from
her chair and walked fretfully to the window, then
rang the bell for a servant. It was Grinling who
arrived. 'Ma'am?'

'All those flowers that arrived the other day.
Please have them taken to the local almshouse
and ask if they would like them.'

'But, ma'am…'

'The scent is too strong, Grinling. I find they
give me a headache.'

'Ma'am.' Her butler bowed.

'Oh, and, Grinling! I shall not be in to any call-
ers this afternoon.'

He looked surprised. 'Ma'am. Had you forgotten your friends are due to arrive this afternoon?'

Oh, no. The Wicked Widows. And they would
surely want to know more about her and Raphael
Lefevre. Especially after that scene at the ball,

involving Lefevre and Jeremy Wolverton... She really was beginning to have a headache now.

Her friends arrived promptly at two. She welcomed them with a sinking heart, though to her surprise, she was not the first item on their agenda.

'I have some very important news!' announced Mary once they were all seated in Serena's first-floor drawing room. And her news stunned them all. 'Lord Gardner has finally agreed to extend our lease. Moreover, he told me, ladies, that he was persuaded to do so by none other than Monsieur Lefevre! Perhaps we all rather misjudged the Marquis.' She turned to Serena. 'Maybe you could invite him to visit our school soon, so we can express our appreciation? I'm afraid I was slightly scathing the other night about his donation of money—but there is no doubt that the securing of the lease is hugely important to us. So unexpected, yet so generous of him!'

It was now four days since Serena had gone with the Marquis to the Duke of Hamilton's ball. Indeed, if it weren't for those flowers or the maddening invitation that had arrived this morning, she might have guessed he'd grown bored with her. And yet he'd secured the lease—why? She didn't understand. Because he was generous?

Surely not—he was too wily for simple generosity. Was he ingratiating himself with her friends in order to put a yet firmer grip on her?

She sat there, dazed.

The rest of the meeting was spent in discussing the school's finances and the problems arising from the fact that extra pupils kept arriving every day. 'You'll no doubt remember the French children who joined us the other week,' Mary reminded them. 'They're homesick, of course, as exiles are bound to be, but I hope they're learning to see our school as a refuge.'

Serena thought again of Lefevre, who was also an exile in his way, but an exile with wealth and the power that came with it. How could he live such a careless and spendthrift life, when so many suffered? Her consternation lingered to the end of the meeting and for once she wasn't best pleased when Joanna stayed on after the others had gone.

'Quite brilliant of you,' Joanna began, 'to persuade that man to save our school's lease! I really am beginning to think that our Marquis might be rather infatuated with you, darling.'

Serena laughed rather shakily. 'I said nothing to him about the lease. And Monsieur Lefevre, infatuated with me? No. No, that is absurd—'

'Is it really?' Joanna drew closer. 'But Lefevre went to great lengths, I've heard. The news is that on Saturday night he gambled well into the early hours with Lord Gardner for that lease.'

'Impossible!' Serena was shaken anew. 'Why on earth should he do such a thing?'

'Because Lord Gardner point blank refused to sell it to him, but Gardner couldn't resist Lefevre's challenge of a wager. Why the Marquis did it, I cannot imagine—but I can guess. Can't you?'

Serena was shaking her head in bewilderment. 'Lefevre and I are enemies, Joanna. Despite his help with the lease, it's a battle to the end, there's no doubt about it.'

'Are you sure? Because at the Duke's ball, I saw the way he was gazing at you when you weren't aware of it. And he looked as though he'd like to do all the things to you that you dream a man like him might do.' Joanna sighed a little. 'Everyone agrees he's probably the most gorgeous man in London, so keep your wits about you, my girl! Lefevre is decidedly alluring—and, I fear, quite dangerous.'

'He presents no danger to me.' Serena spoke firmly. 'As I said, there are private reasons why I have to endure his company now and then. But I haven't seen him for days.'

Joanna put her hand on Serena's. 'You're seeing

him soon, though, aren't you? I saw that invitation lying on your mantelpiece.' Joanna's eyes gleamed with mischief. 'So my advice is to tantalise *him* for a change! Be coy. Be alluring. And wear the kind of attire that will have him wild for you!'

Chapter Eleven

On Wednesday Raphael arrived in Curzon
Street at two, but Grinling asked him to wait in
the hall.

'My lady will be a little while yet, my lord,'
he announced—with a certain grim satisfaction,
Raphael felt. He resigned himself. It was a lady's
privilege, after all, to be late. She must, he assumed, be putting a fair amount of effort into
preparing herself. He passed the time by looking at a rather astonishing console table ornamented with red and turquoise lacquer and was
almost taken by surprise when he heard her light
footsteps on the staircase behind him. He turned
swiftly and blinked. Then he thought, *Oh, yes,
Very clever of you.*

She was wearing a dress of some plain grey
fabric, long-sleeved and buttoned up to the throat.
A small straw bonnet without ribbons hid most of

her lively blonde curls, rather to Raphael's regret. She looked like a governess.

She came swiftly towards him with that defiant look in her eyes. 'Your invitation told me to look my best. I therefore thought I should make it quite clear to you, my lord, that I will dress exactly as I please and not according to your instructions...'

Her voice tailed away as Raphael waited for her to take in his own attire. He was wearing a loose-fitting brown coat, buff leather breeches and riding boots; all clean, of course, all decidedly expensive, but hardly *haute couture*. He could see she was desperately searching for words.

'Have you *ridden* here?' she asked him sharply at last.

He grinned. 'No. My carriage is outside. But I was at Tattersall's earlier, looking over a couple of new mares for my stables. And I didn't have time to change.'

Her rather lovely face was a picture. Her blue-green eyes flashed liked icy diamonds—oh, he enjoyed that. She said at last, 'But you ordered me to look my best!'

'So I did. And I guessed you would take exception to that and act accordingly. Therefore I decided there was no need for me to go to the trouble of more formal attire.'

She remained speechless for a moment before saying, rather faintly, 'Where are we going?'

'To the Royal Academy.' He was already pointing to the door. 'Shall we be on our way? There's a special exhibition opening today.'

'Which means half of the *ton* will be there!' She pointedly ignored his outstretched arm. 'This is outrageous of you, not to warn me in advance! Although I am not going to change my gown now—not when you, too, are so unsuitably attired. In fact, my lord, I don't think I'll go with you *at all*.'

Raphael could see that Grinling still hovered in the background, waiting to open the front door for them. He stepped closer to Serena and said more quietly, 'My lady. Must I remind you that our agreement still stands?'

'Fiddlesticks to our agreement! Anyway, surely you won't want me at your side when I look like a—like a dowd?'

He made a point of studying her again thoughtfully.

Her grey gown was demure, admittedly, but its bodice gently cupped her small but perfect breasts and her waist looked delectably slender. Certainly the shade of the silk was muted, but if anything that soft dove-grey enhanced the creaminess of her smooth complexion, as did the two pearl eardrops she wore. Actually, she looked amazing. Several days had passed since he'd seen her. Too many days... *Control yourself, you fool.*

Just then her maid hurried down the stairs with a garment over her arm, curtsying to Raphael, then turning to Serena. 'Your pelisse, my lady!' Swiftly she helped Serena into the slim grey pelisse that matched her gown, then put a furled parasol in her hand. 'Enjoy yourself,' the maid murmured, before bobbing another shy curtsy to Raphael and disappearing again.

This time, when Raphael held out his arm, Serena moved to join him, though her reluctance was plain to see. 'You look perfect, my lady,' he murmured. 'Absolutely perfect.' And he realised that he meant it. The scent of her—lilies of the valley, he guessed, delicate yet sensuous—tantalised his nostrils. Oh, how he could fantasise over breaking down her cool façade and coaxing fire into her veins!

She answered tightly, 'You're lying, of course. But I'm afraid—' and she glanced down at his riding breeches '—that your reputation as a man of fashion will be ruined.'

He grinned. 'On the contrary, I shall probably set a new fashion. From now on, looking as though one has just come from the stables will become obligatory.'

He heard her mutter, 'Ridiculous, arrogant man.'

He bowed and pointed to the front door, which Grinling held open. 'My carriage awaits, Lady Serena.'

This was getting a little dangerous, he realised as he escorted her outside to his waiting carriage. He was beginning to succumb to the effect of her combination of beauty and *hauteur*. Of course, pretty faces were commonplace among London's elite; but with Lady Serena, there was something more. The way her eyes blazed when she was angry. The tilt of her firm little chin that challenged him even now—*You dare to try to get the better of me, Raphael Lefevre?* Yes—it was the defiance she offered that set fire to his blood and his loins.

'Do try to look as if you like me,' he reminded her casually as they left the house. 'No doubt your servants and your neighbours will be watching avidly to see how our love match is progressing.'

She turned to him with a look of mild surprise. 'Is it? Progressing, I mean? But I haven't seen you for days, though I imagine you've been busy. Occupied with—how can I put it?—the usual activities of a gentleman with too little to do with his time.'

Raphael's mind flashed back to the hours he'd been spending daily with Dominic, examining

Home Office lists of the known French refugees in the capital and visiting the cheap lodging houses where the exiles lived.

Poor Dominic always wore an expression of weariness on his good-natured face by the end of each outing. 'Raphael, you've got to prepare yourself. She might not have made it here. She might not even be...'

'Alive?' Raphael had supplied the missing word. 'She has to be alive, I tell you.'

A gentleman with too little to do with his time. With a slight bow he moved to help Serena climb into his open barouche, while Jacques sat impassively waiting on the driver's seat.

'Very smart,' she said, indicating the barouche.

'It's a lovely day, so I thought to myself, why not enjoy the fresh air?'

'Ah. So it's nothing to do with ensuring that everyone sees us together?'

He laughed. 'All part of our bargain, Lady Serena.'

She made no reply; but as soon as they were settled side by side, she patted down her skirts and turned to him. 'Tell me,' she said. 'Did you buy those horses you examined at Tattersall's?'

'I did indeed. They were a bargain.'

'Ah. You're fond of bargains, aren't you?' She regarded him steadily. 'Monsieur Lefevre. Was it part of our bargain that you'd involve our charity school in your scheming?'

He called out to Jacques to proceed, then turned to her and raised his eyebrows a little. 'I beg your pardon?'

With rather a crisp gesture, she put up her silk parasol against the sun. 'I'm talking,' she said, 'about your sudden impulse to gamble with Lord Gardner for the lease of the charity school.'

He shrugged. 'What's your objection? The school's been saved, hasn't it?'

'That is *not* the point—'

'Oh, you object to me gambling? Actually, it's a quite enjoyable way to pass the time. You should try it one day. Plenty of ladies of your rank do so.'

He saw her struggling to suppress her annoyance and grinned to himself. Presumably, Lady Serena did not enjoy being associated with such ladies. She said at last, 'You must have played Lord Gardner for high stakes.'

'Indeed, I did.'

She turned on him. 'But what if you'd lost?'

'There was always that chance, but I'm really quite skilful. I'll teach you my methods some day, shall I? Faro is a popular game with the fairer sex.'

Her eyes were glinting dangerously now. '*Monsieur*, I think it would take me a few years to

match your experience of—how shall I put it?—
life's lower pleasures.'

He smiled. 'I take it we're still talking about
the card tables?'

This time she really looked as if she'd like to hit
him and he couldn't help but laugh. 'Sorry. Sorry,
that was really going too far. But I don't happen
to like Lord Gardner very much. And I thought
your school needed that lease rather badly.'

She was starting to look upset. 'But you have
already donated to our school. And we would have
sorted the business of the lease ourselves, eventually—'

'Would you?' he broke in. 'I doubt it. Gardner dislikes ladies he calls "do-gooders". Gardner
says,' he added helpfully, 'that they remind him
too much of his wife.'

'We're not "do-gooders"! And I still think you
are doing all this to deliberately make me look
foolish in front of my friends!' Her pretty cheeks
were flushed with indignation.

'We're in an open carriage,' he reminded her.
They were leaving Curzon Street now and about
to turn right into Clarges Street, where her illus-
trious brother lived. He pointed to the carriages
thronging the road and the many pedestrians.
'You'll observe,' he went on, 'that there are people everywhere and at this moment quite a few of

them are looking in our direction. You can tear me to pieces by all means. But try smiling at me while you're doing so, will you?'

She obliged, but swiftly added sweetly, 'Is it all right if I slap you on the face at the same time, *monsieur*?'

He laughed aloud. 'Most couples save those kinds of antics for the bedroom, Lady Serena. Though I must say I didn't guess your tastes lay in that direction. Do they?'

'You are *impossible*—'

He reached across to touch her cheek, very lightly. How smooth her skin was and how tempting, even when she was furious with him. 'It's a beautiful day,' he said softly. 'The sun is shining, so I suggest you sit back and relish the moment.'

She positively seethed. Raphael laughed to himself. He knew he was being wicked, but he was rather enjoying this. She made such a change from the usual sycophants who gathered round him, hanging on his every word.

If she could have turned her back on him, doubtless she'd have done so, but instead she had to content herself with wielding her parasol as a partial barrier between them while gazing out of his barouche in the pretence of taking in the passing street scene. Raphael decided to thaw the atmosphere, just a little. He began, 'Look. I apologise if you're angry because I gambled for your lease—'

She spun round to face him before he could say any more. '*Yes*. Yes, I am angry! There was no need to indulge in what I suspect is a pitiful attempt to make my friends admire you.'

'It was you who asked for my help with the school in the first place,' he pointed out reasonably. 'You said it would make our relationship look more convincing. Anyway, far from trying to persuade people to admire me, I don't care in the slightest what anybody thinks of me.'

She faced him full on. 'Tell me. Did your fellow aristocrats in France boast a similar arrogance? If so, I'm forced to the conclusion that those men who overthrew your royal family were quite justified!'

'The leaders of the Revolution weren't all heroes, you know.' His voice was quiet now. 'Some of them were extremely brutal.'

'Perhaps they had to be, after suffering centuries of poverty and oppression!'

At that moment they were turning into Piccadilly and Raphael, instead of answering, pointed to a ragged young woman with a baby in her arms begging at the roadside. The well-dressed passersby hurried on as if the woman and her child didn't exist. 'I believe you have a saying in this country.

Something about the pot calling the kettle black,' he said quietly.

She coloured. 'I know. I know. And my friends and I are trying, with our school, to help some children at least to escape a life of such poverty. But we still have a long way to go.'

'You do indeed.'

After that they travelled on in silence and he could see Serena pretending to absorb the passing glimpses of St James's Street and the busy shops of Bond Street—the familiar territory of the very rich. He leaned forward when the entrance to the Royal Academy came into view and called to Jacques, 'Please stop here.' Then he turned back to Serena. 'Here we are, then. Ready and eager to participate in a genteel appreciation of art, in the company of some of the most privileged people in all of Europe.'

She was clearly still seething from his criticism and yet, he suspected, understanding it, too. 'I meant to say from the beginning that I'm rather surprised by your choice, *monsieur*. An art gallery? Isn't that rather intellectual for you?'

'It's not my usual kind of haunt,' he said cheerfully. 'But maybe I wanted to show you that I do have some appreciation of the finer things in life. It's not all gambling and drinking with me, oh, no.' His voice altered slightly. 'Though, of course, to that woman we saw begging, the price of just one of the paintings we shall see inside would be wealth beyond her dreams.'

She was silent, fastening her hands rather tightly around the handle of her parasol.

He stretched out to put one finger briefly to her lips. 'Enough,' he said almost gently. 'You can tell me exactly what you think of me later, when we're alone. But for now, please smile—because, once again, everyone's watching us.'

Really, Raphael told himself as he helped her alight from his carriage, it was wrong of him to chide her so. The rich believed themselves to be entitled from birth to their privilege and wealth, his own family included. Lady Serena still looked rather pale as they approached the lofty colonnades of the Academy and he suddenly thought to himself, *She does not deserve this. I am a wretch to treat her so.*

He put his arm through hers to guide her up the steps and said quietly, 'You look exquisite, by the way. You will outshine the other women here by far. Now, might I suggest we declare a truce and concentrate on the paintings? They tell me there's a rather fine new Gainsborough on display.'

She jerked up her head with a slight hiss of indrawn breath and he couldn't help but notice how her colour had heightened and her eyes blazed lambent. *Delicious*. And her lips looked as good as they'd felt in that kiss—silky-soft and full, with a slight hint of moisture where she'd just licked them with the very tip of her tongue...

He moved closer to put his hand on her waist, only lightly, but he felt the way her whole body shivered at the contact. Then they were inside the first room and found themselves surrounded by people, dozens of them, thronging the place from wall to wall so you could hardly see the paintings. Half of the *ton* appeared to be here, particularly the gossiping kind.

'Keep smiling,' he ordered in a low voice. 'Imagine you're on a theatre stage, putting on an act for the general public. Pretend you've decided you were completely mistaken in your previous opinion of me, Lady Serena.'

'If only,' he heard her murmur bitterly under her breath.

But she held her head high as they moved through the crowded room, though he guessed she was restraining herself from uttering the words of scorn she longed to utter. The effort was clearly making her as fragile as a piece of fine glass. And as sensitive, he guessed, to the slightest touch. Just briefly he allowed himself the luxurious torment of imagining how she would feel in his arms. In his bed. How she might be as responsive as the finest musical instrument to his every caress...

A crowd had gathered round them now, making no pretence of their interest in London's most unlikely couple. People were even hurrying in from other rooms to stare and the curator of the gallery was stepping forward. 'Monsieur le Marquis! Lady Serena! How honoured we are to welcome you both here today!'

Raphael saw her graciously smiling and after the curator had gone he leaned down so he was close enough to inhale her delicate scent. 'Like it or not, my lady, we look perfect together. Do you realise that?'

He thought he heard the slight intake of her breath. And something—her scent, or maybe a sudden appearance of vulnerability—made him nearly forget that today's outing was part of a ruthless and necessary strategy to silence a woman who'd made her enmity towards him dangerously clear.

Just as he'd expected, their arrival together was causing far more of a stir than any of the new paintings hanging on the walls. Serena had no need of peacock colours to flaunt her beauty—it was there for all to see. As for his own unorthodox attire, well, he was the Marquis of Montpellier and everyone knew to expect the unexpected. People were gushing openly. 'How delightful to see the two of you together! And at an art gallery, of all places— dear Lady Serena, are you attempting to civilise our wicked Marquis? What do your friends, Lady Joanna and the others, think of your mission?'

Raphael waited, holding himself very still. Then she tilted her chin in that way he was already familiar with and declared with amusement in her voice, 'Oh, my friends adore the Marquis. Really, who can help it?' She half turned so she could gaze up at him. 'Raphael is such a mischievous creature, isn't he? Truly, he is impossible to resist!'

'But how do you explain all the things you've said about him?' A harder voice this time, from a young lordling Raphael had recently clashed with at White's. 'Once, my lady, you declared the Revolution in France was inevitable if the country was filled by rich wastrels like him!'

Raphael quickly stepped in. 'Lady Serena,' he said, 'has announced her intention to reform me. In her own, very special way.'

There were more chuckles. Someone called out, 'And are you happy to be reformed, Monsieur le Marquis?'

He tightened his arm around her waist. 'By Lady Serena?' He arched his brows. 'My friend— who wouldn't be?'

* * *

Afterwards Serena couldn't remember any of the paintings. Indeed, she could hardly have named anyone in the crowd that buzzed around them, because all that filled her head was the constant speculation in the air. 'The Marquis and Lady Serena—together, again! You know they were seen driving in the Park last week and they attended the Duke of Hamilton's ball, too. How astounding, when we thought they were sworn enemies!'

But most of all, Serena recalled the Marquis's cool comment: *Lady Serena has announced her intention to reform me. In her own, very special way.*

Oh, that silky voice of his. It was devilish. It was totally dangerous, in the way it slid like purest silk over her skin. His words made her shiver, because they hinted that he was wicked. Unredeemed. Experienced in all kinds of pleasures...

Serena had to face up to facts. There was no way for now that she could escape her situation and, until she could think of something, she had to play her part. So for the benefit of all the onlookers she had allowed him to escort her around the various rooms full of paintings. She conversed with him about any that particularly caught her eye and laughed a little with him over the most peculiar ones. It must have looked to the outside world as if they were completely at ease in one another's company, and yet…

'Look at that one,' Lefevre murmured to her. He was pointing to a life-size portrayal of the Greek god Pluto welcoming the innocent Persephone to his underworld kingdom. Persephone was watching Pluto with an almost horrified fascination because he was striking and muscular and altogether too male, but the young Persephone clearly could not resist him. The picture had attracted almost as much attention as Serena and Lefevre.

And Serena could not miss the obvious comparison. Because *she* was like Persephone—and Pluto was the devilishly handsome Marquis.

'It really is a most eye-catching painting,' Lefevre went on. 'Don't you agree? And Persephone obviously cannot wait to find out what her new lover has to offer her—' He broke off. 'Stop. Stop, Lady Serena!'

But she was already marching towards the main doors and was halfway down the steps by the time he caught up with her.

She whirled to face him. 'You find all this amusing, Monsieur le Marquis? I have to say that I do not!'

'A pity.' The corners of his mouth lifted a little. 'I've discovered that one has to find amusement in life's various trials.'

With increasing agitation she realised there was a glint of mockery in his eyes. 'I hate all this,' she said in a low voice. 'I hate being subject to so much speculation and gossip. I hate having to pretend to enjoy your company, when you are clearly determined to destroy my reputation!'

There was a moment's silence. Then he said, 'I thought you were quite set on destroying your reputation anyway, by going to Covent Garden on your own that night.'

She stood there, heart sinking into her shoes. He was right. She'd got herself into the mess because she was so fearful of her dead husband being exposed as a coward.

She was getting herself deeper and deeper into trouble, just like Persephone being led into the underworld. And like Persephone, she couldn't drag her eyes from the man who tormented her so—the Marquis himself. His informal clothing in such an elite environment didn't detract one jot from his charisma.

It was the fact that he didn't care, realised Serena rather wildly. Didn't care in the slightest how he looked or what people thought of him. And unfortunately for her, *she* thought of him far too often. She was finding that a kind of sweet, yet almost painful, ache of need unfurled inside her whenever he was near—and it made her desperately afraid. Desperately ashamed.

She couldn't handle this. It was like being trapped and her heart knew it as it thumped wildly inside her ribcage. *Escape,* it was urging her. *Escape!*

But she couldn't and there were two very good reasons for that. Firstly, Lefevre was aware of the full story of her husband's miserable death— aware also how desperate Serena was to conceal it. Secondly, half of the *ton* knew she'd been seen that night in Covent Garden submitting to Lefevre's kiss and he was right: there was no way to overcome the scandal of it except by pretending that they were indeed enjoying a romantic relationship. She could not maintain her previous hostility to him without appearing utterly ridiculous. But in her head—and especially in her heart— she must always hold Lefevre in the contempt he deserved. For her own sake.

She pulled herself away from him and said coolly, 'You'll excuse me, I'm sure, but it really is time for me to leave. I have another appointment this afternoon. I'm sorry—did I forget to mention it?'

He stepped closer and rested his hands on her shoulders. 'An appointment? Do you really? Where is it?'

'I can't see that it's any business of—'

'It certainly is my business,' he said calmly, 'if it's an occasion at which I might be expected to appear with you. Remember, Lady Serena, you've just as much interest as me in keeping up our appearance as a couple. I repeat: Where is your appointment?'

She looked rather desperately around the fore-court of the Academy as if seeking escape, but of course there was none. At last she said in a low voice, 'It's at the charity school. Of course, you will laugh at that. You'll pour scorn on our "lady bountiful" act, no doubt.'

He looked slightly exasperated. 'I'm not pouring scorn on your school—far from it. Listen, why don't you take me there with you? We're supposed to be sharing one another's interests and aims. Remember?'

She said rather desperately, 'But what if all this is in vain? What if after four weeks Silas Mort turns up again? How am I better off? All this… *humiliation* I'm enduring might prove to be completely in vain!'

At first she thought he wasn't going to reply at all. But then Lefevre said, 'Mort won't be back.'

Something caught in her chest. 'What do you mean?'

He was watching her with his inscrutable gaze.

'He won't be back. You can be sure of that, Lady Serena.'

An appalling thought struck her. 'You told me at the ball that you'd dealt with him. Have you killed him, *monsieur*?'

'There was no need, since somebody else did the job. It was a case of gangland rivalry, I gather. Men like him have countless enemies. Mort was found the other morning dumped in the Thames with his throat cut.'

She was suddenly too aware of his eyes still burning into her. She said at last in a low voice, 'Would you have killed him, if he'd threatened me again?'

'Do you know,' he said, 'I rather think I might. Because, you see, I don't like cowards who taunt defenceless women.'

He said no more. So Silas Mort was dead—but Serena knew Lefevre could still ruin her by revealing her meeting with the man and the reason for it. Lefevre was an equal danger, her heart told her so. And she had yet more unanswered questions, so many of them, but she didn't ask any at all, because his very nearness was kindling her most intimate senses and her heart was full with the desperate sense of wanting something from him that she could never have.

So instead she said at last, 'Come, then. Come to visit the school with me. Why don't you?'

'So you can expose me for the superficial wretch I really am?' he said lightly. 'Very well, then, I'll come. Especially since I can now regard myself as one of the school's foremost benefactors.'

'You are unbelievably arrogant,' said Serena.

'Yes. Aren't I?'

And she was able to summon up a façade of scorn for him again, telling herself that her moment of weakness had been merely a clouding of her normally clear judgement, an aberration as unwanted as it was ridiculous.

But her defences were crumbling. And she was frightened.

Chapter Twelve

Raphael did indeed learn more than he'd expected during his visit to the school in Spitalfields that afternoon. He realised, for a start, that he was seeing a very different Serena. It also occurred to him that she'd dressed as plainly as she did not only to only put him in his place, but also to be suitably attired in order to travel on to Spitalfields afterwards.

It was as well, then, that he was plainly clad also.

Jacques was waiting with the barouche outside the gallery and his face was a picture when Raphael came up to speak to him. 'Spitalfields? My lord, you're not taking her *there*?'

'No.' Raphael patted him lightly on the shoulder. 'You've got it the wrong way round. The lady is taking me.'

'But I can't drive this carriage of yours there!'

'Indeed you can't. So you drive it home, there's

a good fellow. And Lady Serena and I will find ourselves a hackney cab.'

He was able to hail one within minutes and, after giving the driver instructions, he helped Serena inside. 'Your friends won't be expecting me,' he remarked as the cab moved off. 'I trust they won't be too startled.'

She shrugged slightly. 'They're certainly expecting me. They also know you and I have struck up a friendship, of sorts—and as you pointed out earlier, at present you are the school's prime benefactor. You saved our lease.'

She was offering him a wordless truce, he realised as they progressed eastwards through the city. To call their liaison a friendship was inaccurate, but it was a term which for now, at any rate, he was content to accept. 'Tell me a little more, if you will,' he said, 'about your school.'

So she did. And he realised how she became more animated, less reserved as she explained how the charity had been set up by Mary and how the four friends between them searched for donors and patrons to support the cause.

'These patrons are perhaps our most important benefactors,' she explained earnestly. 'Much of the money, of course, we provide ourselves— with the aid of some generous friends. But what we really need is more influence over the people who hold power. We need to persuade the government that the children of the poor deserve an education, just as much as the children of the rich.'

'Worthy thoughts indeed,' he said when she'd finished.

She flushed slightly and he saw her gloved hands tighten in her lap. 'You are mocking me, *monsieur,* and I cannot blame you. There could not be a greater contrast between the lives led by myself and my friends and the lives of these poor children. I'm making a feeble gesture, I know.'

'Wrong, my lady.' His voice was gentler. 'I wasn't mocking you. You are giving them your time and your heart, as well as your money. You are also, thanks to your rank, drawing attention in the highest places to the cause of educating the needy. No doubt you and your friends face opposition—hostility, even—from certain quarters, which you should take as a compliment to the brave stand you've all taken.'

She didn't answer and he said after a few moments, 'Forgive me. You must be thinking that I'm in no position to make any kind of judgement on another person's moral stance.'

Her eyes had been downcast, but now she faced him with something like passion. 'No! It's not that,' she blurted out at last. 'It's just that—this is how I *thought* you would be!'

He was mystified. 'What do you mean, how you thought I would be?'

'The night that we first talked, at the ball last November. The night when we danced. I thought you were honest—honourable, even, until...'

Ah. 'Until that fool of a man burst in with his comment about a wager?'

'I wish,' she whispered, 'you could have explained to me at the time that he was telling a lie.'

And Raphael thought, *Damn it all. Surely to God she wasn't beginning to feel something for him?* And wouldn't that, on his part, be the vilest trick of all? Shouldn't he explain everything to her, *now*?

No. It was too early—besides, though her own hostility to him appeared to be lessening, she still had dangerous acquaintances. He steeled himself. 'Perhaps,' he said, 'it was as well you recognised my devious and untrustworthy nature from the start.'

'Perhaps,' she said in the same low voice.

And as the cab rolled on through the city to Spitalfields, she said nothing more.

The school building stood on Crispin Street. Raphael climbed out, instructed the driver to wait for them, then took in their surroundings—rows of narrow tenement houses interspersed with ale-houses and small shops, together with the premises of tradesmen like blacksmiths and barrel makers. Serena pointed the school out to him and when he commented that it was a larger building than most, she explained that it was once a hospital built by the French Huguenots who'd fled to London over a hundred years ago. But it had become dilapidated, until Mary led the charity's efforts to repair and re-use it.

By the time she'd finished her story they were both inside and Raphael was welcomed by her friends with surprise.

'Monsieur Lefevre!' Mary was the first to step forward to shake his hand. 'This is unexpected. Though of course I'm glad to have the chance to thank you personally for persuading Lord Gardner to renew the school's lease.'

Raphael was dismissive. 'I was glad to be of help,' he said.

Mary showed him round, the others following. Mary was businesslike, Joanna's eyes were speculative, while poor Beth was considerably flustered by his presence.

The children, he was told, had already finished their lessons for the afternoon, but now they were filing into the school's kitchen and he saw how the ragged and unkempt urchins headed eagerly for the buttered bread and cups of milk that were laid out for them.

'We feed them before they go home,' Mary explained to Raphael, 'and they are given a more substantial meal at midday, because it's impossible for them to concentrate on anything when they're poorly nourished. It's difficult for any of us to imagine true hunger, isn't it? These poor children. We do what we can. And you may be interested to know, Monsieur Lefevre, that we have some French children among our pupils.'

'Indeed?'

'Yes, their parents are exiles from your homeland and they're penniless. Fortunately there's a nearby lodging house that provides free board for such people, paid for by a generous but unknown benefactor. And we've found a teacher, Miss Murphy, who knows some French, though since you're here, maybe you'd speak with them? Let me introduce you—'

But she stopped, because as they approached the children one little boy was already grabbing his friend and calling out in French, 'Look who it is! It's the rich *monsieur*. We know him! We know him!'

Silence fell as, one by one, every person in the room turned to look at him—the children, Serena, her friends. As well as—what was her name?—Miss Murphy, who'd hardly taken her eyes off him anyway.

There was no help for it. He would have to tell them the truth. He said, 'On my arrival in London last year, I heard about the lodging house you mention. It was a new venture and was struggling, so I felt obliged to offer some financial help.'

'Some?' said Mary a little faintly. 'Or all of it, Monsieur Lefevre? As I mentioned, I have been told of a very generous benefactor.'

He bowed his head. 'All of it. You see, I know what it's like to be a stranger in a foreign land. But I must make it plain that I would prefer my connection with the place to be kept a secret.'

'So you are their saviour!' said Beth a little breathlessly. Serena looked stunned and he noticed how her friend Joanna had moved close to her.

He shook his head. 'I'm afraid I'm very far from being a saint,' he said quietly. *I am not what you want me to be*, he was saying silently to Serena. *And I never can be.*

And so, yet again, Serena found herself badly shaken. Lefevre was a benefactor, but wasn't happy with it being revealed. Why not? Who *was* this enigma of a man who presented himself as an idle pleasure-seeker, but was hiding so much else? Of course her three friends were clearly seeing Raphael Lefevre in a new light. Even Mary had completely melted. But Serena wasn't sure of anything now. Of her own tumultuous feelings least of all.

Her friends expressed their eagerness to show him round the entire school and did so, describing the lessons and their plans for the future; but she could see he looked rather distracted and after a while she intervened. 'Monsieur Lefevre,' she said, touching his arm. 'I wonder, would you kindly take me home now? I have other commitments and I'm sure you must have too.'

'Of course,' he said.

She believed he was just as relieved as she to escape from her friends' avid interest. As the two of them climbed into the waiting cab he was silent, which confirmed anew to her that he had never wanted his benevolent actions to be exposed. She shook her head. He was a rakehell. A pleasure-seeker. Some would claim that even his support of the refuge for French exiles was just another boastful gesture—yet he'd wanted it kept quiet! There was so much about him she didn't understand. *The Marquis of mystery,* she whispered to herself. And his unexpected tenderness towards those children had caught at her heartstrings.

The space inside this cab was confined, making her far too aware of his physical power. She was too conscious also of the subtle scent of his fresh-starched linen and his spicy cologne; even worse, she was conscious of that utterly frightening sense of vulnerability, together with a yearning to be closer to him.

How close? Just how close, you fool?

No doubt about it: her world was being turned upside down. All she'd wanted after Lionel's death was to be independent, with no need of any man to prop up her life, let alone a notorious rogue who'd manipulated her into a disastrous agreement in order to bolster his own pride and to crush hers. She gazed out of the cab's grimy window, seeing little. But then—quite unexpectedly—he spoke again.

'I'm sure you'd rather I was an outright villain. It would be easier for you, I imagine. Perhaps it might help if you remind yourself you have only a limited number of days to endure my company, Lady Serena.'

She'd stopped breathing at his words. And he was watching her, as if he knew how her heart pounded.

'Are you crying?' he asked suddenly.

She dabbed furiously at her eyes. *Stupid. So stupid of me.* Trying to collect her scattered senses she replied, 'No. No, of course I'm not. You make our four weeks sound like a prison sentence, *monsieur*.'

He gave an apologetic smile. 'That bad?'

'Maybe. But we made our bargain, so I must keep my side of it.'

His eyes went darker. 'I'll just say this,' he replied. 'Keep up your scorn for me by all means, if it makes this easier for you. As I've said, you don't have to endure our liaison for much longer. So—no more tears, I hope?'

She struggled a moment, then she looked straight at him. 'It was the children,' she whispered. 'Those poor children. Their plight. Their courage. They always make me cry a little.'

'You have a tender heart. It must have been a personal tragedy that you never had a child to remember your husband by.'

'*What?* What are you saying?' Each word was choked with emotion. Raphael looked bewildered.

'I said,' he repeated, 'that you must have been sorry not to have children. Yours was a very happy marriage, wasn't it? Which is why you are so desperate to protect your husband's name.'

Enough of pride. Enough of pretence. The unhappiness of the past rose up from her soul and could not be stopped. 'Monsieur Lefevre,' she said, 'my marriage was never a happy one. And when

Silas Mort told me my husband was running like a coward when he was shot, I didn't even think to doubt him. Do you know why? Because that was exactly what Lionel was like. In fact, he'd done all he could to avoid active service.' She lifted her eyes to his and now they were quite clear of tears. 'I felt no grief whatsoever at his death, but as you've told me before, I'm too proud—and it was my pride that forced me to keep up my pretence of devotion. For Lionel to be revealed publicly as a coward was something I could not endure. So you see, I'm a coward, too. And now you can feel free to despise me just as much as you like.'

Raphael had always thought his understanding of the English language to be good, but now surely he had misunderstood. Of course, there were tales that Lionel Willoughby had enjoyed all the usual male frivolities. But Raphael had assumed that Lady Serena, like many aristocratic wives, forgave her husband his foibles because she loved him—and her often-repeated declaration that she would never marry again was seen as proof of her devotion.

'You said just now that your marriage was never a happy one,' he said carefully. 'May I ask why?' He saw her emotion betray itself in the way she twisted her delicately gloved hands together.

Then she said with what was clearly an effort, 'There were the usual reasons. He had affairs. He preferred his friends' company to mine.' She shrugged. 'I'm afraid I'd built up this foolish image of married life and, in doing so, I'd deceived both myself and him.'

'So you thought the failure of your marriage was all your fault?'

She nodded. Once more he remembered the way she'd spoken to those urchins at the school: drawing them close, touching their grubby hands, consoling them. She'd been tender. Caring.

She surely had a heart full of love, with nowhere to bestow it.

Just at that moment a ray of sunlight arrowed through the cab's window and he saw how several silky strands of her hair had tumbled from beneath her plain bonnet to be transformed into spun gold. He also saw how her skin was like cream, her lips as pink and lush as crushed berries.

And suddenly Raphael wanted to make her believe in love again.

A crazy idea; because he had no right to. But how he longed to banish that sadness from her eyes, if only for a while.

And destroy her trust in men for ever? There was no future for him here. Mentally cursing his stupidity, he said, 'I don't think you're a coward.

I do not despise you and I don't see how anyone who truly knows you could do anything but admire you. At the risk of repeating myself, let me tell you that I think your charity school is actually rather wonderful.'

She appeared to have regained her calm. 'I'm glad you agree that the education of the poorer classes is vitally important. But I still feel that I'm doing far too little.'

'Lady Serena, most women of quality don't even notice the existence of anyone below their own rank unless they happen to be servants or dressmakers! You and your friends are different— you actually feel for the poor and you're helping them in the most practical way possible—' He broke off and grinned. '*Mon Dieu.* You must remind me that if I continue with this worthy talk, I'll be in danger of losing my devilish reputation.'

She smiled back and he was glad. She said impishly, 'So you're not going to declare that you're a reformed character from now on?'

He laughed. 'No. Oh, no.'

'Then I can't raise my hopes that you might decide to cancel the remaining days of our agreement?'

'Now, that,' he replied, 'is equally impossible. Though rest assured that I'll say nothing of what you've just told me about your marriage. It helps me understand why you've never encouraged any admirers.' His voice hardened a little. 'But there's a certain gentleman—a Mr Wolverton—who appears to entertain hopes in your direction. Tell me, do you offer him any encouragement?'

She looked surprised and a little annoyed. 'Jeremy Wolverton? Goodness, most certainly not. And even if I did, it's none of your business!'

'I'm rather afraid it is,' he said softly. 'For the duration of our agreement, I'd prefer you to keep your contact with Wolverton to the minimum.'

She stiffened. 'Do you know, you've made me feel like embarking on a mild flirtation with Mr Wolverton the very minute I see him again.'

'He's an extremely earnest man, though, isn't he? I can't imagine him indulging in anything as light as flirtation. His intentions would be far more serious.'

She still looked rather heated. 'Are you jealous of him?'

'No, but I'd prefer you to keep away from him. Is that understood?'

Her eyes flashed defiance. 'I calculate there are around two and a half weeks left of our agreement,' she said softly. 'I shall draw up a calendar and mark off the dates, Monsieur Lefevre.'

He was still thinking up a reply when he realised the cab was slowing down. 'I do believe we've reached Curzon Street,' he pronounced. And moments later he was climbing out to help her on to the pavement outside her house.

He led her to her front door, where she smiled brightly up at him. 'Well, Monsieur le Marquis. I declare, I have had such a delightful time! Indeed, I cannot wait for our next outing together!'

She was turning to go, but he kept hold of her hand. 'Let me ask you. What would you really, truly like to do, Lady Serena?'

She looked surprised. 'Why, whatever you suggest, of course.'

'No. What would *you* enjoy?'

She said, rather hesitantly, 'My brother once took me to Richmond Park in his carriage. And I loved it.' She looked up at him as if she was embarrassed by her choice. 'I felt as if I was truly in the countryside. It was like…'

'Like Yorkshire?' He smiled a little. 'Well, we shall have to see what we can do about that.' He bent his head to touch his lips lightly to the back of her hand. And with a bow he left her, thinking of her smile. Remembering the softness of her lips when he'd kissed her that night in Covent Garden.

He set off on foot to Grosvenor Square, thinking, *Damn it. Once this is over, I am going miss her*.

He reminded himself that his plan was going

well. Every time Serena appeared at his side in public, she made it look as if the sun shone out of his eyes, just as he'd hoped. Better than he'd hoped. No danger now of her pressing on with her meddlesome enquiries about his past or his present. The trouble was, he did not feel pleased in the slightest.

As he walked he found himself recalling details of the hours they'd so far spent together. He remembered the way her eyes darkened with trepidation if he tried to tease her and the way she sometimes trembled a little when he touched her. He thought he understood now. It must have been her husband's callous treatment that had led to those moments of vulnerability, which he noticed but no one else had ever seen.

He'd always thought she was sophisticated, worldly wise; but it turned out that despite her privileged background she'd been unlucky indeed. Now her ill luck continued, because she had *him* to contend with. As he approached Grosvenor Square, he felt a shaft of self-contempt so powerful that he almost groaned aloud.

All of society knew by now that he'd made a conquest of her. It was yet another feather in the cap of Raphael Lefevre—after all, there'd been whispers in plenty about his *amours* since his arrival in London and he didn't trouble to deny them, since they served to disguise the fact that Raphael had other, far weightier matters on his mind.

Was he proud of himself, for using Lady Serena in such a manner? Was he proud of himself when he observed how her trust in him seemed to be growing day by day? Of course he wasn't. From the first moment he'd seen her he'd thought, *This woman is different.* Different and overwhelmingly desirable. That memorable night when he'd danced with her, he'd felt the silken fragility of her body and inhaled the delicate scent of her skin. He'd noted the fascinating colour of her eyes and the involuntary fluttering of her thick lashes as she defiantly held his gaze.

And today, he remembered how she'd flinched as he'd said, 'Like it or not, my lady, we look perfect together.'

She'd reacted with horror. Yet there was something between them. She couldn't deny it. If only...

If only things were different. Dear God, he could all too easily imagine her resistance melting as he softly caressed her—and that hard punch of desire in his gut clamped even tighter. But then he remembered how today he'd briefly seen a look that was almost despair in her eyes and it had touched a raw nerve deep inside him. *Don't,* he reminded himself. Don't let her get to you. Don't let her ruin all you've worked for. Not even if she is the first woman to make you feel not only physical need, but the desire to protect and to comfort her.

He reminded himself that she despised him, so the words *need* and *desire* had to be eliminated from his vocabulary as far as Lady Serena was concerned. Yes, he wished things were different, but they weren't. And the action he was taking to keep her under control was all too necessary.

Once he was home, he was told straight away by his butler that Sir Dominic Southern had arrived a good half-hour since. 'I've shown him into your library, my lord,' Surtees told him and, indeed, Raphael found him there pacing the floor—good, loyal Dominic, who looked at him anxiously as Raphael closed the door.

'I thought you'd be back long ago.' Dominic gripped his hand. 'Jacques said you'd set off to visit somewhere in the East End with Lady Serena. You surely didn't go to that school she and her friends set up in Spitalfields?'

'I did.' Raphael pulled off his hat and coat and slung them across his desk.

'Was that wise?'

'No, because unfortunately I was recognised. There were several French children there from the refuge in Spitalfields.'

Dominic gave a low whistle. 'Well. That's your reputation as a careless wastrel somewhat tarnished. Isn't it? What did the Wicked Widows say?'

Raphael pointed to a chair and took one himself. 'As you can imagine, Lady Serena and her friends are now in a state of some confusion about the rakehell Marquis.'

Dominic creased his brow in thought. Then he said, 'You know I'm on your side in all this, Raphael. But I've always rather liked Lady Serena. Tell me, just to reassure me—she'll be glad when all this business between the two of you is over, won't she? She's not going to be—you know—*hurt* in any way?'

'She's counting the days till she's rid of me,' answered Raphael as he rose to pour them both brandy from a decanter. 'She'll be heartily glad when it's over.'

Dominic took his drink. 'Regrets, Raphael? About forcing her into this?'

Raphael, seated again, turned his own glass so it caught the light. 'I can't afford regrets. You know better than anyone how I had to stop her asking questions about my past. You also know that she has friends I don't trust.' He looked straight at Dominic. 'Learning about my connection with the refuge startled Serena. But I'm sure she'll easily slot me back into my usual role as a degenerate scoundrel.'

'I think,' said Dominic slowly, 'that you're finding all this rather harder than you first thought.' He placed his glass on the desk and leaned forward. 'Listen. Last time we met, you asked me to see if I could find out more about Wolverton—the fellow you marched out of the Duke of Hamilton's ball last week.'

'I didn't march him out.' Raphael gave a cold smile. 'I merely suggested his presence was surplus to requirements. Did you discover anything?'

'In a word, no. He has the worthiest reputation you can imagine, both in his private life and his business. I discovered that he pays all the taxes due on his fabric imports with great diligence—and I'm really not sure why you have such an objection to the fellow.' He sighed. 'I can only guess it's because he's formed a *tendre* for Lady Serena and you resent it.'

'Nonsense.' Raphael shook his head. 'The man made some damnably rude comments about me in my hearing. Big mistake. Have you any other news for me?'

'Maybe yes, maybe no. As you asked, I've been searching for businesses that take on foreign workers—French workers, you specified. And I discovered there's a garment factory in

Mundy Street, Shoreditch, that makes clothes on the cheap. You know the kind of place.'

Raphael certainly did. Those grim brick buildings spread themselves year by year across the north of the city to the fields beyond. They were built with the intention of making goods at the least possible cost and for the maximum profit of the owner.

'And I've heard things about this factory,' went on Dominic. 'It seems the manager—his name is Turnbull—is particularly eager to hire poor French women who arrive in the city looking for work. Many of them are already skilled in needlework and he says that if they don't speak English, they can't cause any trouble. He also pays scandalously low wages. It might well be worth a visit.'

Chapter Thirteen

The next morning found Raphael standing outside the factory in Mundy Street. Several foundries and a large brick-making yard stood close by and beyond them were rows of workers' cottages. Carts laden with raw materials filled the road and Raphael watched them a moment before heading inside the factory, where he approached a clerk who sat at a large desk.

'Yes?' The clerk rose to his feet. 'May I assist you?'

'Possibly,' Raphael replied. 'I'd like to know how swiftly this establishment could provide me with coats for the men who work in my offices in the city.'

'Would that be many coats, sir?'

'Three dozen? Maybe four?'

The clerk was all ears. 'In that case, I'll take you to Mr Turnbull right away. Follow me.'

Raphael found himself being led up some stairs to a huge open workroom, at the far end of which men were cutting out pieces of fabric with large shears, while nearer to him were rows of women stitching intently, never looking up from their work tables. Their concentration, he noted, was aided by the presence of three burly overseers who walked up and down the aisles, watching to make sure no one dared to pause in their labour.

A rather stout man with a florid face and small, suspicious eyes came marching towards him. 'I'm Elias Turnbull,' he said. 'Manager of this place. What's your business?'

Turnbull was as rough and ready in his speech as he was in his appearance. The clerk who'd accompanied Raphael spoke to him with nervous eagerness. 'Mr Turnbull, this gentleman is enquiring if he can place an order for quite a number of gentlemen's coats.'

Turnbull's expression softened, but only slightly. 'Depends when you want them, of course. And what quality of cloth and so forth. Any order could take upwards of three to four weeks, since we're mighty busy here. Though I suppose I could get these sluts to work a little harder.'

Raphael looked at the women he was pointing to, bent over their sewing tables while those men tramped up and down making sure they never rested. The sluts. He guessed they'd be paid pennies for long hours of working their fingers to the bone. They were absolutely silent now, but as he'd come in he'd heard them whispering to each other—until the overseers marched up to them and brusquely told them to get on with their work.

Which they did. But for just those few moments, he'd noted their speech.

He said casually to Turnbull, 'I see you have some French women working for you. So they come knocking at your door, do they? For work like this?'

The man's expression changed instantly. 'What business is it of yours?'

'None whatsoever. I was merely commenting on the fact that you employ foreigners.'

'And they're glad of the work! These Frenchies, they spend their last coins on their passage to England. Then they reach London with no money and nowhere to live and they're mighty grateful, you understand?'

'Is that why you feel justified in offering them starvation wages?'

The hovering clerk shrank back in dismay. Turnbull squared up to Raphael. 'Are you a government man? Or some other kind of busybody? They get honest wages for an honest day's work!'

He looked over at the women and snorted with contempt before turning back to Raphael. 'Now, do you want to place this order of yours or not? I tell you, you won't get a better price!'

Raphael took one last look at the women bent over their sewing tables. 'Perhaps I don't want to place my custom here after all.'

'Give me patience. As if I'm not busy enough without time-wasting tricks like yours...'

Turnbull's voice faded as Raphael drew closer. 'Are you saying, perhaps, that you want further dealings with me?'

'No,' the man stuttered. 'No offence meant, sir, I'm sure.'

'Wise of you,' Raphael answered softly. 'I'm leaving now. But before I go...' He walked purposefully towards the women at their sewing tables, ignoring the menacing overseers. '*Mesdames.*' He spoke in French. 'Do any of you know anything at all about a French lady called Madeleine, who I believe arrived in London a year ago and may have been looking for work? She's around twenty-five and slim, with long dark hair and blue eyes.'

One of the older women looked up. '*Monsieur.* There was indeed a Madeleine. She came to work here last summer, but she was taken away—because she was very pretty, you see.'

Raphael found his pulse was thumping. 'Taken where? And by whom?'

'By some men. They visit regularly, to look over any new girls and pick out the pretty ones. And then, poor things, we never see them again.'

Turnbull had come up behind him and Raphael headed out, his brain whirling.

The following Sunday Serena went to church as usual. Since George had travelled up to the Yorkshire estate for a few days, she took lunch on her own and afterwards settled in her first-floor sitting room, supposedly studying some household bills that her steward had presented to her. But in reality, she was gazing out of the window that overlooked her rose-filled back garden and daydreaming—until Mrs Penney came hurrying upstairs, all of a bustle.

'My lady, it's the Marquis! Oh, my goodness, and you weren't expecting him—'

She broke off, because Raphael had followed Mrs Penney into the room. And after making a polite bow, he said, 'My lady. You told me the other day you would love to visit Richmond Park again. I wondered if you might enjoy a drive out there this afternoon?'

He's remembered, she thought rather breathlessly. *He's remembered.* The blue sky had been taunting her all morning. The thought of green open spaces and rural pathways made her heart leap. As did he, she warned herself, for he looked ridiculously handsome in his caped driving coat of dark grey and for once, that mocking look appeared to have vanished from his eyes. Yes, he looked as calm and confident as usual, but his expression was almost warm as he waited for her answer. Mrs Penney had beaten a hasty retreat, closing the door behind her. It was four days since that visit to the school and it dismayed her how much she'd missed him.

'I rather think I would enjoy the drive, Monsieur Lefevre,' she answered at last. 'Would you give me a few minutes to prepare myself?'

Soon they were heading out of London under a sparkling blue sky. Raphael was driving the curricle himself and Serena resolved to let all her cares evaporate for the moment. She had always adored Richmond Park, but to Lionel rural scenes were only of interest if you were either shooting game or riding with the hunt.

Forget Lionel. Her spirits rose as they left London's busy streets behind and when the grassy slopes and majestic woodlands of the park came into view, she leaned forward and clasped her hands in delight.

She could see that Raphael was smiling. 'Like Yorkshire, I think you said?'

'Indeed.' She glanced at him shyly. 'Only a little warmer. And what about you? Where you grew up, in France—there must have been countryside?'

'Oh, acres of it,' he said casually. 'But I can't say I yearn after it. Which is just as well.'

After that he was silent and Serena asked no questions, because she didn't want to break the spell that had somehow descended on them. The sun glittered on the birch saplings and fronds of unfurling bracken. The ancient groves with their bright new leaves were alive with the sounds of birdsong and in the distance a herd of deer were moving like a ripple of light along a ridge of higher ground.

Then suddenly, as the track led them out of a dusky copse, she heard a scrabbling sound to her left and caught sight of something struggling in a thicket of brambles. 'Raphael. Stop. Please! There's an animal trapped in there. I think it might be a young deer!'

He'd already pulled up and was putting the reins in her hands. 'Hold them steady,' he said as he climbed down to head for the stricken animal. Her heart in her mouth, she watched as he carefully drew away the tangle of brambles with his gloved hands and calmed the fawn's desperate struggles. At last it was free and, when Raphael set it on safer ground, it scampered off towards the distant herd.

She couldn't help it. When he climbed back into the driver's seat she clasped his hand and blurted out, 'Oh, my goodness. Thank you! The poor thing might have died if you hadn't saved it!'

He shrugged. 'Anyone else would have done the same. Wouldn't they?'

She let go of his hand and said, in a different voice, 'Certainly, Lionel would have freed it. But only because he'd think it would make good sport for the huntsmen once it was grown.'

Raphael was still watching her. 'I've no time for hunting myself.'

'No?' She was surprised—it was such a popular pastime with men of all ranks.

'No. My father was obsessed. He and his friends would hunt or shoot any creature that moved. I prefer a more equal battle myself.' He pointed into the distance. 'There's the little fellow now, see? Back with the others. He'll have forgotten all about his adventure soon.'

'But I won't,' she said. 'Thank you.'

'Don't mention it. Shall we drive on?'

And so they completed their tour of the park while Serena tried to occupy her mind with the lush scenery. But her heart was full of emotion.

If only. If only he and I had not become enemies from the start.

What Raphael was thinking she had no idea, because again he was almost silent except to point out any wild creature or bird that might be of interest to her. Only once did he make a more personal comment, when they were setting off home. The sun was losing just a little of its warmth by then and he halted the carriage so he could help her to wrap her silk shawl around her shoulders.

'Forgive me for mentioning it,' he said, his hands lingering on her arms just for a moment. 'But I can't help thinking your husband was an almighty fool to value you so lightly.'

A sudden, bone-deep longing crushed her. *If only,* she thought again. She shook her head firmly. 'No. Perhaps Lionel was right.' She looked up at Raphael. 'I was so very young when I married him, you see. I fear I was quite foolish.' *And still am,* she told herself in anguish. Because what did she want at that very moment? What had she been thinking of during this idyllic afternoon?

She wanted him to kiss her. And something stupidly impulsive inside her made her say, 'Raphael, I've truly enjoyed this afternoon. And I want you to know that I find it hard to believe all the things that are said about you.'

A shadow crossed his face then. 'Lady Serena,

I took you to Richmond this afternoon as a way of thanking you for the patience with which you've borne my deeply unchivalrous conduct towards you since that night in Covent Garden. But I'm afraid you would be wise to believe everything— and I mean everything—that's said about me.'

Her heart plummeted. Now, there was a warning indeed. 'Oh, but I do believe everything,' she said lightly. 'Don't worry, Monsieur Lefevre. I'm not in any danger of joining the ranks of your female admirers, numerous though they are.'

He bowed his head, giving that slightly sardonic smile of his.

From then on their conversation was light. Trivial. He drove them back through the crowded streets of London and pulled the carriage up outside her door. 'I won't come in,' he told her.

Already one of her footmen was emerging to assist her. She stepped down from the curricle and a moment later it was setting off down the road. She stood there just for a moment before at last turning to go inside. *I am quite calm,* she told herself as Mrs Penney and Martha fussed over her, taking her pelisse and bonnet and exclaiming over what a lovely outing she must have had. *I know he is using me. I know he feels nothing for me.*

But she had begun to hope and perhaps to

dream; though now, thanks to his warning to believe everything that was said about him, the whole golden afternoon was tarnished. Her emotions were in turmoil. She liked to think she was stronger by far than the girl who'd married Lionel; she'd vowed to herself that never again would she fall under the spell of any man. Yet what had happened?

She'd believed that Raphael Lefevre bore exactly the same faults as her dead husband. He was arrogant, he was vain and he expected women to fall at his feet. She'd thought he was someone she could easily despise. But more and more he was weaving his dark magic over her body and her mind. She knew he was merely amusing himself by having her in his power. Getting his revenge for her insults. But goodness, how her treacherous body longed for him. How she longed to be kissed by him, and wickedly caressed...

She was so angry with herself she wanted to cry.

Raphael was a blue-blooded aristocrat who'd escaped France with his fortune intact, enabling him to lead a life devoted to pleasure. But remembering his gentleness with that trapped deer had driven a fresh arrow deep into her heart. The Marquis, some kind of hero? Impossible! Yet this afternoon—like at the charity school—she

could have sworn she was in the company not of
a philanderer, but someone of honesty, of integrity, who occasionally revealed an inner sadness
in his soul that made her ache to comfort him.
Ridiculous of her, because he was still the man
who'd forced her into four weeks of…what? Of
hell, she'd thought at first. Of utter humiliation.
Yet now all she could think was how empty her
life would be after the four weeks were over.

As for Raphael, he drove home in a state of
cold rage with himself. *You must tell her soon,*
he kept saying under his breath. *You must explain to her what your true purpose is in London.*
But it was still impossible. There were good reasons why he hadn't yet confided in anyone except
Jacques and Dominic. He could not let anyone
else in on his secrets, until Madeleine was found.
Until Madeleine was truly safe.

As the days went by, Serena found that Raphael's behaviour towards her was meticulously
polite and he always kept his distance. But try as
she might, she found she was beginning to await
his arrival at her house with a sense of tingling
anticipation and was starting to miss him when
he left. *It's because he makes me feel alive,* she
told herself—and perhaps anything was better

than the emptiness she'd endured as her marriage took its weary toll.

In the evenings they attended parties together, while on fine afternoons he drove her round Hyde Park. When it rained, they visited more galleries or attended chamber music concerts and soon people grew used to seeing them together; indeed, Serena almost persuaded herself that she was playing her part with skill, listening to Raphael's words with close attention in public, even teasing him lightly now and then over some point he'd made.

When they were surrounded by company, she was able to banish any dangerous thoughts, especially since he never touched her except to lightly hold her as they danced at some grand ball. But at night when she was in her bed, she would think of him in other ways. Dangerous ways, which reflected the yearning she experienced when she found herself looking at his strong hands or his tantalising lips, imagining them touching her and caressing her in ways she shouldn't be thinking of. Imagining that powerful, all too male body close to hers, intimate with hers even...

She reminded herself that of course Raphael must find her unattractive, as her husband had done. *Prim. Tight-laced.* Those were just some of the words Lionel had used. And as she'd heard them, day after day, she'd come to believe they must be true. But in Raphael's company, she felt as if her senses had been woken from a deep, deep slumber—though it was to no avail whatsoever, because soon, their brief alliance would be over.

As the month of May came to an end and June took over, golden sunshine and cerulean blue skies greeted Londoners day after day. Prominent figures of the *ton* gathered in the Park each afternoon and whenever she was there with Raphael, they were welcomed as London's newest, most fashionable couple. 'Lady Serena! Monsieur le Marquis! A fine day today, is it not? How very well you look, Lady Serena!'

She did—she knew she did—her mirror told her so—and it was because he was casting his spell over her.

In public, she could cope. In private it was another story, because as soon as she was alone she couldn't help but sink her head in her hands in despair. How could the lightest touch of his hand have the power to shake her so badly? How could the way he looked at her sometimes—thoughtful, almost regretful—arouse in her a longing that almost forced her to recognise her secret yearning for their relationship to be something other than mere play-acting? More and more she was starting to think, *Surely he cannot be the rakehell everyone thinks him to be?*

But of course he was, she reminded herself bitterly. He'd pushed her into this charade of a relationship in order to get his revenge for the many stupid ways in which she'd tried to denigrate him in the past. Dear God, the physical desire she felt for him was muddling her brain. She had to keep believing he was a worthless pleasure seeker, because to let the relationship go any further made her shockingly vulnerable to yet more heartache. Only her friend Joanna guessed at the torment she was in.

'Be patient,' Joanna whispered to her one night at a party when Raphael briefly left her to talk to some of his friends. 'And be prepared for miracles.'

'Miracles?' Serena was confused. 'What on earth do you mean?'

Joanna squeezed her hand. 'He likes you, you know. He really does.'

Serena laughed out loud. 'Nonsense,' she replied.

Nonsense, she kept repeating to herself. Raphael Lefevre was a rake and a rogue, and she could cope. But then—when less than a week of their agreement remained—came the night that he took her to Vauxhall's Pleasure Gardens.

Chapter Fourteen

The first she knew of Raphael's plan was when George called one afternoon in a state of consternation. 'Serena,' he began, 'I've just run into that dratted Frenchman at my club.'

Oh, no. Serena's heart sank. George had been up to Yorkshire, so he'd not had the chance lately to reprimand her over her apparent dalliance with Raphael. But now she feared her brother was about to lay down his objections anew.

'You mean Monsieur Lefevre? You didn't actually argue with him in front of everyone, I hope?' she queried lightly. She was working on a piece of cross-stitch which was boring her to tears, but at this moment she found it a useful distraction.

'It was neither the time nor the place.' George sighed. 'I felt obliged to exchange a brief word of greeting—after all, you've made it plain you feel the man has *some* good points. But then he informed me of his intention to take you to Vauxhall Gardens tonight. Vauxhall! Did you know about this?'

Serena's heart leapt. Always she'd longed to go to Vauxhall, to watch the jugglers and the musicians she'd heard so much about and to see the summer evening set alight by fireworks. But Lionel would never take her, pronouncing it tedious beyond words—while George wouldn't escort her there either, because he thought it unsuitable for a lady of quality.

Now she said, 'Is it so very shocking, George, that I go to Vauxhall? Plenty of my friends visit the place frequently.'

'Perhaps they do. But, Serena—with *that* fellow!'

'He is a marquis,' she reminded him, 'and rather liked by most of the *ton*. So if Raphael does ask me to accompany him to Vauxhall tonight, I think I shall accept.'

'Very well. It's your decision, after all. But I'll tell you what, Serena.' His face suddenly lightened. 'I shall come too!'

Serena laughed aloud. 'Playing gooseberry, George? I think not!'

'I don't intend to tag along with the two of you! I shall take my own guest!' He paused a moment, considering it. 'I know. I shall ask your friend. Lady Joanna.'

Serena almost laughed aloud. 'Do you know, I'm beginning to suspect you really rather like her.'

'Complete nonsense,' he said swiftly, but he also looked slightly embarrassed. 'It merely seems a good idea for us both to go, if only to be on hand to keep an eye on *you*!'

'You've always done your best to look after me, George, and I'm grateful.' She pressed his hand. 'We'll no doubt meet with you there, but Raphael and I will travel to Vauxhall alone. That is—*if* he asks me.'

Indeed, Raphael did ask her. A note of invitation was delivered soon after George's visit and that evening he arrived at her house at eight. 'My carriage is outside,' he told her. 'I hope you'll forgive the short notice, but I thought a visit to Vauxhall would be a pleasant surprise for you.'

She was ready and waiting, dressed in a plain cloak with a hood. Martha had protested. 'Ma'am, surely you want to look your very best for a night out with the Marquis!'

That had been Serena's own initial thought—in fact, she'd allowed Martha to dress her in a beautiful green silk gown. But then she'd thought with a sinking heart, 'Perhaps I've been a fool to start thinking that he invited me because he actually likes me. What he wants tonight is to put me on display again, so people see me as his conquest. His triumph.'

Indeed, nothing had really changed since that afternoon at Richmond. He'd not opened up to her any more about the secrets he surely hid and why should he, when she'd as good as told him his life was a matter of complete indifference to her? All this was a pretence, one that she had to keep up also, so she defiantly concealed her pretty gown with a voluminous dark cloak and as she joined Raphael in the hall she said, primly, 'Vauxhall is certainly an excellent place for us to be seen together, Monsieur le Marquis. Which is no doubt your intention.'

'No,' he said, 'it isn't, actually. I think the cloak is an excellent idea. Less conspicuous.'

Surprise thudded through her. 'You mean you don't *want* us to be noticed?'

'Not particularly.' He smiled. 'Besides, I know you have a taste for secret adventures. Especially by night.'

She felt the heat rising in her body. Of course. He was thinking of that kiss in Covent Garden. 'Don't say it,' she warned him. 'Don't you dare say it!'

'I can't imagine what you mean,' he said innocently. 'I'm only suggesting that if you manage for once to forget your wounded dignity, you might even enjoy yourself. Both Vauxhall *and* my company.'

Unable to think of a suitable retort, she allowed Raphael to escort her out to his coach and settled inside, smoothing down her cloak with a rather tight flourish. 'Goodness, Monsieur Lefevre,' she said, 'I've never been ordered to enjoy myself before. I always thought pleasure was something that had to arise naturally, from circumstance or from engaging company. I didn't realise it could be *imposed* upon one.'

'Didn't you?' he asked silkily. 'You maybe have some lessons to learn.' And as he surveyed her in a cool way that sent all her senses into a *beware danger* mode, she felt the colour invading her cheeks as she suddenly imagined the physical delights a man like Raphael might bestow... *Stop it, Serena.*

The carriage moved off—driven, she'd noted, by Jacques, who'd looked at her with his usual disapproval. 'I must warn you,' she said, 'that we're likely to come across my brother and Lady Joanna there.'

'Really? Your brother's idea, I'd guess, to defend you from the almighty peril posed by me.'

'Exactly.' Serena's eyes glinted. 'But of course

I told George that I'm perfectly capable of looking after myself, Monsieur le Marquis.'

'Of course,' he echoed politely. But the way he was looking at her did strange things to her that made her feel hot and awkward and furious with herself—and to make matters worse he was now gazing calmly out of the window, which meant that she had an outstanding view of him.

She was well aware that he never favoured the extravagant style of the fop, all stripes and satin and adornment. Tonight he was dressed like a well-to-do man about town, without ostentation. Yet even so, his superbly tailored grey coat and fawn breeches emphasised not only his natural grace, but also the perfection of his powerful body. His starched white neckcloth looked almost carelessly knotted, but it was a style that served to define the strong slant of his jaw and his cheekbones. And by now he'd removed his hat, so she could see how his rich black hair gave an almost Mediterranean look to his lightly tanned skin and strange silvery-grey eyes.

At that very moment, he turned to meet her gaze and her heart thudded to a stop.

'Considering ways to kill me, Lady Serena?' His voice was an amused drawl.

'Oh, *monsieur*,' she said with a sigh, 'it's hardly

worth the bother, since so very soon I'll be rid of you anyway.'

He smiled again. 'So you're still eagerly counting off the days. But you'll miss me a little, won't you? I'm beginning to feel you secretly relish the consternation caused by our appearances in public.'

'Consternation for me at least,' she retorted, 'since you have, for the time being at any rate, ruined my reputation as a woman of taste.'

'Touché.' His eyes sparkled with humour. 'But I'll tell you what. Let's pretend we're truly friends, just for tonight, shall we? As long as we can steer clear of your brother, there should be no one watching our every move, so let's try to just enjoy ourselves. I really would like to see you happy.'

And it was as if she'd fallen headlong downstairs and knocked all the air out of her lungs. This hardened *roué,* who'd trapped her into a brief and scandalous liaison, was speaking as if he truly cared about her. She fought for control and succeeded. 'My enjoyment of our trip would mark a significant victory for you, I suspect.'

'You underestimate yourself,' he said quietly. 'Always.'

She was shaken yet again. But giving a slight shrug, she replied, 'Well, I assure you, I shall not be happy until I have seen all that Vauxhall has to offer. The dancers and acrobats, the musicians and the fireworks. Everything!'

'And so you shall,' Raphael promised.

For the next two hours as dusk softly fell, Serena felt herself to be in a wonderland of lantern-lit woodland walks and glades. The gardens were thronged with people, but as Raphael had promised, no one took the slightest notice of them: not when they ate their supper in one of the booths, not when Raphael paused at a row of stalls to buy her ribbons, not even at the hoop-la stall where he won a gingerbread cake which she ate with delight, licking the sticky crumbs from her fingers afterwards. So far there had been no sign of her brother. Nothing occurred to spoil her enjoyment.

Once more she thought dangerous thoughts. *If only I could be someone else. If only he could be, too.* Then they could be like the many carefree couples who strolled around delighting in the entertainments and the music that drifted through the trees before stealing away into dusky copses for secret kisses...

If only. Serena had to squeeze her eyes shut against the sudden, purely physical longing that tore through her—the longing for this to be real and not just a pretence. Almost in a daze, she allowed Raphael to lead her uphill along one of the lamplit paths. 'We should get a fine view of the fireworks from this point,' he told her. 'Though, of course, we could have stayed with the crowds.' He glanced down at her. 'Are we too far away here, do you think?'

'No,' she answered quickly, 'no. It's absolutely perfect.' And indeed it was. She was bewitched by the way the fireworks bloomed like flowers in the black night sky, hurling out gold and silver showers of petals. Then suddenly, everything was more than perfect, because she found that his arm was around her.

She should have pulled away, of course. She knew that. But instead she leaned into him, not only because the spectacle of the night sky alight with sparks of fire made her feel giddy, but because she longed to be closer. And she felt his hold on her tighten.

'Now, don't tell me,' he said in that gently mocking way of his, 'that you're joining the ranks of my female admirers, even though you denied it so vehemently at Richmond?'

'No.' She laughed. 'Oh, no.'

But his words still curled around her, velvety and warm like the night sky, catching at her very heart. Her physical responses were under assault also; his body was so near, so warm! And his mouth, his beautiful lips… She guessed the sound of her heart drumming against her ribs must be even louder than the fireworks and she wanted to say, *I've fallen for you, Raphael. Can't you see that? I'm heartsick with wanting you—and I want you to kiss me. Now.*

But, of course, she couldn't say that. It couldn't be true, anyway, because she didn't enjoy kisses— and besides, Lefevre was her enemy. Yet at this exact moment all she wanted was for him to enfold her in those strong arms of his; indeed, her breasts ached for the pressure of his body. And with her very soul, she wanted his mouth to caress her face, her lips and more…

Stop it, you fool.

'Sensible Serena,' he said, almost with a regretful sigh.

He was still playing games with her. The trouble was, though, that he was doubtless used to this kind of charade, but she wasn't. He was also far too good at making her body as well as her brain react in ways she couldn't control.

She moved away from him, instructing herself fiercely that it was time to get the situation— and her stupid heart—restored to order. 'Yes,' she said. stubbornly. 'I am sensible. Maybe because a woman on her own has to be. But I don't think you quite understand that these few weeks have seemed like an eternity to me, not least because I feel you are hiding so very much!'

He rubbed his hand against his temple as if suddenly weary. Then he said, 'Let me tell you about one particular time in my life. Some weeks that seemed like eternity to me—every single day of them.'

Something in his voice shook her to her core, but she kept her reply light. 'Really? Maybe you were forced to wait for a new carriage you'd ordered? Or perhaps you'd fallen for some new mistress who was clever enough to elude you for a while?'

He pointed to a bench half hidden in a nook, where a cascade of white-starred clematis spilled through a weeping willow. 'Sit,' he said. 'Please sit with me a while.' After hesitating a moment, she sat and he joined her.

'When I was a boy,' he began, 'my father the Marquis used to take what he called a personal hand in the education of my brother and myself.'

She scarcely breathed, because this was the first time he'd said anything at all about his family. 'I didn't know,' she said at last, 'that you had a brother.'

He nodded. 'He was two years older than me. His name was Guy. He was often ill when he was a boy and my father despised him for it.'

'I would hope that your mother loved him?' She spoke hesitantly. 'Loved both of you?'

'She died,' he answered shortly, 'soon after giving birth to me. I was stronger and fitter than my brother even though I was younger, so I tried to protect him from my father's rages. Fortunately, my father was often away, living the high life; but every so often he would resolve to take a hand in his sons' education. Guy and I always knew what was coming, because he would dismiss whoever had the misfortune to be our tutor at the time.

'One August, when I was twelve and Guy fourteen, he drew up a list of physical challenges for the two of us, every day for a month. For example, we had to swim across the local river, where there was a fierce current, or we were made to ride his most headstrong horses. He even brought in some big village boys to test us on our boxing skills. I managed the challenges. I was lucky enough to be strong and quick. My brother suffered though, on every count. He wasn't a strong swimmer and he was afraid of the high-bred horses we were made to ride. As for the boxing, the village boys beat him time after time.' He paused, then said almost wonderingly, 'After that, my father would beat him, too.'

Serena couldn't suppress a low cry. 'Oh, *no*.'

'Once,' Raphael pressed on, 'I tried to stop

him. So my father said to me, "Every time you plead for your brother, I will double the tasks I set him."'

Again Raphael was silent and Serena waited. 'For all of that month of August,' Raphael went on at last, 'I had to watch my brother endure and fail the physical tests my father set us. I did what I could. I stole money from my father's study and bribed those village boys to let my brother win at least some of the boxing matches. I asked the grooms to tire out the horses my father had chosen for Guy to ride. But Guy still suffered, though he never cried or complained. And I hated my father. I counted the days until I was sent back to school in England. When he died, I came back to Montpellier for his funeral, but I could not mourn him.'

She waited before speaking. The nearby sounds of music and laughter seemed to belong to another world, but this man was all too real—this man and his haunting past. She said quietly, 'How did your father die?'

'He was thrown off his horse when he was out riding with the hunt one day.' He looked straight at her. 'I told you he loved the sport, didn't I? Apparently he was blind drunk, so it was a fitting end.'

'And then your brother Guy became the Marquis? But…'

'He died, too.'

'I'm sorry. So sorry. Was it some illness?'

'No.' His voice was still curt. Unemotional. 'He was murdered two years ago by the Revolutionaries. And I thought, *Let these bloodthirsty fiends get on with it. From now on, my country is not fit to live in.*'

He looked directly at her. 'So now, Serena, you can call me a coward by all means for fleeing my homeland. But in the course of my life I've seen enough cruelty and slaughter to conclude that anyone, be he aristocrat or peasant, has the capacity to behave like the lowest beast. You can therefore feel free to set me as low as you wish in your estimation. Who could blame you? Has anyone ever told you you're too saintly for your own good?'

She longed to cry out her reply into the dusky night air. *But I don't want to be good! I don't want to be saintly, Raphael. I want you to take me in your arms and make love to me!*

Just as she wanted to make love to him, because the magic still pulsed in her veins, together with the sudden blinding clarity of her belief that here was a good and noble man, to whom, if she wasn't careful, she might lose her carefully guarded heart.

'No, Raphael!' The words left her lips without her even thinking about them—instinctive, heartfelt. 'I'm not saintly! But I know you still have secrets you're keeping from me. You've told me about your father, and your poor brother, but there must be more. Please help me to believe in you by telling me the truth. That's all I ask!'

'Serena? Is that you? *Serena?*'

She jumped with shock, because her brother George had appeared from one of the paths leading into their glade with Joanna at his heels. And the moment of intimacy was over.

Joanna hurried to Serena's side as George confronted Raphael head on. 'You've no right, Lefevre. No right at all to lure my sister into this secluded place! What the deuce were you thinking of?'

Raphael had tensed beside her, but Serena was the first to reply to her brother. 'George. Please listen, will you? It was I who asked Raphael to bring me here—I wanted to explore the woodland walks!'

By now some onlookers had been lured by the raised voices and George looked even angrier. 'Serena, don't you realise this man is making a public spectacle of you?'

It was Joanna's turn to enter the fray. 'George, it's you who's making a public spectacle, not the Marquis! Please, everyone, calm down.'

But Serena felt a primeval urge to defend the

man she was supposed to hate. Why? Couldn't he defend himself a hundred times over? He was clearly ready to. By now, his usual polished veneer of indifference had vanished; anger made his mouth harsh and uncompromising while his silver-grey eyes looked almost black. She said in a low, urgent voice, 'George, I appreciate you're saying all this out of concern for me. But you're making completely false assumptions about my relationship with the Marquis—besides which, I'm twenty-five years old and I can take responsibility for myself! So please don't treat me like a foolish seventeen-year-old!'

She swept to Raphael's side and thrust her arm through his, aware that her heart was thumping badly. At last George said stiffly, 'Maybe I should escort you home, Serena.'

'No,' she said, her chin tilting defiantly. 'No, George. I'm sorry. But I'm with Raphael, not you.'

Even more passers-by were stopping and Joanna was tugging at George's arm. 'Come along, George. You're making a public scene. Your sister is quite right—she's well able to take care of herself.'

There was a tormented silence before George said, 'Very well. I'll speak with you tomorrow, Serena.' He gave his sister a curt bow, regarded

Raphael with acute dislike and said, 'Come along, Joanna.'

Joanna mouthed regretfully to Serena, *Oh, dear. What a pickle you're in, darling!* Then George headed back along the path with Joanna following, but Raphael didn't move.

He said quietly at last, 'Serena. May I ask exactly why you took my side and defended me against your brother?'

Because I'm falling in love. With you.

Dear Lord, the thought terrified her. Joanna was quite right—what a pickle she was in. But she said calmly, 'What else was I supposed to do? I thought George was quite wrong to say the things he did. I know I was unhappy with our agreement, but you've not made me a laughing stock—which my brother nearly did just now with that unpleasant scene.'

The group of watchers had moved on, but a party of boisterous revellers were strolling along the path in their direction, some of the men drinking from bottles of champagne they carried. Raphael instantly drew her aside. 'Those men,' he said. 'I don't know them, but I'm afraid we might be recognised. And if they talk—'

She silenced him by reaching up to put her arms around his neck and clasping the back of his head.

'I think,' she said defiantly, 'that in that case, we should give them something to talk about.'

And she stood on her tiptoes and kissed him.

Fireworks? The ones they'd seen earlier were nothing compared to this.

She thought, *This is what I have been waiting for. This is what I've dreamed of ever since I was a girl.* She forgot to care if anyone was watching. She forgot everything. She tasted him, but it was like having a tantalising fragment of a feast, because it meant she wanted more, so much more of the silken pressure of his lips on hers, more of the intoxicating scent and feel of him.

He pulled away, just enough for her to catch her breath and steady herself, though she was still dizzy, because his mouth was so temptingly close. His hands rested on her shoulders, clasping her lightly but possessively, as if he might reclaim her lips any moment and enfold them both once more in that wild, dizzying heat.

He caressed her jaw with one tender finger. 'Serena. Why…?'

Why, indeed? Her heart thudded with desire still. What was happening to her? One thing was obvious—her feelings for this man were running far deeper than she'd ever meant them to. When George had insulted Raphael, she'd not hesitated to defend him; just as when Raphael had told her the story of his brother, she'd longed to somehow take his pain away.

Those revellers had moved on, but somewhere in the distance she could hear musicians playing a haunting tune that spoke of loss and love. She said on impulse, 'Take me to a place where nobody knows us. Where neither of us has to pretend.' She tugged at his hand. 'Where we can just be *us*. Please?'

'But your clothes. Even in that cloak, Serena, you can't help but look wealthy!'

She drew her cloak tighter across her bosom and pulled her hair from its pins. 'There.'

He was shaking his head. 'Oh, my God. You still look expensive.'

'Then people will think I'm your mistress,' she said. 'Let them.'

Chapter Fifteen

When they'd arrived at Vauxhall Raphael had sent his carriage home, intending to take Serena back to Curzon Street by hired cab. Now, though, everything had changed unbelievably. And so on leaving the Gardens he hailed a cab to take them not to Mayfair, but to the Strand, from where he led Serena to a lowly tavern in King Street. Serena's brother would be truly appalled.

Afterwards, when his brain had cleared just a little from the impact of what this honest and beautiful woman had said to him earlier—*Help me to believe in you*—he had asked himself: Why did he take her there, of all places?

The answer came to him as soon as he led her through the door. She'd wanted to know more about him and maybe this was the best way. The tavern was one that many French exiles had made their own—the poorer ones, to be precise. In fact, he guessed the rich Frenchmen in London didn't even know places like this existed, but to Raphael it was like home, filled as it was with the scents and sounds of his native land: the food, the wine, the tobacco—and, of course, the voices of his fellow countrymen.

Their talk reminded him of his army days, of old tales and jokes shared with long-gone friends, bringing back memories of the world that existed before the Revolution overturned the life they'd all known. There was music, too, provided by a fiddle player and someone on a flute. As he and Serena entered a dozen or so of the younger folk were dancing in a ring, stamping their feet as they moved and clapping their hands in time to the beat. Guiding Serena past them to one of the few empty tables, he ordered red wine, bread and cheese.

Mon Dieu, he thought to himself. Was he truly taking a lady of such aristocratic lineage to a common tavern? Yes, he was. Had he gone mad? Quite likely. But she hadn't run—yet—so he said to her, 'I don't know about you, but that supper we ate at Vauxhall Gardens was like bird food and I'm ravenous.'

Then he tried to assess her mood.

Tonight he'd been astonished by the way she'd stood up for him against the head of her family, to whom everyone said she was devoted. And after that she'd actually kissed him—only briefly but, dear God, her kiss was so sweet that he could almost have believed that theirs truly was a love affair.

Cynic though he was, he had been rocked by a wave of extraordinary desire for this woman. Even more worryingly, physical lust was only the part of it. A rather overwhelming part, admittedly, but Raphael also realised that he wanted to find ways to light up her eyes again with pleasure. The pleasure known only by intimate lovers…

For God's sake, man. Furious with himself for his lustful imaginings, his mood darkened anew.

His initial plan had all seemed so simple. He'd resolved to entangle Serena in the appearance of an *affaire,* with the very robust intention of halting her persistent enquiries about his past. After the stated four weeks he would casually discard her, thus ensuring that any future criticisms of hers would be seen merely as the snipings of a bitter ex-mistress. It should have been easy. But, of course, life had a habit of never making things easy.

They were sitting side by side at a corner table, both with a full view of the crowded hostelry's occupants. Raphael was looking out of habit for potential enemies, though Serena clearly had no such worry. Having eagerly eaten her bread and cheese, she was watching the dancers and for once

her lovely eyes were unclouded by doubt or uncertainty.

She'd loosened her cloak so that her green silk
gown was on show. 'Don't worry,' she said when
she saw his frown. 'As I said, people will think
I'm your mistress, that's all.'

He sighed. She was enjoying herself, he realised. If only briefly, she was free of the burden
of being Lady Serena Willoughby with a reputation to uphold. And he was light-headed with her
presence at his side, intoxicated by her beauty.
He'd realised tonight that he didn't want all this to
end once the time was over. Had realised it the moment he saw the fire in her eyes when her brother
had insulted him—and he certainly would never
forget the words she'd used to defend him. He'd
wanted to take her in his arms and kiss her, though
somehow—God knew how—he'd managed to resist. Only then, she'd broken down all his carefully
built defences by kissing him instead.

Again and again he relived the shy but passionate kiss she'd offered, imagining he could still feel
her warm and silken lips on his. He'd been warned
by his companions that she was cold and proud.
But ever since their paths had crossed, she'd taken
Raphael by surprise, every single step of the way.

He'd seen beneath the mask she wore in public.
Seen how she could be warm and funny with her

female friends and deeply affectionate with the children at that school. She'd unwittingly probed his own hard-won defences, for not even to Dominic had he spoken about his boyhood or those other memories which still caught at him every so often like an unhealed wound.

But he had not told her why he was here in London. Initially he'd had no intention of explaining his search for Madeleine, partly because of her hostility and also because of her apparent friendship with some of his enemies. He'd not, so far, had to worry about her feelings because she'd declared, on frequent occasions, her utter indifference to him.

But tonight, that indifference had melted away. She'd kissed him—and it had been exquisite.

You treacherous bastard, Lefevre, he rebuked himself. *You are the one who should be exerting some willpower, because you're getting in too deep.* And try as he might, he'd reached a dead end in his search for Madeleine. What if he never found her? Damn it, he had—he simply had—to tell Serena everything. But now? Did he have to spoil the magic between them now?

He suddenly realised that Serena had drunk almost all her rather large glass of red wine and her eyes were sparkling in the light of the tallow candles fastened to the rough-cast walls. She put her hand on his arm. 'Raphael,' she said, 'please, could we join the dancing?' She was raising her voice to be heard above the sound of the music. 'I want to dance,' she repeated. And the next minute she'd shed her cloak and was on her feet, pulling him up with her. So what could he do? Already people were making room for them in the ring; already he saw her delight as she picked up the rhythm and the movements.

Raphael had often danced like this in his homeland with a pretty girl on his arm. This, though, was different. This was Serena.

'No wager this time,' she murmured to him as he took her hands in his.

He said, 'No wager. And there wasn't one last time. It's very important that you believe me.'

She nodded. 'I do.'

As he swept her into the dancing she clung to him at first, unsure of herself. But her confidence grew, even though the pattern of the steps meant that from time to time they were separated. Of course, she encountered partners who were delighted to dance her round the ring; indeed, one of the Frenchmen said to Raphael, as he handed Serena back to him, *'Votre dame anglaise. Elle est belle, n'est-ce pas?'*

'Yes,' he replied, 'she's beautiful.' Beautiful indeed in her ravishing green gown, with all her golden hair tumbling to her shoulders. *And she's mine*, he wanted to add.

But she wasn't. Could never be. And that was the trouble.

Such a perfect two hours together, though. They shared the simple pleasures of the wine and the dancing and the companionship of the tavern's other customers, who sat with them for a while. 'I'm afraid my schoolgirl French is atrocious,' Serena apologised to Raphael. But she listened and tried hard to understand those people in the tavern, as they talked not only about the tragedy of the Revolution, but also told tales of the vineyards and the villages they'd left behind. The happy times that they hoped would some day come back.

Raphael translated for her and she said earnestly in French to them all, 'But of course they will.'

He saw how her beautiful smile cast more light around that dingy tavern than a hundred fine wax candles could have done. And then he danced with her again, realising he could easily become addicted to the feel of her in his arms; addicted to that intoxicating shiver of delight that he would swear ran through her every time he clasped her close. Not only did he ache to kiss her, he felt an even more powerful need pulsing deep in his loins...

Stop there, he told himself fiercely.

And at that very moment, his attention was riveted elsewhere, because a young woman came up to touch him on the shoulder. She said, in French, 'You have been looking for Madeleine, haven't you, *monsieur*?'

He froze. '*Oui, madame.* Yes, I have.'

'Then call at my lodgings in Cheapside, above the haberdashery shop. Ask for Therese.'

A moment later the woman had gone and Raphael stood there, his brain reeling, his heart pounding like a drum.

The hour was late. Many couples had already left the dancing and were finding dark corners in which to exchange kisses. Serena hadn't understood what the woman said and she glanced at him uncertainly.

'Raphael. You look anxious. Was that someone you know?'

He shook his head. 'She mistook me for someone else.' He forced a smile. 'And now, Serena, I think it's time I took you home.'

'Of course,' she said. 'Of course.'

He saw her try her best to hide it, but as she fastened up her cloak she looked crushed, no doubt because she knew that once again he wasn't confiding in her. Loathing himself, he led her from the tavern with the intention of heading for the Strand to hail a cab, but she'd drunk two large glasses of wine. And as they stepped out together into the cobbled street, she stumbled on an uneven stone and he had to catch her.

'Too much wine,' she said, laughing a little. 'Too much wine—but oh, Raphael, it has been a *lovely* evening!'

She was in his arms. She was gazing up at him with such yearning in her eyes. What could he do but kiss her? Only lightly at first, but she sighed with happiness, then reached up almost wonderingly to touch his cheek. 'Raphael,' she murmured. 'My Marquis of mystery.'

He crushed her slender body to his. Once more their mouths met, only this time he wanted more, plundering her soft lips until they drifted open. He deepened the kiss, exploring her mouth properly this time. The taste of her was addictive and sensual and heady, just as before, but this time her tongue twined boldly with his, demanding still more, and Raphael thought, *I'm falling headlong for her. Falling badly.*

He wanted to say something, to acknowledge that the unthinkable had happened. To warn her that the nature of their relationship was changing, only he knew that it couldn't and he must think of some way to explain that reality without making her hate him again. He'd barely begun to concoct the impossible words when out of the darkness three men came charging towards them, carrying clubs.

Their clothing was rough and the lower parts of their faces were concealed by black woollen scarves. There was something about them. He'd seen them recently, but damn it, where? He whirled to confront them, his fists raised, his body planted firmly in front of Serena's.

He was already admitting that, this time, the odds were dire.

One moment Serena was standing outside the tavern in Raphael's arms, her lips warm from his tender kisses. *So few days to go,* she was warning herself. But this couldn't be the end yet. It couldn't be...

The next minute she was crying out in horror as the three men appeared out of the shadows. 'Well, my fine French lord,' came the voice of one. 'We're here to tell you to stop your damned meddling. Your interfering. Got it?'

And then they launched themselves at him with their cudgels. She saw how Raphael managed to knock aside the first two with his fists, but of course the odds were impossible. Whenever one stumbled, another ran up to rain more blows. What could she do?

Suddenly she realised that music was still coming from the tavern behind her and, after heaving the front door open, she ran inside, calling out to anyone who would listen. 'Please. They're attacking Raphael out in the street. I'm afraid they're going to kill him!'

The English landlord leapt into action. 'What, my pretty lass? Pickpockets, are they? Damn them! Come on, lads, look lively! Let's show the blackguards what happens to villains who lurk outside my tavern!'

And out they flew, the landlord and his barmen and the drinkers, too. They fell on those three men, pulling them off Raphael, then continuing the attack until the ruffians hurried off down the street, no doubt feeling lucky to escape alive. Meanwhile Serena, heedless of her gown and cloak, was kneeling in the gutter at Raphael's side, horrified by his closed eyes and the blood on his forehead. She could hear a voice from somewhere—was it *her* voice?—calling out into the night, 'Is he dead? Oh, dear God, no. Please, no...'

The landlord crouched quickly beside her, checking Raphael's pulse. 'He's had a nasty knock on the head,' he told Serena. 'Rest is what he needs. And maybe a doctor to check for broken bones.'

Rising to his feet, he told one of his barmen to run and hail a hackney cab from nearby Leicester

Street. When the cab at last came into view, several of the men hoisted up Raphael's still-prone figure, ready to lift him inside, but the driver blocked their way.

'Don't normally take on fellows who've been brawling,' he said stubbornly. 'No indeed.'

'Please!' Serena rose from Raphael's side. 'I need to take him to my home in Mayfair and I promise I'll pay you well. He's not drunk and he wasn't fighting. He was attacked!'

'There'll be a reason for that,' the driver said, but Serena's plea and the mention of Mayfair had clearly softened him. 'Well, we'd best get him inside the cab, then. Don't want the gent dying on the street, do we?'

'Thank you. Oh, thank you!' Serena could see that the landlord's friends were already lifting Raphael in and laying him across one of the seats inside. After that she climbed in, too. He was starting to stir, just a little, though his eyes were still closed.

Dear God, all this was her fault. After Vauxhall, he'd wanted to take her back to her house, but she'd dragged him here despite his reluctance. Her fault indeed, so, yes, she would take him home—and she would be the one to take care of him.

Chapter Sixteen

When they arrived at Serena's house, the two footmen watched, astonished, as the driver tried to help the barely conscious Raphael out of this cab. 'Come here, both of you!' she spoke urgently to them. 'You must carry the Marquis inside—he's been injured.'

They snapped to attention. 'Which room, ma'am?'

Serena thought quickly—not upstairs, he was too heavy for them to carry all that way. 'To my sitting room,' she declared. Mrs Penney had now arrived, all of a-fluster, so Serena added, 'Mrs Penney. Please take some fresh sheets to the sitting room and make up the day bed in there.'

Her housekeeper was regarding Raphael with horror. 'But, ma'am… His head—it's bleeding!'

'Do you think I don't realise it? Do as I say and tell the maids to bring in several bowls of

hot water and some linen strips. One of the footmen must go to summon Dr Phillips in Wimpole
Street.' Late though it was, she knew the doctor
would set off speedily at the mention of her name.

Mrs Penney still looked shocked. 'My lady.
You surely won't tend to the gentleman yourself?
It isn't fitting!'

'It's perfectly fitting,' Serena retorted, 'since
Monsieur Lefevre was defending me from street
robbers at the time of the incident. So, yes, I will
stay with him.'

And please, God, she whispered, *please let him
not be badly injured.*

That hour she spent sitting at Raphael's side,
waiting for the doctor to arrive, was one of the
longest of her life. His eyes had briefly flickered
open as the footmen carried him into the sitting
room, but now he'd drifted into unconsciousness
again. She felt quite sick with fear.

One of the footmen had removed his outer gar-
ments while she spoke to Mrs Penney and now
Raphael wore only his shirt and breeches and was
covered to his chest by a sheet. The day bed was
one of George's most expensive purchases for the
house—it was French, he'd told her proudly, with
gold scrolling, It was at least a hundred years old,
but little did Serena care. She flinched when she

saw how the candlelight picked out the gash high on Raphael's forehead, but she braced herself to do what was necessary, using the hot water and linen a maid had brought to bathe away the blood that matted his hair.

The doctor, on arriving, asked her to wait outside and came to her ten minutes later to make his report. 'Fortunately, nothing has been broken, my lady, but the Marquis has suffered quite a blow to the head and has lost blood, as you've noted. The wound is minor, but he will, for a day or two at least, be better staying where he is. Moving him would not be wise. You'll inform his household?'

'Of course,' she said.

There was no sleep for Serena that night because she was busy, either watching over Raphael or supervising her servants in caring for his needs.

The next day, too, she insisted on being in charge; but by nine that evening Mrs Penney was begging Serena to take some rest.

'I'll stay through the night with His Lordship myself, ma'am,' she urged. 'You've had no sleep and I'd swear not a morsel of food has passed your lips since you brought the poor man home. If you wear yourself out, what use will you be to either him or the rest of us?'

But before Serena could reply, a visitor was announced.

'Mr Jeremy Wolverton is waiting to see you in the reception hall, ma'am,' her butler Grinling informed her.

Serena's heart sank. *Why?* Why now, so late in the evening? Wolverton was a worthy man, undoubtedly. His support of the charity school was invaluable and she felt some sympathy for him, since, despite his successful business and his generosity to good causes, he would never be fully accepted by London's elite.

Then she also remembered that the last time she'd seen him was at the Duke of Hamilton's ball, where he and Raphael… *Oh, Lord.*

It was with considerable reluctance that she went to meet him. 'Mr Wolverton. Is the matter urgent? I'm rather occupied at present.'

'It is urgent, as a matter of fact. May I speak in private?' He frowned at the hovering Grinling.

'As I said, this really is not a good time—'

'Very well, then!' The normally reserved Wolverton appeared quite agitated. 'I'll say what I must say right here. It's about that man, Lefevre—'

Swiftly she led him into the small salon to her left and closed the door. Immediately Wolverton started talking again. 'Yes, it's about

Lefevre. I've heard he's involved in something
underhand—'

'Really?' she interrupted. 'My goodness, in-
venting stories about the Marquis's misdeeds
seems to be one of society's chief occupations
at present. I thought you were above all that, Mr
Wolverton!'

'Lady Serena, listen, please. He's been seen
entering the most shocking places in lowly parts
of town. I hate to risk offending a person of your
delicacy, but he's known to frequent the houses
where young women are for sale!'

Serena's brain was reeling. Was Wolverton
mad, to come to her with such a tale? She knew
Raphael was no saint. Everyone did. But what
was Wolverton trying to do?

Poor Wolverton. He's smitten with you, Joanna
had warned her. She said now, 'I believe this is
neither the time nor the place for these stories of
yours. And, yes, you are offending me.'

'But he's here!' The man sounded desperate.
'I've heard he was attacked on King Street by
three men who knew who he was. This surely
proves to you that the man mixes in the most sordid company—and yet you've actually offered
him shelter here, under your roof!'

Her mind whirled again. How did he know all
these details? Who else knew them, other than her

and Raphael? 'You have it completely wrong,' she declared. 'Monsieur Lefevre was injured while defending me from some street thieves. As he was unconscious after the attack, I had no alternative but to bring him here. And now, I must insist that you leave.' She was already heading for the salon door, but he put out his hand to stop her.

'That's not all, Lady Serena. I've heard that he's been looking in particular for a young French-woman who was familiar to him in his former life. He's been asking in the most unsavoury places for her and I imagine her protectors don't like it. This is surely why he was attacked! You *must* banish him from your house immediately and put yourself at a considerable distance from the wretched man!'

Serena was shaking inside. But somehow she managed to coolly reply, 'Thank you, Mr Wolverton. That, I believe, will be all. Kindly allow my butler to show you the door.'

She began to walk out of the room and he followed. 'Be careful, I implore you. I know you're besotted with the Marquis. But he's using you to give himself an air of respectability, while he's secretly laughing at you!'

Her butler was waiting in the hallway. 'Grinling,' she told him, 'please show Mr Wolverton out.'

Mrs Penney came to her side after that. 'Ma'am,'

she urged, 'do take some rest now. As I told you, I will sit with His Lordship through the night!'

So Serena retired at last to her room. After attempting to eat the light supper Martha brought her, she tried to sleep and succeeded, because she was exhausted. But her dreams haunted her all night—and this time they were not of her dead husband, but of Raphael. She dreamed he'd taken her in his arms and so vivid was the reality of his presence that even when she woke she was pursued still by the passionate images that had invaded her sleep. Memories of his caresses. His lips on her skin, her breasts, everywhere...

She woke, her heart thudding. Lionel used to tell her she would have suited a nunnery better than the marriage bed, but there was nothing restrained about her emotions where Raphael was concerned. She'd expected to feel humiliated being seen in his company, but it hadn't been long before she'd found herself counting the hours until his arrival at her front door. Found herself becoming entranced by his presence, because he made her feel alive in a way she'd never felt before.

For many months now, she'd believed him to be exactly what the rest of society thought—a man of easy morals who was indifferent to the plight of his fellow countrymen and intent only on personal pleasure. Yet these last weeks had revealed someone completely different—an intelligent, deeply humane man who she guessed hid dark secrets and perhaps had good reason for his cynicism.

Yes, he was sardonic; could indeed be cutting at times. But to her, he had so often been kind and understanding, tender almost. And so Jeremy Wolverton's accusations had shaken her to her core. Who was this woman Raphael was supposed to be looking for? Someone he'd once loved and still did? The pain she felt astonished her.

She reminded herself that whatever secrets Raphael hid from her, she'd always known he would be leaving her life very soon. But still she felt a great emptiness at the thought. Of one thing, she was sure. Whatever she'd let him do to her emotions, she must never, ever let him know it. There must be no more kisses, no more intimate conversations. She'd been a fool to have opened up to him so much about her life and marriage and it was time to build her guard again, since there were only a few days to go before she returned to the solitariness of her life before Raphael. Yet her heart constricted, because she'd grown to like him. To really, really like him.

Just for a brief moment, she buried her face in her hands. She'd tried so hard to convince herself she was happy being single, happy with her friends and her work with the school. But now that she'd had a taste of what life and love might just maybe offer her, could she ever be happy again?

It was only four in the morning, but she knew she would never get back to sleep. So she rose and wrapped herself in her dressing robe, lit a candle and carried it downstairs through the silent house to the sitting room.

Mrs Penney was dozing in the chair at Raphael's side, though she jumped to her feet when Serena entered. 'Ma'am!'

Serena saw that Raphael had not moved and the bandage gleamed an ominous white against his forehead. Dear God, how long would it be before he opened his eyes?

Mrs Penney was flustered. 'I'm sorry, ma'am. His Lordship seemed to be peacefully sleeping and I must have nodded off, though I'd have been up in a flash had His Lordship wakened!'

'I know you would,' said Serena gently. 'You go and get some proper rest, Mrs Penney. I'll stay with the Marquis for a while.'

'But…'

'I'm insisting on this. I shall stay with the Marquis.'

As soon as the housekeeper had gone, Serena took her place on the chair at his side. The crisp sheet had been pulled up to Raphael's shoulders. His hair was raven black against the pillows and his jaw was dark with stubble. He lay so still. So frighteningly still. She found her mind drifting back remorselessly to that kiss outside the tavern and the way she'd melted into his arms, revelling in the warm strength of him while gazing up into his darkly handsome face…

He's been asking in the most unsavoury places for her and I imagine her protectors don't like it. Wolverton's words tortured her.

The servants would be gossiping avidly come morning. *She's refusing to leave him,* they would be whispering. *We've never seen her so anxious.* She was being crazy to let herself get so involved with this man of all men. And yet she couldn't forget the expression on his face last night as he'd brushed his fingers over her cheek. Couldn't believe he'd been pretending when his lips had captured hers, for she'd seen the dark yearning in his haunted eyes.

Outside in the hallway the big clock was chiming five and she glanced at the window, wondering when the first glimmer of dawn would creep through the curtains. That was when she realised that Raphael was stirring. His eyes were still closed, but he'd pushed back the bedsheet; his hands were gripping at the fabric as if it imprisoned him and he was muttering, through dry lips, 'Not again. Not again.'

Dear God. He was in the throes of a dream, she guessed. A very bad dream. She rose from her chair, her heart knotting, because something about those simple words—the anguish in them— tore at her. She put her hand on his shirtsleeve, feeling the warmth of his muscled arm beneath. 'Raphael,' she urged him. 'It's all right. You're in my house now. You're safe here.'

'The clock. You mustn't...' His eyes had opened, but they were wild and unseeing.

'Hush! It's only the grandfather clock, in the hall of my house. You remember?'

He sat up abruptly, eyes wide open now. 'Where have you taken me? Where have you taken her?'

Her? Serena backed away. 'Raphael, it's me, Serena. You were in a fight outside a tavern and were injured, so I brought you to my house. The doctor came and he says that you'll be all right. There's no serious harm done.'

Slowly his eyes focused on her, recognised her—and he lay back against his pillows.

'Those men outside the tavern,' he said in a low voice. 'I shouldn't have let them get the better of me.'

She could almost have laughed if it wasn't so heart-wrenchingly brave of him to think he'd failed in some way. 'There were three of them, Raphael, with weapons! Rather impossible odds, even for you, don't you think?' She tried to speak lightly.

'I don't run,' he said, 'ever.' He tried to pull himself up again and she yearned to help him. What was this man doing to her? Why was she *letting* him do this to her? Then he clenched his hands where they rested on the sheet and he said, 'The clock. I heard the clock, Serena.'

And she suddenly guessed that behind that simple, everyday sound lay some enormous clue—a clue that might unlock the mystery of this enigmatic man. She said to him, quietly, 'Raphael, why did that clock disturb you so?'

And when he finally answered her, she realised she was right.

Chapter Seventeen

Raphael had once believed there were certain secrets he would keep till the end of his life. The trouble was that in his experience, evil memories tended to come crawling out in the darkness of the night, whether you willed it or not.

The chiming of the clock had penetrated his uneasy dreams and he'd woken to find himself in a strange bed with his head and ribs aching like hell. *Dieu.* Those three blackguards who'd attacked him—he was sure he'd seen them before, but where? Where?

After they'd felled him, all was dark. Yet to see Serena sitting by his bedside with her anxious yet beautiful face softly illuminated by candlelight was enough to banish that darkness, if only for a short while.

'Why,' she'd asked, 'did that clock disturb you so?'

'Do you really want to know?'

'Of course I do,' she said steadily. 'Raphael, at Vauxhall you asked me why I took your side against my brother. I told you it was because I believed George was quite wrong to say the things he did. I still want to believe, so very much, that he was wrong. But once more, I beg you, please *help* me to believe in you by telling me at least some of the secrets you're hiding from me. Tell me about your life, Raphael!'

Wearily he pulled himself up on one elbow, then hesitated, because, damn it, he was only semi-clad in shirt and breeches. But then he realised she was scarcely more decent, sitting a mere two feet away from him with her fair hair tumbling in disarray and clad in a flimsy night robe that did little to disguise her delicious curves. Lady Serena—as lovely as ever. His head ached anew with the sheer impossibility of his situation. But it was, he acknowledged with a bone-deep resignation, time to tell her some of the truth. He owed her that at least.

'You want to know about my life?' he said at last. 'I told you about my father. Here's a little more.' He adjusted the pillows behind his shoulders so he could sit straighter—and he began. 'After my father died,' he went on, 'I joined the French army and was posted overseas. When the

Revolution broke out I was in the Caribbean, so at first my regiment wasn't affected in the slightest. But gradually I heard news that France was descending into chaos, so I sailed home to see how my brother and his wife were. Guy had recently got married, you see, to a girl he loved very much.

'I travelled back to Montpellier and found the situation even worse than I'd feared. The Revolution was poisoning the lifeblood of the entire country and I could see that Guy was in danger. I tried to persuade him he should flee abroad with his wife, if only for a short while, but he refused. Unlike me, Guy believed the best of people, but I knew he was wrong. I'd seen, in Paris, how other noblemen were sending their money overseas, because the banks were no longer safe from the grasp of the Revolution's manic leaders. I urged Guy to do the same, but again he refused—so I went to Paris myself and pretended to be my brother. I arranged for a large sum of money to be sent to London for him, then I travelled back south to the chateau.'

He paused. God, how it hurt him still to even think of it. 'I arrived,' he went on, 'with the intention of trying again to persuade him to leave. I was too late. The place was in flames and the peasants who'd stood by Guy's side had been slaughtered wholesale by a Revolutionary mob. I

should have been there. I shall never forgive myself for not being there.'

She was gazing steadily at him. 'You told me
some of this before. Oh, Raphael, to think that
even in his own home your brother wasn't safe!'

'They beat him to death,' he said tonelessly.
'He died in my arms.'

'But even if you'd arrived earlier, you could not
have saved your brother singlehandedly against
so many people!'

He nodded. 'They were bloodthirsty maniacs.
My brother, on the other hand, was selfless and
kind to everyone.' His hands clenched on the bedsheet. 'You know, when I gave the money to that
refuge for the homeless French in London, I told
myself it was for Guy. Guy was a truly good person—which I am not.'

Serena could hardly bear the self-contempt in
his voice. 'You must stop blaming yourself so!'

He looked weary. 'There's more I haven't told
you. More that I *need* to tell you.'

Pulling himself up, he reached to where she
sat by his bed and took her hand. He half expected her to snatch it away, but she let it remain
firm and warm in his—as if she was offering
him something that was steadfast and true. Like
her, he realised. Yes—steadfast and true. After a
moment he continued. 'I set off north again, be-

cause there was something that I'd promised to do. Jacques was with me—he'd been my companion since my soldiering days. But in Lyons, we were captured by the citizens' army and thrown into the gaol there.'

He saw her draw in her breath. 'What was your crime?'

His mouth curled bitterly. 'My crime lay in being wealthy, yet still being alive. Though I tell you, Jacques and I put up an almighty fight before they locked us in chains.'

'Oh, Raphael. How long was your sentence?'

'You don't quite understand, Serena. None of us was given a date when we would get out, because we'd all been condemned to death.'

She pulled her hand from his in her shock. '*All* of you?'

'Indeed, all. Some lasted months in there, some only days.' He closed his eyes briefly. 'There was a big clock tower above the gaol. Every day when it struck noon, our warders came into the cells to drag out a prisoner or two, or even three—it depended on how the fancy took them. Then the prisoners would be hanged in the courtyard. Our gaolers were drunk most of the time. They used to laugh at those who pleaded for mercy.'

He saw her close her eyes briefly. 'How did you…?'

'How did I escape? I was in luck. A bunch of soldiers turned up and told our guards they had orders to transport us all to Paris, so we could be sent to the guillotine as entertainment for the crowds. Our guards, drunken sots that they were, objected and fought them. They'd been enjoying their rule over us, you see. And during the general chaos, Jacques and I managed to escape.'

'That was when you came to London?'

A shadow crossed his face, 'Eventually, yes. My brother's money was there, after all. As you know, I arrived here a wealthy man.'

She said, slowly, 'You told people you'd been travelling in Europe. Staying in Vienna and other cities.'

'I lied,' he said in a curt voice. 'I lied, because the months after my brother's death and the time I spent in prison were not subjects I wished to talk about.'

'Of course. But, Raphael, after your brother's murder, you must have known your own life was in danger. So why on earth didn't you try to escape from France straight away? Why end up imprisoned in Lyons?'

He looked at her very steadily. 'Because I was looking for someone, Serena. I was searching for my brother's wife. Her name was Madeleine.'

* * *

The rush of understanding that filled her was almost enough to make her unsteady. Silently she damned Wolverton and his sly insinuations. 'Your brother's wife,' she repeated. She enunciated the words with great care. 'Why did you never tell anyone? Why didn't you tell *me?*'

'Because I guessed that Madeleine had been brought to London against her will.'

'As a prisoner, you mean? But why?'

His grey eyes were dark as night. 'Serena,' he said, 'you must know that young women without money are vulnerable in ways that you aren't. I'd heard that the mob who killed my brother had sent Madeleine north, along with other prisoners. So I followed their trail and got as far as Lyons when I was thrown into prison. After I escaped, I headed for Paris with Jacques to continue my search—and there I heard that she'd escaped and fled to Calais. So I went to the coast and heard of a smuggling ring which offered to help fleeing aristocrats to reach England. Only these smugglers weren't doing it out of kindness. They only agreed to take certain passengers on their ships.'

He looked at her. 'They wanted women, Serena. I imagine you'll know there are many kinds of predators, many kinds of victims; but young women with no money and all alone in a foreign city are the most vulnerable of all.'

She said, 'I gather you're saying that they're forced into prostitution.'

'If they're young and attractive, like my brother's poor wife, then, yes. And that's why I travelled here last autumn. I've been searching for her ever since, in the kind of places I feared she might have found herself.'

'You've been searching the brothels.' Serena murmured it almost to herself. This explained Raphael's pose as a *bon viveur,* a rakehell—it was to mask his true purpose. 'Though why,' she said, this time reaching forward from her seat to clasp his hand, 'couldn't you have asked someone in authority to help you? If there are other women suffering in the same way as poor Madeleine, surely these evil men should be prosecuted and put in gaol?'

'Of course.' He let his hand rest in hers. 'But for the time being my search for her has to be in secret, because I fear the men holding her might actually kill her if I look likely to expose their trade.'

'I understand,' Serena said quietly. 'But, Raphael, the things you've let people say about you!' She felt bitterly ashamed that she'd not seen through his masquerade earlier. No wonder he'd been so angry that she'd been asking all those stupid questions about his past. How brave he'd been, to endure the slights thrown his way.

He smiled, but without humour. 'I was content to have those labels thrust upon me—rake, lecher, whatever people chose—since they helped disguise my search. I'd always realised the people who have Madeleine might harm her and harm me also, to keep their evil trade a secret.'

She looked up suddenly. 'Those men who attacked you. Do you suspect them of being involved?'

'Definitely. But now I have to ask you something really difficult, Serena. I have to ask you to keep quiet about everything I've told you and to keep up the pretence that we're a couple for the remainder of our agreement. I believe I'm very close to finding her, you see.'

A huge sense of impending loss invaded her whole being. He was reminding her that she was part of his effort to divert attention from his real purpose in London—nothing more. She understood that—after all, she was Lady Serena Willoughby, who'd vowed to guard her heart always. At the moment her heart was all too vulnerable, but her only option was to never, ever let Raphael know he was on his way to breaking it.

When she spoke again, her voice was perfectly calm. She was proud of that.

'Do you know,' she said as she rose to her feet and went over to the tray the housekeeper had left to pour him a glass of water, 'I never could quite believe the things that were said about you. I know I turned against you after that stupid ball last year, but that was because I was…' She thought a moment. 'Disappointed.'

'Disappointed?'

'Yes.' She handed him the water. 'You see, I'd heard people maligning you, of course. But I'd always imagined you to be somebody different. Somebody courageous and forthright and full of…*integrity.* Yes, that's the word—integrity.'

He sipped some water, but then said bitterly, 'You couldn't be more wrong, because I'm worthless, Serena. I've lied to you constantly.'

She reached across to take the glass, at the same time pressing his hand lightly. 'I think, Monsieur le Marquis, that you are the bravest, most noble man I have ever met.' She tried to smile. 'Only look at the way you saved me from that ridiculous tangle I'd got into with Silas Mort—'

'Don't,' he grated out. *'Don't.'*

She felt fresh hurt lashing through her. Why was he so angry? What had she said this time?

He drew his hand across his forehead. 'Serena. I'm afraid I lied to you about that also.'

And then he told her. He told her how he'd known all along that she was due to meet Mort that night in Covent Garden; how he'd organised his arrival as if by chance and had made arrangements for his companions to witness that scandalous scene. 'Serena,' he said heavily, 'forget what I said earlier. You must consider our agreement cancelled, from this minute. Perhaps you'd do me the final favour of sending one of your servants for Jacques to take me home. In the meantime I'll get myself dressed. I see my clothes are over there.'

He swung his legs out from under the covers and planted his feet firmly on the floor. Loose shirt, breeches—they were enough to cover his modesty, but even so Serena realised that this was Raphael Lefevre in the raw, stripped of his fine tailoring and his mask of indifference.

She said, trying to keep her voice light, 'I'm afraid you can't leave my house yet, Raphael, because the doctor is due this morning to check on your progress. You were knocked unconscious the other night—remember?—and he ordered that you must stay exactly where you are, to rest.'

He spoke more fiercely this time. 'I *must* go. Then this nightmare I've imposed on you will be over!'

She rose to face him. She hoped her gaze was still steadfast, though inside she was tense with the effort to repress her emotions. 'You claim you deceived me by knowing in advance about my meeting with Silas Mort. But you still saved me from him, Raphael. Try as you might, you can't dispute that.' She said it almost flippantly; even tried to smile. 'Soon enough, I'll go back to being a Wicked Widow and I'll be perfectly happy in that role, believe me. But I want you to know that I trust you. You keep telling me not to, but I do.'

He was shaking his head. 'Serena. I think it's you who took that blow to the head, not me. You don't know what you're saying.'

'But I do, Raphael,' she said softly. 'I know this has to end soon. But you see, in our time together you've made me feel…*different*.' She hesitated, struggling for words. Maybe silence would have been wisest, but she wasn't wise—how could she be at this moment, knowing that this man had trusted her with some of his darkest secrets?

If you can't be wise, she lectured herself, *be sensible.* But she was weary of being sensible, so she went on, 'You've actually made me feel that perhaps some day I could learn to love someone again.'

He gripped her shoulders so hard he was almost hurting her. 'Serena. Listen to me. I've been a gambler and a wretched idler half my life. My father judged me as worthless and I obliged him by fulfilling his every expectation. So you're still correct in your assessment of me and, for your own sake, you should hold fast to hating me.'

Hate him? Her hand reached up to tentatively touch his jaw and the faint rasp of his unshaved beard sent a shock tingling to all her most sensitive parts. An almost physical ache squeezed her chest and she felt her blood pounding. He'd gone very still and was gazing at her with that darkness in his eyes so she lifted her hand a little further, to brush one finger across his lips. *You fool, Serena. Whatever do you think you're playing at?* The air in the room seemed charged with tension, like the stillness before a thunderstorm. He would reject her, of course. She knew that. He would move her hand aside while making some muttered excuse and she would flee from the room in embarrassment, her heart shrivelling as she cursed her own stupidity.

But instead, what did he do?

Raphael Lefevre, the most notorious rakehell in London, let out a half-sigh, half-groan, and reached for her face, cupping her cheek with his right hand. Then he pulled her towards him with both strong arms. He was going to kiss her. She knew he was going to kiss her and she longed for it, but she tried to push him away. 'Raphael. You were hurt. They tried to kill you…' The bandage on his forehead signalled *Danger. Danger.*

And what did Raphael do? He laughed. He took her in his arms, reclaiming her. 'They tried,' he said, 'but now I'm well again, apart from the scratch on my forehead. Come here, Serena.'

The command was low but compelling. And when he pressed his lips to hers, Serena felt her entire world shaking around her. Shaking and shattering, just like the time they'd kissed at Vauxhall Gardens, only this was more, so much more—indeed, after this, nothing could ever be the same again. She also realised that she didn't care. She was deliciously intoxicated by the feel of his mouth on hers as he gently prised her lips apart; she was entranced by the teasing of his tongue that made her shivery yet hot at the same moment. She loved the way that his tongue went on tantalising, then began thrusting slowly but surely between her lips, until she felt her whole body thrilling with sensation.

She'd been married for three long years. Her husband had taken his pleasure with her on occasion, but the question of what *she* wanted had never arisen. She hadn't known what she was missing. But she was learning fast.

Somehow—was it her, or him? She suspected

it was *her*—both of them were seated on the edge of the bed, their bodies entwined. She buried her hands in his thick hair and kissed him in a way she hadn't known she was capable of—wild, unrestrained, greedy. He uttered a low moan at the back of his throat and at the same time he was running his hands up and down her body, stroking her breast through the fabric of her gown until she felt her tautening nipple leaping exquisitely to his knowing touch. She closed her eyes and let out a soft cry as a sense of wild abandonment possessed her.

She heard him whisper, *'Ma petite perdue.'*

Her eyes flew open. 'Raphael. What does that mean?' Her voice was hoarse with the tension of the sensations rippling through her.

'It means *My little lost one*.' And then he was kissing her again and she revelled in the fact that she'd found him, she'd found this, and because she wanted—no, needed—so much more, she was tugging at the edges of his shirt and running her hands down the glorious contours of his chest while feeling her nightgown slipping away as he pressed kisses on her throat and her breasts. She experienced a rush of pleasure that was as sweet as honey melting her insides.

And then he stopped.

Her eyes had been closed in bliss, but now they

were wide open. She saw how his gaze had darkened. How his mouth had thinned.

Her heart beat steady hammer blows of doom. What was wrong? Did he think her too eager? A slut even? Perhaps he was right. She had indeed been shameless to bring him into her house like this, to tend him herself like this. *Making a fool of yourself again, Serena.*

Feeling cold and stupid, she began to slide away from him rather shakily.

He grabbed her and pulled her back. 'What in the name of God is this?'

He was pointing to her right breast and she quickly tried to draw her gown up. Her heart was chill as she said, 'It's nothing. Nothing at all—just an old scar.'

'How did you get it?' His voice was almost a growl. 'For God's sake. It looks like a knife wound!'

She tried to moisten her dry mouth before whispering, 'Not a knife. Scissors.'

'And who the hell used scissors on you?'

'It was,' she said, 'my husband.'

Chapter Eighteen

Life was cruel. Raphael knew that. But to have this glimpse of the suffering endured by a beautiful, warm-hearted woman shook him to his core. His emotions were in tumult.

He'd been fighting against his feelings for Serena from the moment he'd cruelly forced their pact on her. He'd only managed to maintain his emotional detachment by using grim determination, for he knew this attraction between them must not be allowed to develop. It would be disastrous for her, for him, for everything he'd planned with his life.

But *Dieu,* he wanted this woman. He'd wanted her, if he was honest, from that very first dance last November, when she'd struck him as so lovely, yet so vulnerable. She'd hated him after that, he knew; she'd sought any way she could to denigrate him in the eyes of society, so much so that she'd endangered his sole purpose in life: to find his brother's wife and fulfil his vow to make her safe.

But he'd not been able to put Serena from his mind. God forgive him for the fantasies he'd entertained time after time, the fantasies of silencing her insults by kissing her beautiful mouth and melting the frost in her soul. Well, now the ice had melted to reveal the fire beneath. The barriers she'd put up to guard herself were in tatters and her sensuality was laid bare. Already the deliciousness of her was driving him wild. What stopped him—yes, what really stopped him in his tracks—was the scar. It was about two inches long and scarcely more than a faint silvery seam. *Inflicted by her husband?*

'Was it an accident?' he asked, more harshly than he meant.

'No.' She spoke without meeting his eyes. 'We were arguing. He was drunk. And I thought he was going to hit me.'

Again came the low, almost feral growl from his throat. He knew theirs was not a happy marriage. But this...

'I was afraid of him,' she went on, 'because he'd hit me before and done other things. He'd come into my bedroom. He was shaking me and I broke free—I told him not to touch me again, *ever*, but he laughed and picked up a pair of scissors from my dressing table and lashed out at me. I was wearing only my shift. I tried to protect myself, but the scissors caught me, here, as you've seen.' She pointed, then closed her eyes briefly. 'I told my maid Martha that my hand had slipped and I'd done it myself. I don't for one minute think she believed me, but she never said anything else about it, either to me or to anyone else. Because Martha knew as well as I did that there was nothing I could do.'

She looked up at him then. 'Lionel was my husband. He lied and drank and cheated on me, but he was my husband. And I think a great deal of the problem was me. You see, I was very innocent when I married him and when Lionel took me to bed that first night, I—I did not know how to please him.'

Her voice had broken for the first time. *That bastard of a husband of hers,* he thought. He said, sharply, 'Did he not know how to please *you*?'

She was clearly surprised by the question. 'He must have done! He was older than me and far more experienced. I was a disappointment to him, I was bound to be.'

Raphael set his jaw grimly. No doubt Lionel had bedded plenty of whores in his time, but he'd decided to grab at the chance of marrying Serena for her money and status, while making her think herself worthless into the bargain.

A disappointment in bed? This beautiful, spirited woman? Never. He'd see the longing for physical love in the darkening of the pupils of her eyes and in the deepening colour of those deliciously sensual lips of hers. He'd noted all her hungry responses, the tremors she couldn't hide and the subtle yielding of her body. No woman could fake that.

Still sitting at her side, he touched her hand as carefully as if he were touching a highly strung racehorse. He let his thumb caress her palm and he saw the ripple of shock travelling to her eyes, then he lifted her hand to press his lips to her fingers. And he said, 'I think you're trying to tell me that you're incapable of feeling passion. Let me tell you that I do not believe it. Not for one minute.'

Her eyes widened.

'Look at me,' he went on, still gripping her hands. 'I'm telling you. You are brave and beautiful and also extremely desirable. I've always thought that.' He gave a half-smile. 'Even when you were telling other people—or maybe saying it directly to my face—that I was an odious brute.'

He saw her blink with outright disbelief. 'Even then?'

'Really,' he assured her. 'Here, I thought, is a woman in a million.' A wave of powerful emotion surged through him again. The urge to defend Serena from any who would harm her.

The room was growing lighter. Outside, dawn would be rousing the sleepy city. He sighed. 'You're cold,' he said gently and put his arm around her. 'Serena. I hope to God you rejoiced when the news came of your husband's death.'

She faced him steadily. 'I played the part I was expected to play. I spent my time of mourning as was expected. But, indeed, I was glad he was dead. He used physical violence against me sometimes, yes, but the worst of it was that he humiliated me at every turn, whether we were in company or alone. He took delight in finding fault with me, until I didn't know if what I was doing was right or wrong any more.'

She looked up at him, so straight and honest that it pierced his very soul. 'And then,' she went on, 'I met *you,* at that dance. And just for a while, I thought, here is someone who is good and honest and true. But then that man came up to you and he made me believe that you'd sought out my company for a wager.'

For one heart-shaking moment Raphael felt that

he'd lost her again. And he experienced the rebellion of all his body, all of his senses, at the thought of this woman once more slipping from his grasp. He was in deep, he warned himself. Far too deep.

'I told you,' he said. 'That business of the wager was a complete lie.'

She nodded. 'And so our punishment of one another began. My public denunciations of you were quite wrong—of course I realise that now. In return you forced me into four weeks of being seen with you, of having to silence my criticisms of you.' She touched his hand. 'Oh, Raphael. I would have been silent straight away, if only you'd told me about your brother's death and your search for his lost wife. I would have believed your story. How could I not?' She looked up at him with emotion-filled eyes.

Raphael felt flayed. Scourged. She trusted him—what an awful, awful reprimand. 'Come here,' he said, holding out his arms.

Her eyes flew again to his, this time almost haunted. 'No. No—you were quite right to turn me down a moment ago! This is not what I should expect from you. Our agreement is for public appearances only and—'

'Be damned to our agreement.' His voice rasped with emotion. 'If it was written on paper, I'd tear it into pieces this instant. Come here.'

He saw her looking at his arms as they reached out to hold her. Her face was so expressive, reflecting every subtle hint of the early morning light that crept through the curtains. When at last she placed her hands on his, he fastened his fingers around them and felt her tremble slightly.

Right, he told himself. This was the furthest he could go before he started inflicting even worse damage on her than that damned husband of hers. He wished with a fierce passion that things had been different. He felt racked by the harsh regret deep down in his soul. More than ever he had to be strong and let her go, *now*—but he couldn't release her hands just yet, it was impossible, because how could he dash the trust from her eyes? How could he banish the flicker of hope that was lighting up her lovely face, after she'd been drained of self-belief for so very long?

He told himself he could stay holding her like this for one moment, yes, just the one; then he would tell her that it was over and he was releasing her early from their bargain. It was for her sake, not his, he would assure her. He would use that old, time-worn phrase, *I am not worthy of you...*

Then she leaned into his arms. And kissed him, full on the mouth.

His resolve vanished into thin air.

* * *

For so long now Serena's heart, if not her common sense, had been telling her that this was the only man for her, whatever the dangers, whatever the risks. Even if it was just for a short while.

Logic be damned. She'd had enough of all social niceties—she was a widow, therefore free to do as she willed. Even if it was for one night, just the one, she needed this man, needed something to remember him by. And it was looking as if she might have her way, because he'd begun to kiss her back, so she felt again that sweet ache stirring in her breasts and tingling through her veins. She belonged here, in Raphael's arms. She had never been more certain of anything.

A thrill of delight rippled through her on the realisation that he'd taken charge of matters. His kiss was long and delicious and the pleasure of it rolled through her in waves, making her want even more. She made a small sound at the back of her throat and lifted her hands to cup his face, loving the feel of that strong, sculpted jaw with its shadow of beard scraping against her sensitive palms. She'd never realised she could feel so much pleasure just in her hands! What he could do to the rest of her, she hardly dared imagine.

His eyes never left hers. 'Serena,' he said, 'you've had many griefs in your life. And I don't want to be the cause of yet another one. I think you'll understand what I'm trying to say and I'm saying it because I respect you so much. This— between you and me—we both know it's real, the attraction we've always felt for one another. But it cannot develop into anything more.'

'You're telling me that it will end soon?' She met his gaze steadily.

'Much to my regret, *ma chère*—yes.'

She listened. She pondered it. At least, she was pretending to ponder it, because all she really knew at that moment was that if he left her now, she would be destroyed. She needed his loving like she needed air to breathe. She thought a moment. Then, *Don't think,* she urged herself. *You know that too much thinking is fatal.* This was Raphael, who was perhaps the one man who could make her whole again.

She said at last, 'I don't want you to believe that I'm using you to prove anything, you know. I don't want you to assume that I'm weak and needy and using you as some kind of support to my battered self-esteem.'

His laugh rumbled low in his throat. 'You, weak and needy? You, who with your friends the Wicked Widows have proved yourselves among the bravest, wittiest ladies in town? You, who once very neatly described me as "one French luxury London could do without"?'

She blushed, but smiled a little. 'I said that, yes. I apologise. But it was quite neat, wasn't it?'

'Actually,' he said, 'I've not laughed so much since I left France.'

She looked at him in wonder. 'You didn't hate me for it?'

He shook his head decisively. 'I admire someone with spirit. And in my experience, a woman possessed of wit and humour makes a fine bed partner. A fiery bed partner.'

He smiled again. And at his words, at that smile, she felt the same delicious, sweet ache low in her abdomen. This man was making her feel sensual. Desirable. 'Then try me,' she whispered. And she said, in shy French, 'Please, Raphael. I wish very much for you to make love to me.'

'You're sure? Absolutely sure?'

'As sure as I've been of anything.'

He let out a low sigh. *'C'est mon plaisir,'* he murmured. He kissed her hand almost reverently. 'And Serena, I will, of course, take all the necessary precautions—'

'No need.' She was already emphatically shaking her head. 'I was examined by my doctor a year after my marriage, because Lionel was disappointed I wasn't yet with child. The doctor told me I was infertile.'

'That,' he said, still holding her hand, 'must have been sad for you.'

'In a way, yes. But it was good, too, because it meant that Lionel gave up all pretence of interest in me and turned to his mistresses for consolation.'

'The fool,' he said quietly. 'The fool.'

And then—at last—he made his move. He enfolded her in his strong arms, he laid her on that atrociously ornamented day bed George had bought—who would have dreamed what a delightful use could be made of it?—then he arched himself over her and kissed her again. Her heart shook and her body was on fire. Fresh desire pulsed through her as he pulled her close and she felt her entire being tingle with delicious anticipation.

He shifted his legs carefully so that their thighs were entwined and she could feel the hard proof of his desire pressing against her own sensitive flesh. All the time, he was still kissing her—her forehead, her throat—then he was easing her nightgown open and pressing his lips to her breasts. When his tongue began to caress her nipples, each in turn, she clung to his broad back as if without him she would be floating off skywards into heaven. She gasped with delight and at the sound he lifted his head to gaze at her.

'So lovely,' he was murmuring. 'So passionate.'

Passionate? Yes. She was. With *him*. She was arching against him, demanding more, much more. Already his lips were teasing her breasts again and his hand was sliding up under her flimsy gown, stroking her inner thigh, then finding its way to that secret place that was already engorged with passion. She felt the heel of his hand there, pressing, circling against her throbbing bud of need— and then, just as she began to feel herself soaring out of control, he took his hand away.

She wanted to cry out in disappointment. Had she done something wrong? Did he find her too tedious to make love to, as her husband had?

The bitter agony of it churned inside her. Her very soul was cold without his caresses. She realised she was squeezing her eyes shut to hide her pain.

'Ma petite.' His voice—his husky, aroused voice in her ear—made her eyes fly open again. She realised then that he was half-naked, his shirt tugged off over his head, the placket of his breeches undone. She reached to touch him in wonder and desire as his manhood revealed itself in all its strength.

She softly stroked the silken length of him and

heard him catch his breath as he threw back his head with his eyes half closed. She felt a heady rush of power on realising that she, Serena, was doing this to him. 'Raphael,' she murmured. 'Make love to me. Please.'

She remembered how she'd once accused him of treating women as playthings, *Only if the ladies in question ask me nicely*, he'd retorted. And here she was now, not asking, but begging. His dark gaze was on her face, scorching her, inflaming her. Her mind whispered of danger, but the warning swiftly vanished because her body was urging her, 'Now. Now is so right.' Then he was cradling her hips with his hands and with one steady thrust he was entering her. She thrilled to feel the manly strength of him moving deeper inside her, as with mounting delight she began the sweet path to fulfilment. They were as one. Climbing the peaks together.

A low moan escaped her and he froze. 'Serena. Am I hurting you?'

'No.' Her voice was breathy with delight. 'Far from it.' She reached to caress the muscles of his shoulders, revelling in his sinewy strength. 'I want more, Raphael.'

Raphael gritted his teeth to regain control of himself as she wrapped her supple legs around him and eagerly arched her slender body to meet his. He'd half feared that he might hurt her, as her husband, the bastard, must have hurt her. But, no, it was as if this was meant to be, as if they were made for one another...

Wrong. A dangerous, impossible fantasy. But this was now. This was the present, here to be grasped and exulted in and he guessed that to have pulled back now would have quite possibly broken her. What else could he have done but make love to her? Hadn't he been longing to do so for days, weeks even?

Ever since he first laid eyes on her last year, if the truth be told.

And in this moment of rapturous intimacy she wanted him and he gloried in it, kissing her lips, her throat, her breasts as he coaxed her into the full rhythm of lovemaking. She was warm and responsive and yielding, tightening herself like a sheath around his hardness, forcing his desire to surge almost to breaking point as she raked his shoulders with her fingers and threw back her head with tiny moans that drove him wild. Raphael reached with his hand to caress her at the very essence of her need, at the same time giving one last powerful thrust as she clasped him close, calling out his name.

He rasped out her name in turn as she shuddered beneath him, uttering low cries of rapture. He withdrew at last to spend himself swiftly while she lay there, eyes closed, face still flushed with delight. As if they were made for each other...

Dear God. She was even more beautiful than he'd dared to imagine.

Chapter Nineteen

And so, thought Serena as she slowly raised herself from her own bed two hours later, with the morning sun pouring through the curtains of her bedchamber, this was what it felt like to have taken a lover. Not just any lover either.

Thoughts of Raphael flooded her senses. The scandalous Marquis of Montpellier, the man the world believed to live only for pleasure. *The man who also gives pleasure*, a wicked voice inside her whispered. *Unbelievable pleasure.*

She sighed and turned over, missing him already.

Before any of the servants were awake, she'd eased herself from her lover's arms to whisper to him that she must return to her own room. Raphael, protesting sleepily, had clasped her close and the temptation to stay had almost won. But she'd kissed him and left, so that when Martha arrived at her bedside at eight with her breakfast tray, her maid suspected nothing.

'Ma'am,' Martha said. 'I'm so glad that you managed to sleep well.'

Oh, Lord. If only Martha knew. And Serena doubted she'd sleep as well tonight, because already fresh fears were flooding her mind, fears for Raphael. He had enemies who wanted to stop his search for Madeleine. Enemies who'd been desperate enough to attack him the other night. Had they really intended to kill him? Her heart thudded. Quite possibly.

Raphael had plenty of other enemies, too, of course—she'd always known that. Staid matrons who disapproved of him. Elderly noblemen who were jealous of him. Upright citizens who denounced his morals.

She allowed Martha to help her into a sober print gown and to pin up her hair as usual. She went downstairs to take breakfast in her parlour, outwardly as prim and correct as society believed her to be. No one would guess that her body still tingled with the fire of passion that Raphael had kindled in her. Shortly afterwards Dr Phillips called and Serena sent him straight through to Raphael. She pretended to be absorbed in a fashion journal when the doctor eventually came to her. 'The news is good, Lady Serena,' he informed her with a bow. 'As I told you, the Marquis has a strong constitution indeed. The cut to his forehead will take a week or so to heal, but otherwise he appears to be fully recovered.'

Which meant it was time for Raphael to leave her house, or else the gossips would have even more of a field day for their wagging tongues. Swiftly she ordered a message to be sent to Grosvenor Square and soon one of Raphael's grooms arrived with a carriage to drive his master home.

Raphael was ready to depart. Serena had told her staff to provide what he needed to wash and to shave and the bandage on his forehead was scarcely visible beneath his hair. He took her hand as they stood together on the marble steps.

'Thank you,' he said, 'for your care of me.'

She nodded. 'Raphael. There's something I meant to tell you. It's about Jeremy Wolverton.' She saw him tense, but pressed on hurriedly. 'I know I've tried to defend him in the past, but he called here the other night. He was very angry that I'd brought you to my house. I told him, of course, that it was none of his business.'

Raphael's eyes were like granite. 'You were right. Don't speak to him again about me, Serena. Do you understand?' He relaxed a little and smiled. 'You see, the man really doesn't like me very much.'

She bit her lip, remembering also how Wolverton had made false insinuations about Raphael's search for Madeleine. No point in mentioning that—doubtless others had misinterpreted Raphael's actions and whispered the same lies. It didn't matter now anyway, because she knew the truth. 'Yes. I'm sorry I even let him in.'

He shook his head. 'Don't be. It's not your fault.' He hesitated, then said, 'You and I must talk. Very soon. In the meantime, Serena—thank you for everything.'

She nodded, as if he'd been nothing more than an unexpected and slightly inconvenient guest. 'Of course, Monsieur le Marquis. And it's been no trouble at all.'

Yes, she appeared completely untroubled, for she was Lady Serena Willoughby, much admired as a woman who knew her rightful position in society. The servants were already returning to their various duties as she came back inside the house and Serena, on spotting Mrs Penney, declared her intention of retiring to her study to spend an hour or so on correspondence. The household was as calm as ever, but she knew that the servants' quarters would be buzzing all day with gossip and conjecture.

Her husband had called her cold, but her body had been on fire for Raphael. She'd fallen for her

Marquis, badly. She felt that she understood him now and all that he'd suffered; she recognised his steadfast determination to find his brother's widow and understood, too, why she had been a particular obstacle in his way, with her hostile questions and her friendship with his enemies. If Wolverton approached her ever again with his malicious accusations, she would order her footmen to throw him out of her house.

Raphael, she guessed, would be pressing ahead urgently with his search for his brother's widow. Clearly he believed he was very close. Then what? Their shared passion this morning had seemed so real—though she reminded herself bitterly that she had almost begged him to make love to her.

After this was over, she had to return to her previous life. She knew it was inevitable, but oh, how her heart ached at the thought.

Jacques was waiting to take charge as the carriage drew up outside Raphael's house. His greeting was predictable. 'Well, my lord? Been getting yourself into more mischief, have you? Should have had me at your side.'

Raphael closed the carriage door behind him. 'I could certainly have used an extra pair of fists the other night,' he answered, 'but I'm getting close, Jacques.'

'And what kind of trouble are you planning to land yourself in next, I ask?'

'Necessary trouble,' came the answer.

Jacques had a familiar stubborn look on his face. 'Well, this time, my lord, I'm coming with you. Wherever it is you're bound.'

'No, you're not, *mon ami*.' Raphael patted him on the shoulder. 'Someone else is.'

Jacques sighed.

Raphael entered the big house a little warily, knowing he would now have the rest of his staff to deal with. His anxious butler was the first to greet him. 'My lord, we were most concerned to hear you were set upon by footpads! Fortunately Lady Serena sent us regular communications to let us know how you fared. We were relieved to know you were in such good hands.'

'I was indeed.' Raphael allowed Surtees to remove his coat. 'And now I'm completely recovered.'

'I'm pleased to hear it, my lord. And you already have a visitor, but I really wasn't sure it was convenient...'

Wolverton? Raphael wondered, his brow darkening. Or maybe Serena's irate brother?

But it was Dominic. His old friend was in the library gazing out of the window, but he turned the minute Raphael entered. 'Raphael,' he exclaimed. 'Jacques sent me a message to say you were on your way home. Everyone in town's been talking about the attack. They're saying it was street robbers, but what's your opinion?'

Raphael closed the door firmly. 'They were under orders, Dominic. And I think I know who gave them, but as yet I can't be quite sure.'

'Then this,' said his friend gravely, 'might help.' He handed Raphael a sheaf of papers. 'A short while ago you asked if I could find out who owned that garment factory you visited in Shoreditch. I've been searching the records kept by the Home Office. And I discovered that the owner—though he keeps it mighty quiet—is Mr Jeremy Wolverton.'

Raphael was already leafing through the papers, his eyes dark with speculation. '"Shoreditch,"' he read aloud. '"Mundy Street. Manager—Elias Turnbull."' He looked up at his friend. 'This is it, Dominic.' His voice was tense. 'This is it. My belief is that Wolverton takes on French newcomers to London as cheap labour—which, indeed, many do. But Wolverton goes a step further. He makes more money by allowing brothel owners to come in and pick out the prettiest women. All his employees know about it, but they need the work so desperately that they don't dare to act against him. Except, maybe, for one of them.'

'What do you mean, Raphael?'

And Raphael told Dominic about the woman who'd approached him in the tavern shortly before he was attacked. 'Her name was Therese. Somehow she knew I'd been looking for Madeleine at the factory and she told me to call at her lodgings in Cheapside. Which is where I'm heading next.'

Dominic looked concerned. 'But couldn't it be a trap? Those men who set on you outside the tavern—might they be connected with all this?'

'I'm pretty sure they are. But I also feel certain that Therese is on Madeleine's side. Will you come with me to Cheapside, Dominic?'

'I hope you know you don't even have to ask.' Dominic had walked over to an oil painting on the wall and he pointed. 'I've never forgotten her, Raphael. You realise that, don't you?'

The painting was of a young couple in the grounds of a country estate. The man resembled Raphael, though he was a little less stern of feature. The woman had long brown hair and blue eyes and she radiated happiness.

'I thought,' went on Dominic as he gazed at the picture, 'when I saw Madeleine that summer, that she must be the most beautiful girl on earth. Do you remember my visit, I wonder?'

'Of course.' Raphael had come to join him. 'My brother had just married her. I was home on leave from the army and I asked you to visit us at the chateau.'

Dominic turned to him then. 'I was smitten, Raphael, badly. I think I'm that kind of man, you know? She was so sweet. So kind—and of course, Guy deserved her. What he didn't deserve was such an atrocious death.' He took one last look at the picture. 'To be honest, I don't think I've slept one night through since you arrived in London last autumn and told me what might have befallen her. To think of where she might be sickens me to my soul. And now it sounds as if you're in danger, too.' He looked directly at his friend. 'So you think those men who attacked you have some connection with Wolverton?'

'I'm almost certain, now I've remembered where I've seen them: they're overseers at his factory.'

Dominic's face darkened. 'It sounds as if you're getting close. You're definitely in danger, Raphael.'

'As Madeleine might be, if they know I've guessed what's going on. And that's what really worries me.' He indicated the door. 'So—shall we go and find Therese?'

Cheapside market was bustling with servants and housewives haggling for bargains and the air rang with the cries of traders shouting their wares. Raphael and Dominic had come here by cab and they quickly found the haberdashery shop, to the side of which were some steep stone steps. Raphael and Dominic looked at each other, then headed upwards to the door at the top. Therese must have seen them coming, because quickly the door opened.

'Well, Monsieur Lefevre,' she said to Raphael in French, 'you're here at last.' She scrutinised Dominic. 'And who's this one?'

'A good friend of mine,' said Raphael swiftly. 'And, *madame*, I apologise for not being here sooner. I was unavoidably detained.'

He'd already noticed that three younger women were sitting at a large table engaged in some kind of fine needlework. Therese had seen his enquiring glance. 'I would guess,' she said, 'that you're eager for the information I promised you? But let me tell you my story first. I was a fine seamstress in Paris, Monsieur Lefevre. I worked for Royalty—but when the Revolution came I fled before the mob could kill me. Fled to London, in fact, where I worked for a while in that wretch Turnbull's clothing factory. But thanks to my skills, I was able to set up my own small business here and pay several needlewomen who also once worked at that factory.' She indicated her three companions. 'I know why you've come here, *monsieur*. But what have you been up to since I saw you in that tavern a few nights ago?' She was still staring at his face and clearly she'd spotted the marks on his forehead. 'No, let me guess. There was a nasty scrap outside the tavern, soon after you left with that pretty English lady. Were you part of it, *monsieur*? What was it about?'

'I suspect I was attacked, *madame*, because I've been searching for someone called Madeleine. Which clearly you know—but how? What made you come up to me that night with your message?'

She pointed to her assistants again. 'I told you my girls here worked at Turnbull's factory, until I persuaded them to leave. One of them—Annette—was there when you called with your questions about the French girl, Madeleine. Annette also happened to be with me that night in the tavern and she recognised you.' Her hands on her hips, Therese was still scrutinising the two men. 'But before I say anything else—why do you want this Madeleine? Because I warn you, if you're like the others, intending to make money out of that lovely face of hers—'

Raphael heard Dominic at his side letting out a low oath. Raphael said swiftly, '*Madame*, Madeleine was my brother's wife. My brother was murdered by the Revolutionaries—and Madeleine, as she may have told you, was abducted and ended up here in London.'

'*Hélas,*' she murmured, 'that country of ours. It runs with blood. So what will you do with Madeleine, if you find her?'

Dominic stepped forward then. 'Raphael will take the very best care of her, I know he will. I swear he'll do everything he can to ensure a new and a safe life for her.'

Therese turned to inspect him. 'So you think highly of your friend, do you, *monsieur*?'

'Yes. I think highly of him.' Dominic spoke earnestly. 'Please, I beg you. Can you tell us where Madeleine is?'

Therese spoke to the other women at the sewing table and for the first time, Raphael realised there was an empty chair there. 'Ladies,' Therese was saying, 'you are to inform no one that these two gentlemen have been here, or who they've been asking for—do you understand? Continue with your work.'

Then she led them to a door at the far end of the room and they climbed some wooden stairs to an attic that was lit by a single skylight window. Only one person was in there, cowering in the shadows. She wore a shapeless grey gown and her long brown hair was tied back. He'd only seen her in silks and satins and she was thinner than he remembered, but it was her. Madeleine.

As they'd entered, she'd backed up against the wall in fear, but when she saw Raphael her blue eyes opened very wide. And she said in French, quite simply, 'Raphael. I have been waiting for you. I knew you would come.'

He walked steadily toward her and put his hands lightly on her shoulders, then said, 'Madeleine. It's taken me far too long. How can I apologise enough?'

'No need.' Two tears were running down her cheeks and she reached to touch his chest, as if to reassure herself that he was real. 'Raphael, I have lived through a nightmare, but this kind lady—' she indicated Therese '—and other people have kept me safe.'

He heard Dominic clearing his throat behind him. 'Madeleine, I don't expect you to remember me. But we met years ago at the chateau in Montpellier. In happier times.'

'Monsieur Dominic!' She beamed through her tears. 'Of course I remember you!' This time she spoke in broken English. 'You are Raphael's good friend and therefore my friend, too!'

Raphael turned to Therese. '*Madame*, I am more than grateful for your help. With your agreement, I'd like to take Madeleine with me now.'

'Of course.' Therese addressed Madeleine. 'My dear, you must dry your tears and gather up your belongings.' Madeleine nodded and hurried over to a chest in the corner while Therese turned back to Raphael. 'But where are you taking her, *monsieur*?'

Raphael hesitated. To his house? But the word would spread in no time that he had a guest. And there were still things he had to do, people he had to see before the news escaped.

Then Dominic said, 'Let her come to me, Raphael.'

And Raphael thought, *Perfect*. Rural Kensington, where Dominic lived, was far away from the gossip of the *ton*. He knew, too, that Dominic's unmarried sister Amelia was as kind-hearted as her brother and would welcome Madeleine with open arms. She would also provide the necessary chaperonage to stop any foolish gossip about the lovely Frenchwoman who'd appeared so unexpectedly in Dominic's mansion.

'Excellent,' he said to Dominic.

He realised Madeleine was coming back to them, fastening up a small valise. She looked hesitantly at Raphael. 'Where now, *mon frère*?'

'Madeleine,' he replied, 'for the time being, I think you'll be safest living with Dominic. He has a very kind sister, who will take great care of you.'

'And I already know how kind Dominic is.'

Madeleine paused to dash away another tear trickling down her cheek. 'Oh, Raphael, it has all been such a nightmare! The fire and poor, poor Guy. I was taken away, to Paris at first, but then some men told me I would be safer in London. So I let them bring me here and I thought I'd found honest work in that factory. Then some men came and told me I must do things I could not bear to do. I would have killed myself rather—but Therese knew what was happening. She came to me as those men prepared to take me away and she brought me here. She saved me, as she has saved many others, I believe.'

Therese hugged her, murmuring words of comfort. 'There, *ma chère*. You'll be safe now. Completely safe.'

'Thank you, *madame*,' Raphael said quietly to Therese. 'Dominic, I suggest you find a cab to take you and Madeleine to Kensington.'

'Of course. But what about you?'

'There are still some matters I have to attend to. People I have to visit.'

Dominic shook his head slightly. 'Take care,' he warned. Then, lifting up Madeleine's pitifully small valise, he escorted her down the stairs.

Raphael turned back to Therese. 'What do you know about the man who runs the factory, Turnbull?'

'I know, *monsieur,* that the rogue is only the manager. It's the factory owner who employs the poor, desperate French *émigrées* who come to London and makes them work like slaves. Though the young women—the prettiest ones—fare even worse, because this owner permits men to come in and take them to work in terrible places where women are for sale. You understand, *monsieur*? The owner is paid, I believe, to turn a blind eye to what these wicked men are doing.'

He understood all right. All the pieces of the puzzle were fitting together. Those three men who'd attacked him were indeed overseers at the factory where Turnbull was manager. And the owner of the factory, who made money out of allowing the prettiest of his workers to be taken into brothels, was none other than Jeremy Wolverton. As Dominic had informed him.

Now for the final act of the drama that was so rapidly unfolding. He walked along Cheapside to Lombard Street, from where the mail coaches set off on their long journeys around the country. Already several of them, painted maroon and black with the royal coat of arms emblazoned on their doors, were lined up in the road outside the booking office. He walked inside and called for the clerk's attention.

'Ah,' said the clerk. 'Sir, I remember you were

in here a few days ago, asking about travelling to Liverpool.'

'That's right. This time I wish to make a definite booking.'

The clerk was leafing through his timetables. 'For Liverpool. Of course, sir. Just for yourself?'

'No—myself and a lady.'

'Two, then.' The clerk's eyes glinted with curiosity. 'And then, I seem to recall, you wish to arrange a passage to New York?'

'I intend to find a merchant vessel in the port to take us there,' said Raphael. 'How much to reserve our seats on the coach?'

The timetables, he'd studied already. This time, he paid the required fee. They would depart from London in two weeks' time—and from there, he would sail to New York with Madeleine.

It was his final promise to his brother.

He arrived home to be informed by Surtees and yet more pithily by Jacques that the Earl of Stainsby had called, but departed on learning that Raphael wasn't at home. 'I asked him, sir,' said Surtees, 'if he wished to leave a message. He declined.'

Jacques had been a little more descriptive. 'The Earl caught sight of me when he arrived and ordered me to look after his horse. He looked to be in a fine old rage. When Surtees told him you weren't at home, he rode off again, but not before I heard him mutter some interesting things about you, my lord. Want to hear them?'

'*Merci.* But I think you can safely leave them to my imagination.'

Jacques grinned.

Raphael closeted himself in his study and perhaps for the first time in his life sank his head into his hands. He should have heeded George from the very beginning and stayed well away from Serena, but now he feared it was far too late. He guessed she'd fallen in love with him. There would be untold damage from now on, whatever he did, but his path was still unavoidable.

When Raphael had arrived two years ago at the burning chateau and cradled his dying brother in his arms, Guy's thoughts had all been of his young wife. He'd seen her carried away by those brutes and Raphael guessed that the fear of what she might suffer at their hands was worse torture to Guy than any wounds he'd received from the mob.

'Find her,' Guy had begged. 'And make her safe! She has no parents—they died when she was a child.'

'You told me, though,' Raphael had said swiftly, 'that she was brought up by her aunt and uncle in Paris. You said they were like parents to her.'

'Yes. But they sailed to New York, before all this. They wrote to her. Begged her to join them— but I wouldn't let her go...' Guy was struggling to speak now. 'Take her to them, Raphael. Swear to me that you'll find her and take her there. Keep her safe...'

Those were Guy's last words, but he'd heard Raphael swear it, on his life. There was no way Raphael could break that oath to his brother. He had to get Madeleine on board a ship bound for America—and he had to fulfil his promise to go with her.

Chapter Twenty

After Raphael had left her house, Serena spent the rest of the morning dealing with her correspondence and in the afternoon her milliner arrived with several new hats for her consideration. Straw or silk? Trimmed with ribbons, or flowers? Serena didn't care in the slightest. That evening she'd been invited to a dinner party, but she sent her excuses and stayed in, trying to read yet another worthy book that Mary had lent her. But it was hopeless—and the night was worst of all, because she lay awake for hours, missing him. How could she have thrown herself at someone who'd always made it plain that he couldn't be the man for her?

'But he is,' she whispered into her pillow, her heart aching with loss. 'God help me, I've fallen in love with a man I can never have.'

What a fool she had been. She'd been warned

against Raphael from the start by her friends, her brother and by the united wrath of the good and worthy, who unanimously declared Raphael to be an arrogant wastrel.

But he wasn't. Her rakehell Marquis had proved himself to be kind and deeply considerate; yes, he'd lured her into a false relationship, but that was to quell her downright hostility and he'd always been reluctant to draw her in any deeper. He'd always warned her that their relationship could go no further. Yet it had. And their love-making had been miraculous.

She rose the next morning with an aching head and a sorely troubled mind. A message arrived from Mary shortly after breakfast and she opened it warily. Mary had decided to hold a special meeting that very afternoon—*a matter of routine business,* she'd written. But Serena didn't believe it. She was pretty sure that the 'matter of routine business' would be her and Raphael.

Her three friends must know by now—as half of London must know—that she and Raphael had patronised a lowly tavern and Raphael had been attacked, after which Serena had, quite shockingly, taken him into her own house to recover from his injuries. Wearily she prepared herself for the interrogation.

* * *

Indeed, just as she could have predicted, all conversation stopped as she entered Mary's drawing room.

'Serena,' Mary said. 'We almost expected you not to turn up today.'

'Is that so?' Serena tried to speak lightly. 'I wonder why?'

'Well...' Mary was looking to the others for support. 'We heard that after your visit to Vauxhall the other night, there was some kind of fracas involving your Marquis. Naturally, we were all rather worried about you.'

Serena managed to face her friends calmly. 'It's true, I'm afraid, that the Marquis was slightly injured by some street robbers. But all's well now.'

Mary still looked concerned. 'I'm glad to hear it, but really, this is the kind of situation we feared. Of course we're naturally grateful for the help the Marquis has given our school; but even so, my dear, the incident does emphasise that the man leads rather a ramshackle life.'

'Don't worry.' Serena spoke with a nonchalance she was far from feeling. 'I think we've all rather misjudged the Marquis, but I shan't waste my breath trying to defend him. All I can say is that I am having fun.'

Mary repeated, *'Fun?'*

'Yes, fun. Just for a short while,' Serena pointed out. 'Are those the latest charity accounts you were talking about?'

She'd been aware that Joanna had been watching her carefully and, while Mary and Beth examined the accounts, Joanna drew closer and whispered, 'You look different, somehow.' Suddenly she put her hand to her mouth. 'Oh, my! You and the Marquis—he's become your lover, hasn't he? I imagine you had a wonderful time! I'll call on you later, shall I?'

'No, Joanna! There's absolutely no need—' Serena broke off because Mary was looking straight at them. As the business of the meeting proceeded, she found it impossible to concentrate. She was anxious and heartsore. Yes, she and Raphael had become lovers, but she shouldn't have allowed it. She shouldn't have *wanted* it—she knew that. The trouble was, her body and her heart told a different story. And Joanna would want to know more—oh, Lord.

She hurried home once the meeting was over, only to discover that George was waiting for her. Her heart sank anew.

'Serena,' he said as soon as they were alone in her sitting room. 'I must talk with you about your friendship with that man.'

She pulled off her bonnet and laid it down with something of a snap on a nearby table. Indeed, her brother meant well, but these days he was trying her patience sorely. 'George, as I've explained before, I have the perfect right to have a male friend if I so wish. It's not as if the Marquis is married himself, or if either of us had children to consider!' Tired by now, she felt almost on the brink of tears.

And she nearly did cry when George came up to her and put his arm around her. He said, 'Serena, my dear. It's because I care for you so much that I'm saying this. Wasn't Lefevre involved in a brawl the other night outside some tavern? And you were there with him? What really concerns me is the fact that he's just spent some nights under your roof.'

She eased herself away from him. 'I brought him here because he was unconscious. And, George, it wasn't a brawl—Raphael was attacked, by some street thieves! It wasn't his fault!'

'Yes, but...' George hesitated and shook his head. 'Maybe I'm wrong to mistrust him so, though he does attract trouble. I don't want him to hurt you, do you understand? Be careful. That's really all I can say.' He took both her hands. 'I care for you very much, you know.'

'And I you!' She hugged him hard. But after

George had gone, she sank into her chair and closed her eyes.

With Raphael, she'd tumbled headlong into something she'd sworn to avoid for the rest of her life. She'd fallen in love—but very soon she'd have to cure herself of it and the prospect not only chilled her heart, it almost broke it in two.

Now, Raphael had advised her. *Live for now.* The trouble was, that she didn't want her time with him to ever end.

And suddenly, after George had gone, she remembered something else that Raphael had told her, about having to silence her because of her questions about his past. Especially, he'd said, as she moved in the same circles as some men he regarded as his enemies. Who? she'd wondered. And now—oh, goodness. For a moment her heart stopped, then began pounding hard. How stupid she'd been. But now she thought she might have the answer.

She called for Martha. 'I need my cloak, Martha, straight away! Yes, I'm going out, so order the town carriage for me. You see, I have an urgent call to make.'

Jeremy Wolverton was sitting at his desk, studying some paperwork, when she arrived at his office in Holborn. He was surprised, naturally, to see her. 'Lady Serena. To what do I owe this honour?' He'd risen to his feet and was pointing to a chair, but she didn't take up the invitation.

'It was you,' she said. 'You who ordered those men to attack the Marquis. I should have guessed it the night you came to call, because how else could you have known so swiftly that three men attacked him outside the tavern in King Street? And you knew, too, all about his search for a young French woman, when absolutely nobody else did!'

'My dear Lady Serena!' He looked as though he was struggling for words. 'Whatever are you talking about? Ah.' He nodded. 'I think I can guess what's upset you so. You must have heard that your Marquis is planning to leave the country.'

The floor seemed to shake beneath her, but somehow she held firm. *Ignore him. He must be lying.* 'He is not my Marquis,' she said steadily. 'And you didn't answer my question.'

'No, because it's as irrelevant as it's ridiculous. I can only say, my lady, that it's as well for your reputation that the Marquis is about to depart for good. Did you know he's already booked a coach journey to Liverpool and that there he intends to find a passage to New York?'

She couldn't ignore what he was saying now. 'This must be a jest. Why on earth…?'

Wolverton shrugged. 'Seeking new adventures? Who knows? I did hear him once say he was growing bored with London. After all, many of his fellow countrymen have already started a new life in North America. And as a matter of interest, he's found his French woman and is taking her with him. She's very lovely, I've heard—'

It took her some moments in which to register those final sentences. A new life? With Madeleine, his dead brother's widow, for whom he'd searched so ardently? But it couldn't be what Wolverton had just hinted. She *knew* Raphael. His quest to find Madeleine was entirely honourable. And as for his leaving London, hadn't he warned her all along not to let her emotions be engaged? Not to let herself fall for him?

Her fault, all of it. Yes, Raphael had always been clear that their affair could not last; she'd always known the end was nigh. Only she hadn't expected it to hurt, so very, very much.

'The woman you mention is his dead brother's widow,' she answered. 'He's been searching for her ever since he came to London. And, yes, I believe it was you who arranged for him to be attacked, because you hate him, don't you? Why? Why do you hate him so much?'

She suddenly realised Wolverton wasn't listening to her any more, but was staring at the open door behind her. Turning round, she saw that Raphael was there. Her heart bumped to a stop.

'The lady is correct,' Raphael said softly. Dangerously. 'Wolverton, those men who attacked me were your hirelings, weren't they? And you arranged it because I was getting too close to your dirty secrets.'

'I don't know what—'

'You know very well what I'm talking about. You employ desperate French women in that factory of yours and pay them appallingly. Then you deliberately turn a blind eye—in fact, you're paid—to allow the younger ones to be drawn into a world of depravity they could never have imagined. But you went too far, Wolverton. One of the women who begged for a job at your factory was my dead brother's wife. You allowed her to be taken away by a brothel owner, but she escaped. She's safe now. But you're not.'

Wolverton had gone very pale. 'I deny it utterly. Every word!'

'Really?' Raphael still stood in the doorway, his arms folded casually across his chest. 'The game's up for you. I'm going to report your deliberate betrayal of innocent women to the authorities and to the newspapers; so all I can say is that, if I were you, I'd get out of London before the storm breaks. And break it will, you can be sure.' He turned to Serena. 'My lady. Will you permit me to escort you home?'

Raphael noted how she didn't meet his eyes as he led her to the cab he'd left waiting outside and when he tried to speak she shook her head. 'Shall we talk once we're at my house, Raphael? You will come inside, I trust?'

He said, 'Of course I will.' He needed to. His heart was heavy, because he guessed what Wolverton had told her and it was the least he could do to try to explain.

As the cab rattled along Holborn, he remembered his conversation with Madeleine that morning. Dominic and Amelia had left Raphael alone with his brother's widow and he'd realised she was calmer, less tense; though the shadows still haunted her face as she'd talked just a little more about the nightmare that had begun for her with Guy's death.

'I saw what they did to Guy, Raphael. They made me watch, but I could do nothing.'

Raphael took her hand. 'I've been looking for you ever since. I'm only sorry it took me so long to find you.'

'But you did.' She clasped his hand in return. 'You did. And as for your friends who are looking after me, Amelia could not be kinder. And I remember the time Dominic came to visit the chateau with you—I feel he is a truly good man. As are you.'

'No.' He shook his head. 'No, Madeleine, I'm not.'

'Of course you are. You saved me!'

But at a cost, he thought to himself now as he followed Serena into her drawing room. *At such a cost.* He didn't know what to expect from her. He'd arrived in time to hear Wolverton telling Serena that he was going to America with Madeleine, so she must realise now that this was what he'd always planned. Yet he had allowed her to start believing in him. Allowed them to become lovers. *Unforgivable, Raphael.* He waited. Whatever she was about to say, he deserved it.

She sat down, beckoning to him to sit opposite her. She looked pale, but dignified: Lady Serena, sister to an earl and one of the loveliest ladies in London. She'd been treated despicably by her husband and now by him. Yes—unforgivable.

She spoke at last in a voice that was true and clear. 'Raphael,' she said, 'I must apologise for my foolish defence in the past of Mr Wolverton. I understand now how finding Madeleine has been your life's mission and how I was endangering it, both with my insulting comments about your past and my apparent friendship with Wolverton.' Her voice was husky with emotion, but quite steady. She went on, 'As you may have heard, Wolverton informed me that you have made plans to take Madeleine to America. Is this true?'

Dieu. He felt as if every calm word of hers racked his very soul. 'I'm going with her to America, yes. I promised my brother I would take her to New York, because there she has relatives who will welcome her into their home.'

She still appeared to register no emotion. 'This is what you said we must talk about when you left my house yesterday. Isn't it?'

He bowed his head. 'Yes. I cannot let her travel on her own, not after what she's been through. I made a promise and I must keep it.'

She was sitting very straight, the only sign of emotion being the slightly heightened colour in her cheeks. She said to him quietly at last, 'Of course. What else could you do?'

He felt his hands clenching. Heard the hiss of his own indrawn breath. 'What else could I do? Serena, I could have left you out of all this. I *should* have left you out of all this!'

'No. You couldn't, because as I've just said, I was harming your search. For all you knew, I was taking Wolverton's side against you, when I guess you already suspected he might be your enemy.'

'Even so.' He'd stood up now, unable to bear this any more. He walked to the window, then swung round to face her again. 'Even so, there's no excuse for what I did to you. No excuse for inflicting the humiliation you must have felt on finding yourself forced into my company.'

'Some women wouldn't call it humiliation to appear at your side.' She gave that faintly mocking smile of hers. 'After all, I'm a Wicked Widow, remember? Maybe you're *my* conquest, as much as I was yours. And we've had fun, haven't we?'

He felt as if each one of her calm words was squeezing his heart. He could hardly speak. She'd risen also and she stood there, so proud and so brave. *Fun,* she'd said. But he knew it was more, so much more for her. As it was for him, too.

Now she was waiting for him to reply, to tell her that she was right and he'd had no choice but to deceive her, because he'd had a much higher purpose in mind—to find and save his dead brother's wife. But could he really justify treating Serena as he had?

Had he truly been obliged to become her lover?

Of course not. But dear God, he'd found her irresistible. Still did—especially now, as she stood there so steadily, forgiving him. Saying she understood. Ready to let him go without a single word of recrimination, every bit of which he deserved a hundred times over!

'Serena,' he began, his voice hoarse, 'believe me, I didn't intend to cause you any harm.'

'You haven't,' she repeated. 'You're worried that I'll miss you? Not at all.' As she spoke she was moving across the room to hold the door open for him. 'But, Raphael, I think you had better leave, before you say any more. Besides, I have things to do, as I'm sure you have, too.'

She was still smiling, but her voice was brittle and her eyes over-bright. With tears? Again Raphael cursed himself inwardly.

He realised she was speaking again.

'There's one last favour I'd ask of you. Do you mind if we tell people that you'd informed me from the first you'd be leaving soon for a new life in America? It will make me look rather less of a fool, don't you think?'

'Very well,' he said quietly. 'We shall tell people that. Though no one, Serena, would ever think you a fool.'

'In my opinion, that's rather debatable.' She was still holding the door open and he began to head for it, but he turned suddenly.

'Don't forget tomorrow night,' he said.

'Tomorrow night?' She looked blank.

'We're due at Lord Rotherham's ball. Remember?'

For the first time she looked panicked. 'No. *No.* You cannot really still expect me to attend a ball with you?' He saw the physical effort she was making to suppress her emotions; saw the way she briefly pressed her hand to her throat. But then she took a deep breath and summoned a smile. 'Well. Let me think. A party—after all, why not? It will be almost the final night of our agreement, so it's rather a pity to give up our pretence at this point, isn't it? And who knows—maybe while we're dancing, you and I can laugh a little over our stupid mistakes. *My* stupid mistakes, in believing all the lies people told about you.'

'I was the one who ensured those lies were believed,' he said.

'And so?' She waved her hand airily. 'Let's treat all this lightly from now on. After all, it's not as if we're in love or anything ridiculous like that, is it? Now, would you mind showing yourself out?'

He bowed over her hand, with self-contempt churning through his veins. If she'd wept, he would have understood. If she'd ranted at him, he would have understood. But her courage—her sheer defiance in the face of what fate had thrown at her—cut him to the quick. In the aftermath of her unhappy marriage she'd succeeded in making a new life for herself, but then he'd arrived and thrown her world upside down. It was he and he alone who was responsible for that bereft look in her eyes.

Brave, beautiful Serena. She didn't deserve this. As he recognised all her qualities afresh, he realised the enormity of the loss he was facing.

Grinling brought him his coat with deference. 'Save your bows, man,' Raphael muttered under his breath. 'You were right first time. I don't deserve your respect in the least.'

Grim-faced, he stepped out into the London street, remembering Serena's words: *You're worried that I'll miss you? Not at all.* But he would miss her. A new life lay ahead of him, but already it was as if the light had gone out of his world. He walked back to his house in Grosvenor Square then set out directly for leafy Kensington on horseback, to explain to Madeleine that he was making all the necessary travel arrangements and soon they would be on their way to America. She would settle swiftly, he was sure, with the relatives she remembered with such fondness. But how long would he himself stay in that far-off land? '*For ever*' had always been his plan. He'd always intended to make a new life for himself;

to forget the places he'd lived in, the people he'd known. But to forget Serena? Was that possible?

A footman showed him through to the sunny garden room where Dominic and Madeleine were playing a game of chess. With great enjoyment, he observed, because Dominic was chuckling. He also noted that the two of them sprang up almost guiltily when Raphael came in. Then Dominic, after warmly shaking his hand, cleared his throat and said, 'Raphael, my good friend. I have something I need to discuss with you, in private.'

And, very slowly, Raphael began to realise exactly what Dominic was telling him.

Less than half an hour after Raphael's departure, Joanna swept into Serena's private parlour and tugged off her flower-adorned bonnet. 'Now, I promise I shall not interrogate you any more about what's going on between you and the gorgeous Monsieur Lefevre. But you will be attending the ball tomorrow night with him, won't you?'

Serena had been arranging some roses in a vase on the window sill, but now she put down the flower she was holding. 'Yes, I'm going,' she said. 'With Raphael. But it will be our last outing together, Joanna.'

Joanna's expression changed. 'Oh, Serena. And I was beginning to hope...'

Serena shook her head. 'As it's turned out, we've had great fun together. But now we've decided that it's over. Completely.' She tried her best not to sound as if her world had just fallen apart. With anyone but Joanna, she might have succeeded.

'Over!' cried Joanna. 'No! Serena, darling, I thought that you and he were absolutely marvellous together! I thought it was the real thing!'

So did I. Serena felt her heart contract with fresh pain. 'What nonsense,' she said as lightly as she could. 'We'd promised each other it was a temporary arrangement from the very beginning—because, you see, Raphael is leaving London soon. Leaving the country, in fact.' She picked up another rose. 'I'm not sure about this apricot colour. Do you think I should use a yellow one instead?'

Again, Joanna's face was a picture. 'Stop fussing over your flowers this minute and look at me! Surely Lefevre's not returning to France?'

'He can't, Joanna. Under the new laws there, the property of all those who've left France belongs now to the state. No, he's sailing for America—New York. He tells me that hundreds of French exiles have settled there and he's going to join them, to start a new life. Apparently it's what he's always planned.'

'So he's off to pastures new.' Joanna frowned. 'He had us all fooled, didn't he? Though do you know, just lately, I was starting to rather like him.' She looked at her friend swiftly. 'And as for you, my dear, I think you rather more than liked him, didn't you? This really is unforgivable of the Marquis!'

Serena forced a smile. 'My friendship with Raphael was surprisingly enjoyable. But I don't need a man in my life—I'm a Wicked Widow, remember?—and I intend to stay that way.' She pointed at Joanna and attempted a change of subject. 'Talking about men, I rather think you're the one who's in danger of letting the side down.'

'*Me?*'

'Yes, you! I cannot believe you're seeing so much of my brother.'

'Oh, George,' Joanna said resignedly. 'Yes, I'm going to the ball with him tomorrow. I am quite determined, you see, to make him enjoy himself despite all his excuses about business and duty!'

'Then I wish you luck.' Serena let her eyes twinkle. 'But really, what's the attraction? He is *so* predictable and so very particular about everything. You should hear him tell his butler exactly how he wants his breakfast cooked!'

'And he refuses to wear a coat in any shade of blue, only brown or black.' Joanna chuckled. 'He won't wear a cravat in any style other than the very plainest. Yet his taste in furnishings is—oh, goodness, what can I say?' She glanced at two ornate bronze jardinières that towered on either side of the fireplace and both women burst into giggles. 'But...' Joanna sighed '... I do think I'm rather fond of him, you see. I've never met anyone quite like him before, but perhaps that's where I've gone wrong. He's so utterly, boringly...reliable.' She hesitated a moment. 'Serena, so far it's a secret. But he's asked me to marry him—and I think that maybe I'll say *yes*.'

Serena hugged her warmly. 'Dear Joanna, he'll make you a wonderful husband! And I shall be the best ever aunt, visiting you and all your children at birthdays and Christmas time to shower you with presents!'

Joanna hugged her back, for which Serena was grateful, since a tear or two glistened in her own eyes and she wanted to dash them away quickly before her very best friend should glimpse them.

Chapter Twenty-One

❦

It was almost seven in the evening when the message came from Raphael the next day.

I could be late. Forgive me. Please go ahead without me.

By then Serena was in her bedroom and Martha was helping her to prepare for the ball. As she let the piece of paper fall to her dressing table, she felt all remaining hope wither. So their time together really was over. She hadn't realised that she still harboured a lingering hope inside her, but now all thoughts of a future with him were truly extinguished.

He was going to America. He'd vowed it two years ago as his brother lay dying.

She rose from her seat, aware that Martha was waiting for her to decide what she was wearing tonight. 'Will it be the pink or the blue, ma'am?' Martha had already laid out two ornate ballgowns and Serena forced herself to concentrate. *Your priority now*, she instructed herself, *is to remain in control, whatever happens.*

If he didn't turn up at all tonight, it was probably for the best. It would spare her the agonising farewells. But if he didn't appear, it also meant she'd already said her last goodbye to him. And she would never see him again.

Her emotions were raw. She didn't care which gown she wore or how her hair should be arranged. Poor Martha, intent on presenting her in full finery, kept making suggestions which Serena rebuffed with scarcely a glance.

'How about this one, ma'am? The colour looks lovely on you!'

Martha was holding out the peach silk dress that Serena had been wearing on the night she and Raphael first danced together last November. How much had changed since then. How much *she* had changed. A great tide of missing him surged through her and it was with difficulty that she fought it down. 'Not that one,' she said calmly. 'It's a little insipid, don't you think, Martha? Not the blue either. I'll wear the emerald silk. And my diamonds.'

So she dressed and put on her finest jewels. She

sent a message to George's house—*Please will you call for me on your way to the ball tonight?* And after Martha had arranged her hair, piling it to the crown of her head with just a few tendrils artfully trailing down her neck, she looked at herself critically in the cheval glass.

Lady Serena Willoughby—fashionable, independent and wealthy. She moved in an exclusive circle of glamorous friends and aristocratic admirers. She knew that many women envied her. But at that very moment she felt she would have changed places with anyone, however humble, who had fallen in love and was loved in return.

When her brother came to collect her, she halted in surprise as she came down the stairs. Was this *George*? Elegant black tailcoat, white cravat knotted quite daringly… Joanna's doing, she guessed. She was about to express her approval, but George was bursting to speak. And she guessed what he would say.

'Serena, Joanna told me that Lefevre is leaving the country! My dear, I knew he would let you down sooner or later! And—'

'George,' said Serena. 'Not now. Please, not now.'

Shaking his head, he led her out to his carriage, where Joanna made room for her. George helped

Serena in, then tapped on the roof to instruct his coachman to proceed. 'I shall not forgive the rascally fellow,' he went on as he settled himself opposite the two women. 'Not after the dance he's led you, Serena.'

Joanna must have seen the look of desolation on Serena's face because she said rather tartly, 'George, you're not being at all tactful. But then, you never are.'

George sighed and pressed his sister's hand. 'I apologise if I've spoken out of turn. I hope you're not going to miss the fellow too much?'

'Far from it, George!' Somehow Serena forced a smile. 'I enjoyed his company for a while, that was all. So I'm perfectly fine, thank you!'

George nodded, mollified, and turned to look out of the window. But Joanna moved closer to Serena and whispered, 'Fine? Are you sure?'

Serena took Joanna's hand, but found she couldn't say anything. Anything at all—let alone tell a lie.

Lord Rotherham's ball was almost the last grand event of the Season and by the time they arrived, the mansion in Berkeley Square was packed with the *haut ton*. Serena danced, greeted old friends warmly and was surrounded by male admirers. She had feared she would be bombarded with questions: *Where is the Marquis? Why isn't he here with you?* But she wasn't. Perhaps this would be easier than she'd feared. Perhaps everyone else had recognised the inevitability of Raphael's departure from her life, right from the start.

But even so she felt as if there was a great, aching hollow where her heart should be. She realised now that her rakehell Marquis was a man of honour, a man of great integrity—and his vow to his dying brother to find his lost wife, then take her to safety, had to override his own feelings. And, yes, it was unfortunate for Serena that he had to crush her heart in the process, but she completely understood why he'd had to do it.

Though how desperately she would miss him.

She was trying very hard to concentrate on the conversation of a baronet whose name she hadn't fully registered—was it Sir Christopher? Sir Crispin? She didn't really care, although he was making huge efforts to impress her with an account of his estate in Lincolnshire.

She nodded to everything he said, all too aware of the unshed tears aching at the back of her eyes. Raphael was completely noble and nobody knew it except her. He wasn't to blame for her heartache in the least. It was she who had tempted him into that first kiss, she who'd broken the pact that their intimacy was for outward show only. He had known all along where his duty lay. He'd known that his plans could not include falling in love with Lady Serena Willoughby. It was her fault, all hers, that she'd allowed her safe world to be shattered into tiny pieces. Like her heart.

'And in three weeks, I'm hosting a grand ball at my house in Lincolnshire,' Sir Christopher— or Crispin—was saying to her eagerly. 'Might I send you an invitation?'

She knew she ought to say yes, because she was single again now, wasn't she? She was free. A Wicked Widow again—and she couldn't have hated the thought more.

After supper, of which she ate scarcely a thing, the baronet asked her to dance again and she agreed. But when the orchestra started playing that haunting popular melody that she'd heard in the distance at Vauxhall, when she and Raphael had kissed, she broke away from him abruptly. 'I'm sorry, Sir... Christian, but I'm finding it rather warm. I must go and sit down for a little while.'

'It's Crispin, actually. But of course, Lady Serena! Let me offer you my arm...'

Shaking her head, she turned tail and fled through the packed ballroom. He tried to follow her, but she lost him easily enough in the crowd, after which she hastened along a corridor until she came to an unlit conservatory well away from the main reception rooms.

There, in the darkness amid the tall palm plants, she struggled to find that inner core of strength that had helped her to survive her marriage. *And you will survive this*, she told herself. Though at the moment, it didn't feel like it in the least. Because that haunting music still drifted through to her, filling her with such desperately sweet yet painful memories that she felt utterly bereft. She went over to one of the tall windows to stare blindly out into the dark night, hurting so much inside that it was as if a vital part of her had been lost for ever.

That was when she heard someone speak her name.

'Serena.' It was a man's voice, low and husky, with just the faintest trace of a foreign accent. Her heart bumped to a stop. Dear God, she must be going mad, because Raphael wasn't going to turn up, not now. He must know he would only be prolonging her agony…

But she turned round slowly—and, yes, Raphael was there.

His tall, muscular frame was silhouetted by the light coming from the hallway. He looked devastatingly handsome in a dark tailcoat that hugged his frame and a white starched cravat that emphasised the stark perfection of his features. He appeared calm and in control. As usual.

But there was something different about him—some uncertainty in the way he held himself. And was that a look almost of desperation in his silver-grey eyes?

She said with precise calmness, 'Why, Raphael. I gave up hope of your arrival some time ago.'

He shook his head impatiently. 'I always intended to get here. When I arrived, I was told you'd been dancing. But why are you here, in the near dark?'

'It was the music,' she blurted out. To her horror she was unable to keep her voice steady any longer. 'The orchestra began playing the tune we heard that night at Vauxhall, when we were together and we...'

When we kissed.

She didn't say it. She didn't have to, because he realised. He took another step towards her— 'Oh, *Serena*—' and then he stopped. The silence hung like doom between them. She wished with all her heart that she didn't love him so desperately, but, God help her, she did.

She pulled herself together and endeavoured to speak lightly. 'Anyway,' she said in a calmer voice, 'it also seemed a good moment to give my-self a brief rest from the dancing and the chat-ter. It's been such a busy evening and I've met so many friends! You've no idea, Raphael, how much I shall enjoying being independent once more. Being free to do exactly as I wish—'

She broke off because he was putting his strong hands on her shoulders now and she couldn't stop the racing of her blood. Couldn't stop her body's recognition of what he meant to her. For he was the one. The only one and always would be. He stood over her, his eyes burning into hers until she felt her heart clench painfully.

They'd said their goodbyes. She kept remind-ing herself of it, yet still she ached to feel his arms around her and his lips on hers; she wanted it all so much that it physically hurt to hold herself away. This man. This unique, impossible, char-ismatic man. What had he done to her?

He said, 'Serena. I realise I don't deserve an-other single moment of your time after the way I've treated you. Pretending that I came across you and that wretched man Mort by sheer chance. Forcing you into a mockery of a liaison. And worst of all...' his voice became very quiet '...to seduce you was unforgivable of me.'

She looked at him for a moment. Then she said, very steadily, 'You didn't seduce me, Raphael. I seem to recall that I gave you every encouragement. Don't you remember?'

'I didn't need much encouragement though, did I?' His hands tightened on her shoulders; his expression was still haunted and his eyes roved her face. 'Serena, I longed to kiss you from the moment I danced with you at that ball last November. I wanted you in every way: in my arms, in my bed. I can't deny it.'

His words rocked her soul. Silently she was begging, *Please, Raphael. Please don't put me through this agony again. Not when we both know it's impossible.* But oh, how easy it would be to sink into his arms, to let him kiss her and lose herself in the sweetness of his embrace, just one last time...

She stepped away from him, seeing how his arms fell empty to his sides. 'We've been through all this. And I cannot see what's changed. You've explained to me that you have to accept your duty, because you are honour-bound to take your sister-in-law to America, as you promised. And—'

She broke off, because now her voice had started to shake, just a little. 'Raphael, do you mind if I leave you now, to go to find my brother and Joanna in the ballroom? You see, I find all this rather difficult. And surely you have a great deal to do in preparation for your journey?'

He said, 'I haven't. Not now.'

She stared at him, feeling a curious swooping sensation in the pit of her stomach.

He took a step closer to her. 'Serena. I've come to tell you that I'm not going to America after all.'

What was he saying? Oh, dear Lord. Just when she'd resolved to be strong and to live her life without him…

'I'm not going,' he repeated. 'I no longer need to go. Please, will you sit down, while I explain?'

Raphael allowed her the time she needed to settle herself on a sofa by the window. She looked badly shaken and he wasn't surprised. Dear God, how he'd misjudged her and mistreated her from the start.

He hesitated a moment then sat beside her. *Not too close,* he warned himself. *Give her space. Give her time. Because you'd better not mess things up again, you fool.*

When he'd arrived and spotted Lady Joanna across the crowded ballroom, he'd headed straight for her. Of course, she'd been hostile towards him. He couldn't blame her. She'd said, 'What are you doing here?'

'I've come for Serena. Do you know where she is?'

'She was dancing in here a short while ago, so she must be somewhere around. But I'll tell you this, Monsieur le Marquis. If you upset her again, I'll have a few words to say about your behaviour—and in public this time. Do you understand?'

'I understand.' He said it quietly. 'And I deserve it.'

After leaving Joanna staring after him in surprise, he'd renewed his search for Serena, pushing his way among the crowds, ignoring friends who called to him just as he ignored the middle-aged matrons who scowled at him and denounced his ill manners.

At last he found her in that unlit conservatory and she'd not heard him enter, which gave him time to steady his pulse rate. His heart had skipped several beats because she looked so lovely in that emerald silk gown with her blonde hair piled high, although as usual some stray tendrils had escaped that he longed to touch and kiss. Then he'd spoken her name, but she'd flinched as if afraid of him, afraid of what he might do to her. Again, he saw the fragility masked by her defiant façade. Remembered how often her efforts to hide that fragility had tugged at his heart even more than her beauty.

How could he have hurt her so badly?

He drew breath to speak again. Should he try fancy words? A declaration of penitence? *Just tell her the truth, man.*

'I've been to visit my sister-in-law,' he said at last. 'At Dominic's house.'

He registered the huge effort she made to smile. 'Madeleine must be looking forward eagerly to her new life in America. As must you.'

'Not any longer,' he said. 'Let me repeat. I'm not going to America.'

Her eyes flew to his and she looked frightened almost, of how he might hurt her next. 'Raphael,' she said in a low voice, 'this is not right. You made a solemn promise to your brother to escort her there. You once told me that since his death it's been your sole aim in life. The one purpose that's kept you going—'

'Until I met you.' He saw her catch her breath and struggle to find the next one. Indeed, her usual strength seemed to have temporarily vanished.

'No, Raphael!' she said at last. 'We've been through all this, haven't we? I told you—I don't need you, but Madeleine does, very much so.'

'But you *do* need me,' he said very softly. 'Just as I need you, Serena.'

He saw her shaking her head and jutting her chin in that stubborn way of hers. 'How many times do I have to tell you that I'm perfectly content to remain a widow?'

He gave a sudden smile. 'A Wicked Widow? You won't be one for much longer, if I can help it. Though you can be as wicked as you like—in private, with me. And with me only.'

As he spoke he leaned forward to take her in his arms and kiss her thoroughly, cherishing the sweet softness of her mouth and the way her body fitted so perfectly against his. Dear God, there was no one like this woman—which was exactly why she was the only one for him.

She pulled away, looking dazed. 'But your sister-in-law! Your duty, to her!'

'Let me explain,' he said, reluctantly subduing the blood pounding in his veins, the heat rushing heavily to his loins. And he told her. He explained how yesterday he'd gone to Dominic's house to speak to Madeleine about the details of their forthcoming voyage. 'But then Dominic took me aside,' he went on, 'and told me that he needed to speak to me about something very important. Listen, Serena. Dominic wanted to ask my permission to become betrothed to Madeleine.'

At first she looked as if she could hardly speak. Then she whispered, 'Are you saying that Dominic has fallen in love with Madeleine? So very quickly? How is that possible?'

'Dominic actually met her some years ago in France. You know, don't you, that he and I have been friends for many years? He came to stay at our family chateau in the summer before the Revolution, when I was home on leave from the army. My brother had just married Madeleine and I invited Dominic over for a month or so. He's confessed to me that he secretly fell in love with her that summer—and that he's never, ever forgotten her.'

Her lovely blue-green eyes were wide with wonder. 'You mean that all this time poor Dominic's been thinking of her? How incredible! Although, you know, I always wondered why he hadn't married, when he must have had so many chances!'

'Well, there you have your answer. Madeleine is easy to fall in love with if you're the protective and brotherly type as Dominic is. And I think that everything she's suffered in the last two years has made him even more eager to take care of her.'

'But what about her feelings for him?' Serena asked that more tentatively. 'After all, she loved your brother very much, didn't she?'

'Of course she did. She and Guy were completely devoted to one another. So I suggested to Dominic that he give Madeleine a little more time to think about it, and today—this afternoon, in fact—I visited them again. On this occasion, I spoke to Madeleine on her own.' He gave a wry smile. 'She made it quite plain that they'd already decided the matter. She explained to me that though she'd loved Guy with all her heart, she'd always remembered Dominic with fondness. "I think I can be very happy with him," she said. So I told her that she was quite right to think she had found someone extremely special in Dominic and their marriage has my wholehearted blessing. In other words, it's all settled. Dominic and Madeleine are to be betrothed. She no longer wishes to travel to America—and I no longer need to escort her there. All this took some time, which is why I'm late. Please forgive me.'

'Of course. But, Raphael—I thought you wanted to go to America anyway.' Serena spoke very slowly, still taking it all in. 'To start a new life there, you said.'

He took her hand and clasped it. 'That was my intention. And during the last few weeks, I've decided that, yes, I do indeed want to start a new life.'

He felt her hand tremble in his, just a little. 'A new life. Of course. I understand.'

'No.' He lifted her hand to kiss it. 'No, Serena, you don't understand at all. I want to start a new life with *you*. Here in London if you wish—or even among those northern hills and moors you and your brother seem so fond of. We can live anywhere—I feel I can do anything, face anything, as long as I have you by my side!'

He broke off, suddenly terrified because so far she'd shown no sign of responding. He went on in a lower voice, 'Serena. I know I've made many, many mistakes. I've treated you abominably by hiding my secrets from you for so long. Maybe I should give you time to think it over and perhaps some day you can forgive me?'

She put her finger to his lips. 'Raphael. Raphael, you foolish man. I'm head over heels in love with you. Any of my friends could have told you so. You are noble. You are honourable. And after all, if I remember correctly, I practically invited you to seduce me, didn't I?'

He grinned suddenly. 'Yes, thank God.' He was remembering that sweet, sweet night. 'If you hadn't, I couldn't have restrained myself for much longer.'

'Me neither.' Serena smiled up at him, through the tears in her eyes. Tears of happiness. 'I love you, Raphael.'

'And I love you. So very much.'

He kissed her then, a kiss of ravishing intimacy that said everything, promised everything. Time stood still and, as he held her in his arms, Raphael realised that, finally, here was redemption. Here was the love of his life—the woman who could heal all the hurts, wrongs and evils he'd both witnessed and endured.

'Speaking of restraining myself,' the love of his life said a little breathlessly at last, 'Raphael, please can we leave this dreadfully tedious ball? I've had my fill of trying to make polite conversation with boastful men who ogle my figure while the matrons stare at me and whisper about how immodest I am.'

He grinned. 'They'll say even more, *ma chère,* when we announce our betrothal. Only this time they won't whisper. They'll make their disapproval heard all across London.'

'Let them!' Her eyes danced with delight as he drew her lovingly to her feet. 'Shall we tell them now? This minute? I cannot wait to see the shock on their faces! Then, Raphael, will you take me home? *Please?* For more of—this?'

And she stood on tiptoes and kissed him so tenderly, yet with such passion, that he felt whole at last. Complete. Saved. Yes—this woman had *saved* him.

'You'll have all the loving you desire, *ma petite,*' he said softly. 'But first things first. You're quite right. I think now is absolutely the perfect time to tell the assembled company our news.'

The guests in Lord Rotherham's ballroom were speechless when Raphael made his announcement, but then the whole room broke into applause. Joanna had tears in her eyes as she hurried up to Serena. 'My dear, I couldn't be more delighted for you. Didn't I always tell you your Marquis was madly in love with you?'

Serena watched George's approach with apprehension. But her brother shook Raphael's hand and said gruffly, 'Make her happy, won't you? Otherwise you'll have me to answer to.'

'I will.' Raphael returned his gaze steadily. 'You can be sure of it.'

'Good man,' said George. 'Good man. We'll let bygones be bygones, then.'

Serena and Raphael received much the same reaction from her staff when they reached her house shortly afterwards. Grinling was there, of course—and the footmen and Mrs Penney and Martha. Raphael took charge.

'You'll all be pleased to hear,' he said, 'that Lady Serena has tonight agreed to become my wife. Grinling, bring some champagne up to her suite, would you? And then—' his eyes twinkled '—we would appreciate a little privacy.'

All the servants scurried off except for Martha, who bobbed a curtsy to them both and whispered to Serena, 'I'm delighted! So delighted, ma'am!' Then she vanished, too.

'Raphael,' Serena protested, though she was laughing a little. 'Champagne? Privacy? So blatant! Perhaps we should have been a little more subtle?'

He was already leading her up the grand staircase. 'Subtle?' He grinned down at her. 'When by tomorrow morning, all of the households in Mayfair, servants included, will know our news?'

The champagne was promptly delivered, after which the footman beat a hasty retreat. The next moment Serena was in Raphael's arms and he was saying, very softly, 'Let me make this quite clear. I love you, Serena. I love your courage and your kindness and the way you always fight for what is right. I love how you went to tackle Wolverton, on your own. I love how you were prepared to give me up, for Madeleine's sake—indeed, I think that's one of the bravest things I've ever known.'

She looked up at him quickly. 'Raphael. Will you report Wolverton for that attack on you?'

'No.' His tone was contemptuous. 'Because the man's ruined anyway. He knows this all means the end of his pretensions to social standing. No doubt he'll hold on to his factory and his import business, but I'll be keeping a watch on him. And that's enough of Wolverton, because tonight is about you and me and nobody else.' He took her hand and kissed it. 'By the way. Did I tell you I love you? If I did, can I tell you again?'

She thought she was going to cry. She dashed a tear away and whispered, 'I love you, too. So much.'

'I'm sorry for everything I've put you through, Serena. Forcing you into that agreement, when you must have hated every minute—'

'I didn't,' she said calmly. He stared at her. 'I didn't hate every minute, Raphael. I was confused and sometimes humiliated a little, but that was my fault, for being stubborn and proud. You see. I was falling for you from the very start. Though I tried not to, because, yes, you *were* overbearing. And far too handsome for your own good—'

He tilted up her chin with one finger. 'Too handsome for my own good?'

'Indeed!' Her eyes sparkled with laughter. 'Too handsome and you know it!' She lowered her gaze. Said more quietly, 'And I was afraid, because I knew the way I was feeling about you was making me far too vulnerable to—to…'

'To what?' His eyes were searching her face.

'To heartbreak. There. I've said it. So I tried to put up my guard. To be hateful to you at times—because I couldn't bear the thought of the hurt that lay ahead.'

'Oh, Serena.' He drew her close again. 'Are you ever going to be able to forgive me?'

She gazed up at him. 'Only on one condition.'

'And what's that?'

'That you kiss me again.'

'*C'est mon plaisir,*' he murmured. 'Serena, my darling, *je t'adore.*'

After that, they didn't talk much. The need in both was too intense—she felt it and guessed he felt it, too, because his steely eyes were almost black. He kissed her and undressed her from her fabulous gown as if—and she caught her breath—as if she were some priceless work of art. A painting by a master. Then he undressed himself and she watched.

He was perfect in every muscle, every sinew. He was so beautiful he took her breath away. And he wanted her—there was absolutely no doubting it. What they were doing, she thought in her emotion-filled heart, was making love. Yes, love was the word for it, surely. This time there was an extra intensity, an extra dimension to their passion; this time all her senses were tautened to breaking point by the ways he had of pleasuring her. And she, in turn, rose to respond to him, to please him. Daring, adventurous, teasing him with her tongue and lips; taking the lead, which made him gasp in delighted surprise.

Though soon enough he took over again, clasping her in his arms, and she wrapped her legs around his lean hips and was soon engulfed by a crescendo of exquisite, yet nearly unbearable tension. When he'd built her almost to her peak, he stilled himself and gazed into her eyes. *'Ma belle,'* he whispered. She could feel the power of him deep within her. And then he bestowed on her more kisses, more caresses with his hand down between her thighs, where her bud of pleasure responded to his every touch; all the time he was moving himself harder and more inexorably inside her until she was gripping him tightly and she was engulfed by a heart-stopping tidal wave of ecstasy, her body pulsing and her soul soaring as he, too, drove himself to his release.

For those few exquisite moments, time stood still. As they lay in one another's arms, the sheets tangled around them, she thought, *This is happiness. Not for four weeks, but for ever.*

Epilogue

Four months later

'Well, my dear? Are you ready for your big day?' Joanna had sailed into Serena's front parlour wearing an even more outrageous hat than usual, with silk flowers piled high and ribbons trailing.

Serena embraced her. 'I still can't believe it, Joanna. Can't believe I could be so very happy. I know I'm marrying Raphael tomorrow, but I still feel as if it's a dream.'

'And I'm going to be marrying your brother in a month's time.' Joanna laughed merrily. 'Goodness, who would have believed it? But—' and her laughter turned to tenderness '—he's a dear really. And I think I shall be very happy with him.'

'Of course you will. I'm so glad for you both.'

'Though he's hardly a romantic, handsome rake like Raphael!' Joanna pretended to sigh. 'But no one deserves happiness more than you, Serena. Every happiness there is.'

'I believe,' said Serena just a little shakily, 'that there's even more happiness coming my way, Joanna.'

Joanna's face lit up. 'No! You actually mean it? A *baby*? Oh, Serena, I am so truly delighted for you!' She wagged a finger. 'Now, this is really giving George and me something to live up to. Wouldn't it be wonderful if we both have broods of children? They'll be cousins and they'll run rings round us. Yours will be daring and mischievous like Raphael, while mine will be… Oh, Lord. Reliable and dutiful, like George.' She laughed suddenly. 'But I do think George and I will suit, Serena, I really do. I'll be able to teach him to have more fun, won't I?'

Serena laughed. 'You've already made vast improvements. He looks quite dashing in that new high-perch phaeton of his!'

'Doesn't he just? Also, my dear—' Joanna's eyes twinkled naughtily '—I've begun to make him more adventurous in other ways. I believe it won't be long before I'm following you into producing an heir—'

She broke off. 'Oh, my goodness!' She was rushing to peer out of the window. 'There's a carriage pulling up. It's your Marquis, so I'd best be on my way.' She reached for her hat. 'So delighted for you, Serena. And I'm thrilled about being your matron of honour. I shall see you tomorrow, bright and early!'

Joanna scurried off and a few minutes later Raphael entered. 'I can hardly believe it,' he said. 'Do you know, Grinling was almost pleasant to me just then. I think that he's resigned to my presence at last.'

Serena's heart had leaped when he entered the room. 'So,' she said, walking towards him, 'am I.'

He gathered her into his arms. 'Which is what I would expect,' he murmured, 'when we are to be husband and wife tomorrow. Happy, my darling?'

'So happy I could burst.' She laid her cheek against his broad chest. 'Because I love you, Raphael, so much. And I want the world to know it.'

'They will,' he assured her a trifle sardonically. 'Well, all of London at any rate. Believe me, they've been talking of nothing but the two of us for the last few weeks. "The rakehell Marquis and Lady Serena!" they're whispering. "Who would believe it?" They claim,' he added helpfully, 'that you've reformed my wicked ways.'

She brushed aside a stray lock of hair from his forehead, revealing the faint scar that would always be a reminder of that frightening night-time attack. Then she smiled. 'You won't abandon quite all your wicked ways, I hope?'

He shook his head and kissed her tenderly. 'Never. I can never have enough of you, *ma chère*—you'll have no peace, I promise you, once we're married.'

'I'm glad.' Her words were heartfelt. 'So glad. Raphael, you said you were going to visit Dominic this morning. How is he? How is Madeleine?'

He walked across to a sofa and gestured for her to sit beside him. 'Indeed, I rode over to Kensington to make sure my groomsman knows all his duties for tomorrow. And he's asked me if I'll perform the same favour for him, in two months' time.'

Serena clapped her hands in delight. 'So they've set the date for their wedding? Oh, Raphael, what celebrations we shall have! I'm so glad for them.'

'Yes,' he said, but then a shadow crossed his features. 'I think,' he went on more quietly, 'that people will be making the most of the next few months, because very soon I fear that England's war with the French Republic will intensify. It's going to affect us all, Serena. And now that Madeleine is safe, I feel I must turn my mind to the plight of my fellow countrymen.'

Her heart plunged, but she tried to sound

calm. 'So are you thinking of joining the Royalist army?' The thought of losing him again—
of the long absences and the danger war would
entail—was almost too much to bear, especially
now. She felt her hand moving protectively down-
wards towards her womb.

'I won't be fighting,' he said quickly. 'Not in
the foreseeable future. But I received a summons
to the Home Office yesterday. They want me to
help them in the war effort; you see, I can trans-
late for them, I can share with them all my knowledge of France and its cities, maybe provide the
names of people they can rely on in their plans
for a possible invasion of France next year. But
all this is highly secret, Serena. Dominic knows,
of course, but no one else.'

'An invasion,' she repeated slowly. 'Raphael,
this is all too real, isn't it? But I'm proud of you.
So proud.' She leaned against him and he put his
arm around her. 'And I hope,' she went on, 'to
make you proud of *me*.' She gazed up at him. 'You
realise we shall be leading a double life again?
We shall be leaders of society without a doubt,
hosting parties, being seen at all the grand events.
While, in reality, you'll be spending time closeted
in government offices, engaged in making secret
plans. Oh, Raphael, I hope that this war doesn't
last too long!'

'I fear it might.' His expression was grave. 'But we have one another, Serena. We shall have our love for each other, always. And there's something else I've been meaning to say to you. You were honest with me from the beginning—you told me you were unable to bear children. So I hope it won't be too hard for you when maybe George and Joanna start a family, or Dominic and Madeleine—' He broke off. 'What? What is it?'

She'd stopped him by putting a finger to his lips. 'Raphael. Don't say any more.'

'I'm sorry,' he said quickly. 'I shouldn't even have mentioned it, should I?'

'Perhaps you shouldn't,' she said with a mischievous smile, 'because, you see, you're quite wrong.'

Raphael looked bewildered. 'I don't think I understand.'

And so, utterly delighting in the moment, Serena told him. And her happiness—like that of her husband-to-be—was entirely complete.

* * * * *

MILLS & BOON

Coming next month

PORTRAIT OF A FORBIDDEN LOVE
Bronwyn Scott

'You want to watch me paint, Mr Rutherford.' It was a quiet accusation. She might as well have said, 'You want to see me naked.' To her it was likely the same thing. He recalled her earlier reference to the studio as a bedchamber, an intimate space

'Well?' He rose to the argument. 'You've seen me naked in my bath.' Surely, this confident woman was not intimidated by him watching her paint. Her talent was already proven, even if it was not accepted by the Academy at the higher levels.

'You had nothing to lose, it's hardly the same.'

She really believed that. He gave a short chuckle. 'My dignity? My pride? Those are no small things.

'What does it cost you if I watch you paint? You've already said you think it hardly matters what you come back with in March. Perhaps you, too, have nothing to lose.'

She did *not* believe that. She put her pencil away and closed her sketch pad, signalling the end of the session. 'I have everything to lose and you hold all the power. Your words *will* matter, far more than mine. A man's testimony always carries more weight than a woman's.' Her stare was piercing, forcing unspoken truths to surface. They both knew it was true. How many times was a woman believed in a court of law over a man? How many maids didn't dare lay a complaint against the molesting lord of the manor in fear of their jobs? Never and none. His thoughts stalled on the last. It wasn't just men, then, that she referenced in her shrewd comment, but men with status, a subtle reference to the power of his title and perhaps to something more.

'If there is any sway to be had,' Artemisia said with deadly quiet, 'it rests with you, Mr Rutherford.'

Continue reading
PORTRAIT OF A FORBIDDEN LOVE
Bronwyn Scott

Available next month
www.millsandboon.co.uk

COMING SOON!

We really hope you enjoyed reading this book.
If you're looking for more romance, be sure to
head to the shops when new books are
available on

Thursday 24th December

To see which titles are coming soon, please visit

millsandboon.co.uk/nextmonth

MILLS & BOON

THE HEART OF ROMANCE

A ROMANCE FOR EVERY KIND OF READER

MODERN

Prepare to be swept off your feet by sophisticated, sexy and seductive heroes, in some of the world's most glamourous and romantic locations, where power and passion collide.
8 stories per month.

HISTORICAL

Escape with historical heroes from time gone by. Whether your passion is for wicked Regency Rakes, muscled Vikings or rugged Highlanders, awaken the romance of the past.
6 stories per month.

MEDICAL

Set your pulse racing with dedicated, delectable doctors in the high-pressure world of medicine, where emotions run high and passion, comfort and love are the best medicine.
6 stories per month.

True Love

Celebrate true love with tender stories of heartfelt romance, from the rush of falling in love to the joy a new baby can bring, and a focus on the emotional heart of a relationship.
8 stories per month.

Desire

Indulge in secrets and scandal, intense drama and plenty of sizzl hot action with powerful and passionate heroes who have it all: wealth, status, good looks…everything but the right woman.
6 stories per month.

HEROES

Experience all the excitement of a gripping thriller, with an inten romance at its heart. Resourceful, true-to-life women and strong fearless men face danger and desire - a killer combination!
8 stories per month.

DARE

Sensual love stories featuring smart, sassy heroines you'd want as best friend, and compelling intense heroes who are worthy of th
4 stories per month.

To see which titles are coming soon, please visit

millsandboon.co.uk/nextmonth